In *Confessions to a Stranger*, Danielle Grandinetti weaves a tale that is at once mysterious, suspenseful, romantic, and inspiring ... Filled with truths that made me ponder my own life, this novel is a lovely start to what is sure to be a wonderful series!

—Heidi Chiavaroli,
Carol Award-Winning Author of *The Orchard House*

Danielle Grandinetti has crafted a wonderful tale of suspense and romance that will keep you on the edge of your seat. With well-drawn characters authentic to the era, a gripping plot, and a strong message of hope, *Confessions to a Stranger* is a read I recommend!

—Misty M. Beller,
USA Today bestselling author of the Sisters of the Rockies

A Strike to the Heart is a compelling story. From the very first page, I was immersed into the thrilling action and remained gripped with intrigue until the satisfying ending. The romance escalated right along with the winding plot, creating a layered mystery that is sure to delight readers.

—Rachel Scott McDaniel,
Award-winning author of *The Mobster's Daughter*

Riveting from the first scene, *As Silent as the Night* offers a unique, edge-of-your-seat Christmas read ... A beautiful, gripping, and romantically suspenseful Christmas story you wouldn't be able to put down if you tried.

—Chautona Havig,
Author of *The Stars of New Cheltenham*

The Neighbor and the Gifts is a poignant tale that transforms a familiar carol into a stirring journey of faith, love, and danger ... For readers who love historical romance, mystery, and want a deeper meaning in their holiday stories—this one's for you.

—Natalie Walters,
bestselling and award-winning author of *Living Lies* and the *SNAP Agency* series

Investigation of a Journalist

**Discover the Foundation
of Danielle's Bookish World**

Harbored in Crow's Nest
Confessions to a Stranger
Refuge for the Archaeologist
Escape with the Prodigal
Relying on the Enemy
Sheltered by the Doctor
Investigation of a Journalist

Bridge: His Boss's Little Sister

Unexpected Protectors
To Stand in the Breach
A Strike to the Heart
As Silent as the Night

For a complete list, visit
daniellegrandinetti.com/books

Investigation of a Journalist

Danielle Grandinetti

Hearth Spot Press

INVESTIGATION OF A JOURNALIST

Published by Hearth Spot Press

Scripture quotations are taken from the King James Version of the Bible

Kindle Book ISBN: 978-1-956098-31-0
EPUB eBook ISBN: 978-1-956098-30-3
Paperback ISBN: 978-1-956098-34-1

Cover Art: Roseanna White Designs
Author Picture: Abby Mae Tindal at Maeflower Photography
Editor: Sarah Hinkle

To Ann Elizabeth Fryer

Fellow historical romance
author, critique partner, and
friend. I'm so grateful to be on
this journey with you!

"Justice and judgment are the habitation of thy throne:
mercy and truth shall go before thy face."
Psalm 89:14 (KJV)

PROLOGUE

Two months ago …

Unrepentant criminals did not deserve a second—or, in this case, a fourth—chance. Yet here she stood, cocooned within the deepening shadows of Lower Wacker Drive. The growing population of homeless who camped here churned her spirit. She, Caroline Wagoneer of the Di Stasio Giornaliste Agency, wanted to do something. Instead, she was forced to wait for her lowlife informant.

She spotted the man slipping toward her. Stringy hair. Missing teeth. A stench that drove even the rats away. She wouldn't have minded any of that, except he was a rumrunner who exploited the down-on-their-luck people who took refuge here. Men who drank to erase what the economy took from them. Women who drank to forget the abuse they suffered. Children—

Lord, help me shed Your light in these dark places.

"Hey, doll." Ploughshare—that's the name he provided—looked from her black hat down her black dress to her black shoes.

She pinned her lips shut, knowing he couldn't see any definition thanks to the darkness, especially since she'd defied the heat by wearing long sleeves and black gloves to stay better concealed.

"I ain't doing this no more." Ploughshare crossed his arms. Was he trying to look tough? Carrie wasn't that tall, but she still had two inches on him. "Unless you show some gams, this is my last snitch."

"You have provided me no new information, Ploughshare." Just confirmation that her suspicions were correct. His boss's organization had at least one cop on the take. Probably more. "I'm the one who should cut you loose."

"If yous weren't pretty, I wouldn't give ya this." He unwound one arm to flutter a bill from grimy fingers.

"Really?" She battled her voice back to a whisper. "I won't be bribed."

"It ain't a bribe, doll." He wagged it. "Look."

Gingerly, she slipped it from his pinchers, watching his expression in the flickering light of a barrel fire. No glee or anticipation flashed. This wasn't a trap. She rolled out the bill, holding each end, and turned it toward the firelight. "A one-dollar bill?"

"See anything wrong with it?"

She studied it, recalling the lessons her ex-fiancé had taught her. "It's too dark. But counterfeiting ones isn't worth it."

"It ain't more'n a test case. Pass along enough of these, then add a zero or two." He grinned. "Or three."

Carrie rubbed her temple. "Ploughshare, you need to get out while you can. When the G-men find out, you'll go to prison."

"It's good money, doll. And if the boss finds out I snitched, I'm a dead man. No matter where I live." He glanced over his shoulder. "You won't tell nobody 'bout me?"

"I never reveal my sources."

"Then this is goodbye." Ploughshare backed up a step, hesitated. "Watch your back. If he finds out, he'll silence you."

"I'm not scared of a bully." Carrie squared her shoulders. "The truth matters."

"You say that now. You won't once he gets his claws into you. Goodbye, C. C. Wagner."

Carrie held her position, a tad shaken that Ploughshare had used her byline. She made sure her person and her nom de plume were never connected. Plus, there'd been a threat in his tone that she'd never heard before. It wouldn't deter her, though. No sirree. She studied the dollar bill one last time before pocketing it.

She was on the right trail. Excitement coursed through her. This was the closest she'd gotten yet to finding out the real reason Buck Wilson left her a month before their wedding.

CHAPTER ONE

Monday, September 14, 1931
Chicago, Illinois

Buck Wilson did not deserve a second chance. He knew it down to his marrow, yet here he stood, outside Chicago's Union Station, in the very town where he'd left all his hopes and dreams. The detective who wanted to arrest him at his side.

He adjusted his fedora to cover more of his face. "If they find out I'm here, you know what they'll do."

"I reckon so." Michael O'Connor braced his hands on his belt and looked around, neck craning to see the tall buildings around them. "You liked it here?"

"Let's go, O'Connor. Quit acting like a tourist." Buck tugged at his collar. The heat was more oppressive here in the city than up in Crow's Nest. He couldn't wait to leave, to return to the small Wisconsin town that had become home. But first, he had to face the one person he thought he'd never see again.

"I could have done this by myself, you know." O'Connor kept up with Buck's brisk pace.

"I know." Buck turned his back on the Chicago River and headed west down Jackson. He needed the walk, even if it meant arriving looking wrung out. Frankly, he wasn't entirely sure he wouldn't be tossed out on his rear. He deserved nothing less. But he needed to face her like a man, not send the detective to do his dirty work.

Detective Michael O'Connor was around seventy, with blue eyes that could see into a man's soul and a gray mustache that seemed to be a living thing at times. Buck scratched at his own usually clean-shaven chin as his eyes fell on a Beistle Devil Dancer in a shop window. The travel down from Crow's Nest hadn't afforded time to shave, and the scruff provided a measure of anonymity. However, showing up, looking like a hobo—or worse, a Halloween decoration—wouldn't win him any good graces.

He halted. "We need a cab."

"Finally. He has some sense," O'Connor grumbled.

"Yeah. Yeah." It was a longer walk than he remembered, and the Windy City Chicago was not today. He'd give anything for a fishy breeze off the lake. And just as much, he wouldn't breathe a word of that sentiment to his companion. Though, as the older man folded himself into the hansom cab with a twinkle in his eye, Buck suspected the good old detective knew more than Buck wanted.

"Did you tell Matrone where you were going?" Detective O'Connor broke the silence that settled once they were on the move.

Nick Matrone was an Italian doctor who'd befriended Buck this past summer. He was one of the few men in Crow's Nest who saw Buck as a person instead of the head of the Crow's Nest Conglomerate. They sparred every morning. Matrone's fiancée, Mindy Zahn, was the first to prod Buck about facing his past.

"They can't know the truth." Buck watched the old buildings go by, many already donning the orange and black of next month's holiday.

Black cats and witches hats. Pumpkins and masks. "Telling you is dangerous enough."

"I wish you would have told me two years ago," the man huffed. "Two heads and all. We could have solved this before people got hurt."

Could they have done so? He'd been reluctant to risk it. But now, with children getting caught in the cross-hairs and his own step-brother in jail again, the counter-risks were piling up, too. "I guess we'll never know."

Before too long, he recognized the spire of St. Mark's. The sun reflected off the cross that rose high above the surrounding buildings, including the one where the cabbie stopped. Buck paid the driver and sent him on his way. O'Connor stood silently beside him. He appreciated that about the detective. The man didn't rush into things. For a moment, Buck let his eyes linger on the Catholic Church across the street, where a man in a flat cap unloaded crates of food to be carried inside.

On the edge of one of the Italian neighborhoods, smells of sausage and basil wafted through the air and punched him in the stomach. They reminded him of the blissful life he'd been forced to leave behind. O'Connor gripped his shoulder, and Buck shook himself away from the memories. If he wanted to make his sacrifices—her sacrifice—worth it, he needed her help. There was no other choice.

"We're being observed," O'Connor's gravelly voice rumbled.

Buck turned toward the old brownstone, nearly stumbling over a newsboy as the kid darted by, a package of newspapers tied with twine in his arms. Sometimes, he missed the hustle and bustle of the city, but most times, he did not. And there were plenty of children to trip over on the wharf in Crow's Nest.

He scanned the building. A paper apple with a cut-out smile hung below the agency name painted on the picture window beside the door. On the second floor, he spotted the flutter of a curtain. The Di Stasio Giornaliste Agency was home to some of the most dogged female journalists he'd ever met. Curious women who would have no trouble tossing him to the street for what he'd done to one of their own.

Enough stalling. He fortified himself as he climbed the five steps to the brownstone's door, O'Connor to his left. *Lord, please let me find favor in her eyes. Grant me this grace.*

He knocked and stepped back, arms loose at his sides. The confident arrogance he wore in Crow's Nest had no place here. It was but a disguise. One he had worn so long, now he wasn't sure what to do with his hands. Maybe he should have brought flowers? No. This wasn't a date. He wasn't even here to apologize. Though he surely would. Maybe he should begin on his knees in penance. Begging for her help.

"Take a breath, Wilson," O'Connor spoke almost silently. "You're going to Lindy Hop your way out of here."

A laugh jerked up his throat, and his shoulders relaxed. He stuffed his left hand in his pocket and raised his other to knock again—only for the wood to vanish before his fist. He stumbled a step forward, catching himself on the doorframe. For there, before him, stood the most beautiful woman in the world. His heart stuttered, and an ache bloomed in his chest as the realization of all he had given up crashed in on him.

"Caroline." Her name on his lips emerged broken, just like him.

A variety of emotions danced across her round features before she shuttered them away. She was not overly tall, but neither was she short. Indeed, diminutive she was not. Dressed in her typical white blouse and black skirt, a tie at her throat, and a black eyebrow cocked, she looked like the warrior he knew her to be. Her dark hair was exactly as he remembered, pinned up with combs to soften the bob. She shifted. With one hand, she held the door open, but she relaxed a hip, resting her other hand on it as it jutted out in her signature stance. Still, not a word left her unsmiling mouth.

He'd rehearsed this moment in his mind since they left Crow's Nest. No, ever since he'd made this ridiculous plan with Detective O'Connor, his nemesis-turned-partner. Though if this didn't work, the man beside him might have to arrest him, as he had surely dreamed of doing the last few years. Buck could picture the older man's bushy mustache twitching in glee as he secured Buck's wrists in cuffs.

"Did you have something to say?" Carrie spoke firmly, neutrally, showing the skills that made him first admire her. Her gaze took in his companion but focused on him. "Or are you going to stand here in a daze until supper?"

"I need your help." Dunderhead. Those were not the first words he'd planned. Beside him, O'Connor sighed.

The index finger of Carrie's right hand bounced against her belt, the only sign he'd caught her off guard. "The girls think I should slam the door in your face."

"I deserve it."

She huffed and threw the door closed.

"Your eloquence leaves something to be desired," O'Connor growled.

Buck cringed. But before his brain engaged, Carrie flung it open again. "Get your *posteriore* in here, Wilson. And shut the door." She spun on her heels, leaving him gaping on her front step and O'Connor laughing like a crazy old man.

Caroline Wagoneer had used those exact words the first day they met over six years ago.

"I like her." O'Connor pushed into the house.

Yeah. So did he.

And, for the first time in two years, his heart gave a pitiful thump of hope.

Carrie strode directly to the kitchen, unsure whether she hoped Buck would follow her or go on his way. Strike that. For his own safety, he better follow her. The women of the Di Stasio Giornaliste Agency were both loyal and fierce, and they all knew what Buck had done to her. If he dilly-dallied, or worse, left, they'd pounce.

She glanced over her shoulder. Good. He kept close, his older companion on his heels. Beneath the man's gray eyebrows were eyes that saw way more than most. He had to be a cop. The puzzle pieces swirled as her heels clacked on the wooden floor. When Buck left Chicago, he left his job, his life, everything. All supposedly because of unscrupulous dealings—something she didn't quite believe him capable of. So why would he now show up with an officer of the law? Unless the man was dirty.

Another look over her shoulder. This time, her gaze shot past the men to the dark brown gaze that watched from the parlor door. Her boss, sixty-five-year-old Alessandra Di Stasio, gave a subtle nod, and Carrie's shoulders relaxed. Ali had her back, as did all the female journalists who worked for her. If Buck hurt Carrie again, there was no telling what the fearless stunt reporter would do to him.

She still hadn't decided what to do with him. Honestly, the man left her a month before their wedding. Disappeared, leaving only an apology and no explanation in his wake.

At first, she'd been hurt, then angry. But once her curiosity took hold, she'd chased lead after lead, needing to find the truth. She thought back to the one-dollar bill Ploughshare had given her. What she'd found since

Buck left did not match what she'd been told about why he disappeared.

"How's the job?" Buck's halting question reminded her to check the watch that hung from her belt.

Forty-five minutes before she was due to meet the agency's best source: Gio Vella. The handsome Italian could find anything, including information. How one of the doting females he garnered hadn't yet convinced him to marry, Carrie didn't know. Then again, Buck was the only man who had convinced her to set aside her desire to remain unmarried.

She pushed away the memories, not having time to reminisce when Signore Vella would be waiting at St. Mark's for her shortly. He'd sent a note around this morning that he'd discovered a person who claimed to have knowledge of the press printing those unbacked one-dollar bills. She wouldn't be late.

"Not that it matters, but the job is fine." She waved her hand to dismiss the topic and set about pouring three cups of coffee. Hers and Buck's tastes matched: strong, black, and rich, without cream or sugar. Very unladylike, but she was a journalist first, a female second. And no matter how tight finances got, the agency always splurged on quality coffee beans. She slid one cup across the table, aimed her question at the older gent. "Black?"

The man tipped his chin. She turned her back on them and poured.

"You remembered." Buck's voice resisted surprise. Why would he think she didn't remember? She remembered ... everything. The partnership, the dreams, the kisses.

She slid the cup to the older man, leaned a hip against the table, and hid behind a sip. "Why are you here, Buck?"

Standing on the opposite side of the table, he avoided looking at her and turned the cup ninety degrees. The man was nervous. He glanced at the older man, then finally met her eye. "I need your help, Carrie."

"So you said." Another sip. "What kind of help?"

"I'm in trouble." He dropped his gaze again, appearing nothing like the confident man she'd known. Compassion inched up her spine and she shoved it away.

"Oh, for pity's sake." The older man slapped Buck's shoulder. "Be a man and spit it out."

Carrie gaped, and Buck turned as red as an apple.

The older man huffed, held out a hand to Carrie. "Since he hasn't had the decency to introduce us … I'm Detective Michael O'Connor, special investigator in Crow's Nest, Wisconsin."

"A pleasure." She shook the man's gnarled hand, cataloging everything she could about him. From his flat-brimmed hat, which he'd tossed on the table, to his gray facial hair, tall form, and serviceable clothes. "Caroline Wagoneer. Investigative journalist."

His grip tightened, as if testing something. She cocked her head.

"Trust her yet?" Buck grumbled. "She isn't Alistar."

More details revealed. As a journalist, she knew the negative perceptions people in her career received. It frustrated her because, thanks to a few unscrupulous journalists, they all received a bad name. Or maybe it was because the above-board journalists sought the truth no matter the consequences, and powerful people hated having their sins revealed in black and white.

"No, she's not. She's much prettier." Mr. O'Connor winked at her as he released her hand, and she realized she liked him even though she usually kept her opinions of people as neutral as possible.

She sipped her coffee. "I also have morals, which I'd guess this other journalist does not."

Respect flashed in the detective's eyes. Score one for her!

"Alistar has no morals whatsoever." Buck lowered himself into a chair, rested elbows on the table. An ungentlemanly move that raised her concern still more. "Carrie, you know as well as anyone that the truth is elusive, and I need you to find it."

"You know how to pull a gal in. Go on." Her tease didn't cause even a twitch of his lips. *Santocielo,* she thought, using one of Ali's favorite Italian exclamations. He really did need help.

She set her cup on the table and circled around to him, laying a hand on his arm. He stared at where her fingers touched his sleeve, his throat working double time. This close, she could see the black marring the skin beneath his eyes. Eyes that lacked the sparkle she remembered of her fiancé. His skin was chapped, worn, as if he'd aged ten years, not two, since she last saw him.

That tug inside turned into a crack. Buck was indeed in trouble. The evidence filled in a few of the gaps in her investigation, but there was more she needed to know. "Is this a matter for my ears alone, or may I invite Ali into the conversation?"

"Your ears." He met her gaze, his own a shimmering well. The man was crying! "Just telling you could cost everything, but I can't do it alone anymore."

The crack in her heart fissured as pieces fell into place. She glanced over her shoulder at the detective, then lowered her voice to a whisper. "You're undercover, aren't you? You've been undercover this whole time. Over two years. Buck! That's too long!" Her boss set the limit at six months.

"I didn't have a choice." His head sank into his hands. "Over two years, and I can't find the proof I need. Enough to keep my job, but if I don't come up with it soon, my superiors aren't just going to cut me loose. I'll be tossed in a cell beside Capone."

It'd been a few months since the mob boss's indictment for tax evasion, after a lengthy investigation by the Treasury and Justice Departments.

"After all this, they'd still take your badge? Buck, can they do that?" She twisted toward the detective. "Can they?"

"It's the US Treasury, Carrie." Buck brought her attention back to him. "I was found with counterfeit money in my possession without an explanation."

That she'd heard, and didn't believe. "Was it true?"

"That I had counterfeit bills in my possession, yes."

Her stomach twisted. "And the explanation?"

"None. Officially." He rubbed his face. "You know Prohibition Agents were moved to Justice, so my boss doesn't even work for the Treasury Department anymore. One minute, we were about to get married, the next my cover was blown, I was in cuffs, and removed from the counterfeit-prohibition task force."

"Why didn't you tell me?" The question had burned since the day she'd been told of his arrest.

"Because then my uncle would have come after you. Carrie, I have known ties to a suspected bank robber and drug trafficker, counterfeiter, and who knows what else he's done. My history is the only reason my boss—former boss, I don't even know any more—gave me a shot at redeeming myself. My colleagues think I was fired, and the only way I have a chance at saving my career is to drag my sorry, worthless uncle in by the bootstraps."

Carrie's pulse pounded in her ears and she paced the kitchen as she filtered in details from her own investigation. She suspected Buck had been set up, that a dirty cop had played a role. But she couldn't prove it. "It's not right. It's not just. You shouldn't pay for someone else's mistakes."

Buck scrubbed his face again. "You think I haven't told my boss that? Problem is, Perry Baxter is a slippery conman, and my boss is under pressure because his boss and all my colleagues are convinced I'm his partner. And the longer I take to find evidence Baxter is the only one of us that is actually a criminal, the less my boss can protect me."

Carrie stopped in front of Detective O'Connor, hands on her hips. "Do you think Buck is a criminal?"

The man's eyebrow twitched. "I have not found enough evidence to arrest him. Yet."

"Yet?" Carrie tossed her arms out. "Then why are you here? Trying to get me to incriminate him?"

The detective raised his chin, his gaze darting over her shoulder. "Mindy was right."

"Mindy?" Carrie's stomach dropped. Had Buck moved on to another girl? "Who is Mindy?"

Buck glared at his companion. "Shut it. You're not helping."

A gleam flashed in the detective's eye. "Oh, I think I am. Mindy Zahn is the reason you're here. She's the one who convinced you to admit you needed help. And you listened to her."

Buck leapt out of his chair, fists clenched as he launched himself in front of O'Connor. "Your insinuations are not welcome."

The detective crossed his arms with a smug smile. "Maybe it was her pretty smile that finally won you over."

Was it possible to have one's heart broken into so many pieces the dust would simply blow them away?

Buck grabbed the detective by the lapels. "How dare you talk about her like that! She's Nick's fiancée! I have never, never, looked at her as anything other than a friend."

"And why is that, Mr. Wilson?" Detective O'Connor asked, unruffled by Buck's loss of control. Something Carrie had never seen in Buck before.

She stared, stunned, yet trying to snatch up the details of Buck's last few years that these two men unwittingly dropped. The woman—Mindy—wasn't Buck's girl. Did that mean he didn't have someone new? He hadn't moved on from her? Carrie took a gulp of coffee. Not the details she needed to focus on. Still, it hurt to hear he had friends she didn't know, a life apart from her. Even if he was undercover.

Buck deflated like a hot-air balloon whose heat source had run out of fuel. "What do you want me to say, O'Connor? That I still love Carrie? I do. I've never stopped. And you know that."

"You still love me?" Carrie covered her mouth, but that didn't stop the question from slipping out.

Detective O'Connor patted Buck's shoulder, nodded to Carrie, and left the room. He'd goaded Buck into that admission. For what purpose?

Buck pulled Carrie to the chair beside him. "Truth is, I left to protect you. I know I've ruined everything between us. I'm sorry."

Battling the emotions that threatened to overwhelm her, she returned them to the issue at hand. "How exactly do you expect me to help you find proof if you haven't been able to find it in two years?"

"Because I think I finally found Baxter's source. I thought it was my stepbrother, but I'm eighty percent sure it's a journalist."

"Alistar."

Buck nodded. "Greg Alistar of the *Crow's Nest Gazette*. He's unscrupulous, dirty, and plays close enough to the rules that I can't get him fired."

"I can't abide people like that. But you didn't answer ... what can I do to help?"

"Occasionally, your articles get syndicated into the *Gazette*." Buck's thumb rubbed over her knuckles. "You're making a name for yourself. I'm proud of you."

The praise felt too good.

"O'Connor suggested you visit Crow's Nest under the guise of doing a society piece. There's a big wedding—Sorry." He ducked his head.

Carrie ignored him as more details snapped together. "Crow's Nest is where that socialite ended up. What's her name? Parents were killed in an accident. Sister tried to murder her."

"Adaleigh Sirland."

"That's it! Wait, is it her wedding?"

Buck nodded.

"I can work with that." Carrie grinned, the scent of a story coursing through her.

"We can't know each other." Buck broke into her plans. "O'Connor is the only one who knows the truth. Well, and Mindy and Nick. Sort of."

"Mindy." She shouldn't be jealous.

"They only know I was supposed to marry you, not why I left or my real ... job."

The job that took him away from her. It's what she'd suspected, after she got past the anger and hurt. Buck Wilson did nothing without a good reason. And to abandon her a month before their wedding would require a very good reason.

Like the transcontinental railroad, if they approached this investigation from two sides, perhaps they'd find the proof—the golden spike, as it were.

Over the last eighteen months, she'd moved from source to source, digging to find the truth, whether or not she liked what she discovered. She'd needed to know. What she found, however, only brought more questions. Dirty cops. Mafia ties. Counterfeiting rings. Memory of the one-dollar bill she'd tucked away surfaced again. Somehow, Buck's original disappearance was tied to that one-dollar bill. Helping Buck was the next step in her investigation, and his.

Carrie released a long-suffering sigh. Then another thought hit her. "Am I going to like the Crow's Nest Buck Wilson?"

He closed his eyes. "I don't know. But I'm having trouble remembering where he ends and I begin."

Carrie couldn't help herself, she cupped his cheek to bring his gaze to hers. "You've been under too long. We're going to get you out of this so you can have your life back."

"My life was with you, Carrie. I already forfeited it. Yet here I am, begging you to help me. I still would have stayed away except children are getting caught up in this mess. Their lives are being threatened and I won't stand for it. This has to end."

"All right, all right." Carrie checked the time. She needed to leave if she didn't want to be late meeting her source. "When's the wedding?"

"Saturday, the third of October."

"I'll be there." Even if Buck hadn't been there for theirs.

CHAPTER TWO

Two weeks later...
Saturday, October 3

"This is where Buck's been hiding?" Ali craned her neck as she parked her husband's Ford behind the long line of parked automobiles, then shielded her eyes against the bright sunlight. "It's beautiful."

Carrie tried not to bristle at the word *hiding*. Her boss meant well, but like the rest of her colleagues, their loyalty lay with Carrie, not Buck. Why she thought to defend her former fiancé, she didn't know.

Crow's Nest was beautiful. Though also set along the coast of Lake Michigan, it was a quaint little town, not a dirty metropolis like Chicago. As they'd driven through town, she'd noticed the buildings were a mix of weathered and new, especially a swath along Main Street. Made her wonder the cause. The trees also lent a beauty to the area. While not fully cloaked in their autumn colors, there were many more trees with tinges of red, orange, and yellow here than in Chicago.

"Are you sure you're ready?" Ali rested long olive fingers on the navy fabric covering Carrie's arm. "You haven't attended a wedding since

Buck left."

Carrie rubbed her breastbone beneath the fabric bow that hung loosely from her neck, praying the heartache wouldn't be too distracting. She knew seeing another woman wed would hurt, and require all her undercover prowess to keep from reacting. Ali thought she could do it or she wouldn't have approved the assignment. "I'll be fine."

Ali hummed and reached into the back seat for the camera case.

Technically, it belonged to Ali, but Ali called it the Agency Camera. Frankly, most of the Agency's belongings were purchased by Ali's husband. A wealthy man, he funded his wife's business. She did not go by her husband's name within this business in order to keep him and their children from the scandal her work would cause. Few knew the powerful couple behind the Di Stasio Giornaliste Agency.

A fact that had Carrie asking, "Why didn't you send one of the other girls with me? You are rarely in the field." First because she had children who needed her attention, and then because age had slowed her in recent years.

"Because Buck's position is delicate. Detective O'Connor and I thought it best if only the barest few knew the entire operation."

"What about Buck's friend Mindy?" She tried not to let her jealousy bias her against the woman who had become Buck's friend after he'd left Carrie at the altar. Sure, Buck had relented to telling Ali everything, but that was only because her boss wouldn't sanction Carrie's operation without all the details.

Ali didn't miss a trick. "Mindy and her fiancé, Dr. Nick Matrone?" The way the doctor's name rolled off Ali's tongue betrayed her Italian heritage. Usually, her accent lent only an exotic lilt to the cultured tones she'd developed since her marriage. No one would guess she was once a homeless street urchin after her immigrant parents died.

Carrie rolled her eyes. "Yes, that Mindy."

Ali chuckled. "They only know that you and Buck were once engaged. Unless Buck decides otherwise, the four of us will be the only ones who know everything."

Carrie reached into the backseat for her sweater. "Why am I so nervous, then?"

"Because this is important to you." Ali clucked her tongue. "Buck is still important to you."

"He shouldn't be."

"I know, la mia stellina." The nickname plunged the motherly love Ali showered on all her little stars deep into Carrie's heart. "Now, watch yourself. Please. Just because Buck came begging for you to find the truth doesn't mean you'll like what you discover. Are you sure you want to go through with this? I can turn the car right back to Chicago."

Carrie took a bracing breath. "If nothing else, I need closure."

"There's my journalist." Ali winked. "You ready for my mean boss persona?"

Carrie grabbed her satchel and followed Ali from the car, but halted on the walk to the white house where the wedding would take place. Ali went on without her, but the view stalled Carrie's feet. The house overlooked Lake Michigan from a raised cliff. Brilliant blue stretched toward the azure sky, meeting at a small bank of clouds on the horizon. To the left and right, the coast stretched above the waves that lapped at the rocks.

"Breathtaking, isn't it?" a woman spoke from behind her.

Carrie turned. The woman who joined her offered a brilliant smile. Her blonde hair was drawn back in a twisting mass and topped by a small purple hat. Her long-sleeve, knee-length lavender dress fit a perfectly hourglass form. Carrie glanced down at her own serviceable navy suit.

Though the white collar and bow dressed it up, and the skirt was a fashionable knee-length, she lacked womanly curves.

"Are you ... Caroline?" the woman asked. "I'm Mindy Zahn."

This was Mindy? *Mamma Mia.* She was gorgeous in an all-American kind of way. How had Buck not fallen for her? "Yes, I'm Caroline Wagoneer."

Somehow, Mindy's smile grew as she squealed and threw her arms around Caroline's neck. "I'm so happy you're here!"

Carrie endured the hug for a moment, then disentangled herself, utterly mystified by the woman's reaction. She wanted Carrie here? And so enthusiastically. Why? "No one can know that, you know. You haven't told anyone, have you?"

"That I know you? Of course I don't know you." Mindy wrinkled her nose. "Not yet, anyway."

"That Buck knows me." Carrie shook Mindy's shoulders. "If you care about Buck, you'll keep my secret."

Confusion created lines on Mindy's perfect face. "I don't understand. He knows you're coming. Asked me to take you in, show you around."

"He did?" Carrie shook her head. Ali had said nothing about staying with Mindy. Carrie sighed. Probably because she knew how Carrie felt about the woman.

Mindy clasped Carrie's elbows. "I'm taking you under my wing so you can keep your distance from Buck. Detective O'Connor explained that you'll be angling to stick around. No one would be surprised at me for making a new friend. I'm not known for my ... my wisdom."

Carrie blinked. "What?" Who was this woman? Gorgeous, sure, but Buck wouldn't befriend an empty-headed blonde just for her looks. At least not the Buck Carrie knew. There had to be more to Mindy.

Mindy's smile was back. "Isn't it obvious? I saw a lone woman standing here by herself. I came over to say hello and ask if I could help you. Everyone would expect that of me. You tell me you're a journalist here to cover Adaleigh's wedding. Being Adaleigh's best friend, and a naïve woman, of course, I invite a viper right into the dressing room."

Carrie choked on a swallow. "A—w-what did you call me?"

Mindy laughed. "That's what everyone will think of you because they hate Mr. Alistar."

Lovely.

"Truth be told?" Mindy lowered her voice. "You're the reason my fiancé is a free man. I pay my debts, so you're stuck with me."

None of this made sense, and it made the whole situation a lot more complicated. Why hadn't she pressed Buck or O'Connor or even Ali for more information about Mindy? Because Carrie didn't want to know anything about Mindy. She'd let her jealousy color her preparations.

Of course, Ali had to know. She approved every undercover plan in order to keep her journalists safe, even though she understood such assignments were, by necessity, fluid. Still. No wonder her boss had laughed in the car at Carrie's reference to this female friend of Buck's.

"Smile, Miss Neary." Mindy used Carrie's undercover name. Another surprise. "It's a happy day. A wedding between two of our town's favorite residents."

A wedding might be a celebration for some, but not for Carrie. However, she allowed Mindy to weave their arms together. What choice did she have? Apparently, this was what Ali had agreed to, even if she'd kept Carrie in the dark.

"Now, come on, let me introduce you to the wedding party." Mindy shot her a sly look. "You're here to write an article, aren't you?"

"I suppose I am." Then why did she feel like she was being swept into a fairytale that didn't have a happy ending?

Buck watched Mindy lead Carrie along the cliff, pointing to the trellis arch where David would marry Adaleigh. Carrie was gorgeous, even in her understated navy suit. How she navigated the grass in her heels—how Mindy did in even higher heels—he hadn't a clue. However, the knee-length skirt ruffled in the slight breeze, drawing his attention to Caroline's shapely legs.

He yanked at the tie that strangled his neck. Two years hadn't dampened the attraction he felt toward the woman he was supposed to marry. How had he walked away from her? Was his job, his freedom, that important? Fool. Utter rot. All of it. Buck rubbed his face, self-loathing growing with the sun's last hurrah before winter's cloudy skies set in.

Physical magnetism aside, his insides had been a mess since seeing Carrie again. After leaving her, he'd shut off that part of his heart. It added to the deadened side of his undercover persona. But sitting in her kitchen, sharing coffee with her, begging for her help, had awakened that part of him and longing swamped him. If the poets were right and there were such things as soulmates, Carrie was his.

As strong as the desire was to run to her side, he had to keep his distance. The plan he, O'Connor, and Carrie's boss, Ali, had put together was for Mindy to lead Carrie into the house to be introduced to the bride as a reporter. However, a few key confrontations needed to happen first. Ones that might make his case or put Carrie in danger. Maybe both.

"Are you sure Mindy is up for this?" Buck whispered to Nick, who stood beside him in a simple black suit. He withheld a groan. Where had his confidence gone? The Buck Wilson of Crow's Nest never would have asked such a question.

Nick snorted. "Mindy single-handedly subdued your brother. She is stronger than she appears."

"Step-brother." Never again did he want to claim any type of connection to the man who shared a maternal bloodline with him. The same bloodline that connected them both to Perry Baxter. Sleazy criminals, both. "And I know Mindy's strong. She resisted Joe after all."

Nick rolled his eyes, though he didn't take his gaze from his fiancée, who had collected Ali along their way toward the house. "Mindy will be fine. Her inability to tell a lie will benefit us."

"Us. Us. Us." Buck sighed, jamming his hands into his pockets to keep from scrubbing his face again. "When did this become an *us* thing? You don't even know the whole situation."

Nick copied Buck's attempt at casual, matching his stance, including placing his hands in his trouser pockets. "Don't need to know the whole situation. I've seen the toll it's taken on you. Know first-hand what your brother—step-brother—did. I've also treated enough criminals to recognize one. And it's become obvious to me that you are not a criminal."

"I'm not sure Martins agrees with you." Buck forced his shoulders to relax as Mindy drew Carrie and Ali closer to the moment of disruption. He hated to do this at Adaleigh's wedding, but it served as the best cover. O'Connor signed off. But David Martins might never forgive them. The fishing captain was beyond besotted with his bride and would do anything to bring about her happiness.

Nick grunted. "I know full well Martins has reluctantly approved of us both. And since we began as neither Silas nor Gil's favorite people, we still have ground to make up."

Buck couldn't disagree. Silas Ward, David Martins's best friend, and

Gilbert Cox, Ward's sister-in-law's new husband, both had complicated experiences with Nick, who offered a marriage of convenience to both their now-wives while also saving the lives of those they loved as a medical doctor.

However, Buck, well … Buck was persona non grata to most of Crow's Nest. Exactly his goal when he first went undercover. But reaping the reward of his assignment wasn't easy on the spirit, especially now. Seeing Carrie again reminded him of all he'd sacrificed.

Nick shifted, tensed. "Here we go."

Buck clenched his fists, hidden in the depths of his pockets as Greg Alistar showed open … appreciation … for the three women. Nick and Buck trained every day, a mix of martial arts Buck had learned from Chinese immigrant workers and bare-knuckle boxing Nick had learned from an Irishman back in New York City. What Buck wouldn't give to drive a punch straight into Alistar's nose.

Ali struck up an animated conversation, drawing Alistar in with a hand on his arm and a laugh that carried over the open space. A few heads turned from the grassy area where they waited for the ceremony to begin. It made Buck's skin itch to see them drawing so much attention. Even if it was the plan.

David and Adaleigh were both well-liked in Crow's Nest, which was reflected in the number of guests present. Instead of limiting attendance to the space inside their church, they opted to have the wedding outside where anyone could attend. Like Silas Ward and his bride had done last fall. It was just like them, too. Open, welcoming. And with the background of the lake, he had to admit it was perfect. Romantic even.

Buck sighed. He and Carrie had planned a small church wedding. A few friends and colleagues, no family. Over the past two years, he'd put in the obligatory appearance at weddings, as expected of the head of the Crow's Nest Conglomerate. It'd been too painful to pretend to be happy, though most didn't expect him to gush. Thankfully.

Nick scratched his jaw. "How well do you know Carrie's boss? She has Alistar hooked."

"She's that good." He'd missed watching Ali work. The diminutive woman had drawn Alistar in until she had him at her command. Masterful. Growing up on the streets had taught her much about the human condition, and then marrying into the Chicago elite had honed those skills. "Fellow Italian, you know."

"Is she? Should have guessed with her straight Roman nose." Curiosity sparked behind Nick's glasses. "Born here or back in the homeland?

Before Buck could comment, Alistar's raised voice silenced the low chatter around them. "They can go inside, but I cannot?"

"He took the bait." Nick's gaze stayed riveted to the scene, tension flowing from him as Alistar loomed over Mindy. Her words to Alistar were lost across the open air.

Then Ali stepped between them, getting in Alistar's space. Shorter than both Alistar and Mindy, Ali only came up to Alistar's chest, which she poked with her finger. If only they could hear what she was saying. Buck rubbed his neck, wishing he could relax the muscles. He knew Ali could handle the situation, but other wedding guests made this a volatile one. If anyone stepped in, it could ruin the setup. And they needed to let Alistar rail long enough to welcome Carrie's help.

Buck especially willed David and his brother Patrick to keep their distance, but David was Mindy's best friend. Buck searched for the brothers. They watched from the trellis where they had been speaking with the pastor of the local protestant church. David's gaze darted from the scene Alistar and Ali were making, then to Nick, before meeting Buck's eye. David scowled. Then Patrick elbowed him, and their attention was snagged away as Patrick's wife, Meri, chased their baby, who crawled toward his dad.

Thank you, Baby Samuel.

"O'Connor should step in at any moment. Unless Sebastian gets involved." Nick folded his arms and jerked his chin toward the chief of police. The short man stood off to the side, slightly apart from the rest of the wedding guests. In a uniform that barely covered his potbelly, he watched the escalating scene with Alistar, but made no indication of intervening.

Buck shifted his attention back to where it needed to be. Ali held herself regally, chin up, back straight, not backing down as Alistar said something about fairness and journalistic ethics. His words were not loud enough to hear, but certainly not quiet either. Ali's reply, however, was clear for all around her, and Buck couldn't help feeling proud that he knew her, especially when a look of respect filled Mindy's eyes. Carrie stood with her back to them, which was wise in order to not blow their cover story, but Buck wished he could give her a nod of encouragement.

Guests inched closer, as did Buck and Nick. Just in case they needed to intervene. Detective O'Connor stepped out of the shadows of the house, arms crossed. Even David's sister—visiting from Montana—came to the back door. As if sensing the attention for the first time, Carrie glanced around, briefly making eye contact with Buck. His chest squeezed, stealing his breath. This was it.

"I'm a journalist just like you," Alistar shouted at Ali, inches from her face.

Ali smirked. "But I'm a *woman*."

He flung his arms in the air. "And Crow's Nest is my beat."

"Miss Di Stasio." Carrie acted the part of subordinate and attempted to squeeze between the fighting pair.

"Italian." Alistar spat. "I should have known."

Beside Buck, Nick cringed. Mindy opened her mouth, likely to defend her fiancé's heritage, but Carrie spoke first. "Perhaps we should wait like the other journalists. This man is right. It is the fair thing to do."

Alistar preened at being defended.

Ali turned on Carrie. "And that's why you'll never advance in this industry." Carrie dropped her chin, and Buck ached for her. This was a planned ruse, but to hear those words, even if they were fake, would hurt. Especially coming from Ali.

"Please, Miss Di Stasio." Carrie patted the air.

Alistar watched with smug satisfaction as Detective O'Connor stepped forward, motioning the Martins brothers, Sebastian, and the other guests to stay back. Like a well-choreographed play, all the pieces moved in perfect alignment. And for once, Sebastian kept his pompous self out of the way.

Then why did the band around Buck's chest tighten as if a boa had wrapped around his torso? Why was each breath an increasing struggle?

Ali shook her head in disappointment. "You must take every lead available, Miss Neary, every opportunity, and make the most out of it. Now where's the bride? I will have my interview." Ali marched toward the house, a powerful woman on a mission.

"Wait!" Mindy hurried after her, leaving Carrie and Alistar behind as designed.

Detective O'Connor calmed the crowd, acknowledged David's worried expression, and made a show of returning to the house. The people around Buck and Nick muttered about arresting that "Italian woman" and how all journalists were "nosy good-for-nothings." Buck clenched his teeth from responding. Ali was a good woman and there were ethical reporters making a difference in the world.

"Might want to wipe the scowl off your face," Nick muttered. "You look like you care, and Sebastian is still watching too closely."

Buck struggled to school his expression, to relax his jaw, but his muscles only coiled tighter. Ali and Mindy were in Detective O'Connor's hands now. The rest was up to Carrie. Would Alistar connect with her? Would she be able to hook the man into letting her help him? This put her in the lion's den. Not that she couldn't handle it—she'd faced dangerous mafiosos and powerful politicians without blinking an eye.

But if something happened to her because Buck begged for her help? He'd left her to keep her safe, and here he'd dragged her right back into the middle of his mess. What was he thinking? He needed to call off the whole charade. No undercover work for her. Ali needed to take Carrie back to Chicago. They needed to forget about him. He'd figure this out on his own.

Before he could take a step to disrupt their carefully laid plans, the happy squeal of children met his ears. Usually, Marian Ward Cox's two girls would be chasing the other children who now dodged through the wedding guests, but Gil had taken his family west to keep them safe. They now lived in Blue Spruce, Montana, near Crooked Tooth Ranch where Silas Ward was foreman.

Quietly standing off to the side, watching the children race by was Nick's sister Bella who held hands with Mindy's little sister, Mabel. The poor girl had uncovered a counterfeit ring that had stolen her voice. As far as he knew, she still hadn't spoken more than a word or two. She should be running after the other children, not watching from the edges.

Buck rubbed the heel of his palm under his left collarbone. This had to end before more children were put in danger. Even if it meant putting

Carrie's life in danger. He had no qualms risking his own, but Carrie? She knew the costs, of course. Still, if something happened to her ...

Nick moved to block Buck's view of her. "You okay?"

"Yeah." He ground out the word, hauled in a bucket of air only for stars to dance across his vision. He stepped sideways. What was going on?

"You nauseous?" Nick's voice scattered the darkness. "Light-headed?"

"No." But his heart might explode if it beat any faster. He staggered again. "I'm fine."

"You're not." Nick grabbed his wrist, his fingers pressing Buck's pulse point. Buck tried to pull away. Couldn't. He needed to get to Carrie. Couldn't leave her without backup.

"Why are my hands shaking?" And why were his face and hands going numb? Carrie needed him.

"Inside with you. Doctor's orders."

"I can't." Yet Nick easily pushed him toward the house. "Carrie ..."

"Will be fine." Nick gripped Buck's biceps as they mounted the back steps. "I'll send Mindy out. You, sir, are going to sit down."

Buck wanted to protest. If only he could get enough air in his lungs in order to speak.

CHAPTER THREE

As Ali and Mindy disappeared into the house, Carrie turned her back on everyone. Especially Buck, who looked handsome in his tailored suit. She couldn't let herself be distracted. This was the most crucial part of the plan, as she knew it. It didn't help that Ali's comment about never advancing in the industry struck a bit too sharply.

She forced a huff, determined to use her angst to reel in Alistar. "I have a byline, too, you know."

"Oh?" He sidled closer. The man was a creep. That was easy to spot. Or should she say, feel? The way his gaze had wandered over her left her wishing for a bath.

"Women can be journalists." She infused her tone with a dose of petulance. His reaction to being out-scooped by a female wasn't an uncommon one. Women had been making strides in the workplace for years, and during the Great War, doors opened that hadn't been available before. But since then, and especially thanks to the economic downturn the politicians couldn't figure out how to fix—an article for another day—women were getting forced out. Female journalists especially. Which made her even more grateful to work for someone like Ali Di Stasio.

"They find scoops, sure." Again with the wandering gaze. "But women need to know their place."

"My boss doesn't. She's always trying to scoop stories from men." Carrie toyed with the strap of her satchel. Frankly, none of the women working for the Di Stasio Giornaliste Agency knew their so-called place, at least what Alistar would consider it to be. But Ali encouraged them to use the gifts God had given them in whatever avenue the Lord opened. There was no agenda involved. Usually.

"You deferred to her well." Alistar patted her hand in a patronizing way that had her imagining smacking him with her satchel. "Having a more understanding boss might help."

"Oh?" She drew out the word to hide the zing that shot through her. She had Alistar on the hook! Now to reel him in. She raised her chin just enough to show backbone, but not enough to threaten Alistar's masculinity. "How might my boss become more understanding?"

"Not your current one. A new one."

She pretended to deflate. "I'm not looking to leave my newspaper." Letting Alistar convince her to stay would allow him to think this was all his idea.

"What about temporarily?" Alistar rounded in front of her. "I have a big lead I'm working, and I could use a gal like you. I need someone who can get men to talk. You seem capable."

Carrie couldn't decide if that was a compliment or not. She cocked her head, allowing a calculating gleam in her eye. "What's in it for me?"

"Your own article in the *Crow's Nest Gazette*."

Carrie feigned excitement. Little did Alistar know she'd already been featured in that little paper because her investigative articles were occasionally picked up by big city syndication services. But he didn't know mousy Carrie Neary was big-hitting C. C. Wagner. Frankly, most people thought Wagner was a man. Carrie didn't mind because it allowed her better undercover protection when going up against crooked politicians, dirty cops, and mafioso types. Her bread and butter.

"What do you say, Neary?" Alistar waggled his brows. "First assignment is to get me the scoop on Adaleigh Sirland's wedding preparations."

Carrie made a show of considering, then allowed a speculative smile. "If I give you the bridal story, what wedding-related byline can I get?"

Alistar tossed his head back with a laugh. "I like you."

Carrie pursed her lips, waiting.

Alistar leaned too close. His breath smelled like stale coffee. "Find out why Buck Wilson clutched his chest like he might keel over."

Carrie narrowed her eyes to keep away any other emotion except the calculation she wanted Alistar to see. But her pulse raced. Was Buck suffering a myocardial infarction? Those could kill. If only she had seen what happened. But she had purposefully kept her gaze away from him. Didn't want anyone to guess they knew each other, let alone that they were once in love. Her reaction now whispered that *once* wasn't so long ago.

She faked confusion to hide the unnatural pause and jutted out a hip on which to rest her hand. "You going to tell me who in the world this Buck Wilson person is and why he's my assignment?"

Alistar's mouth quirked in an approving grin. Heavens! That had been a test. And unless Alistar was a phenomenal actor, she passed. "He's head of the Crow's Nest Conglomerate and a thorn in my side."

"Okay. Guess I'll find out what that means on my own since you insist on being cryptic." Carrie pulled out a notepad and pencil. Did that mean Buck was actually ill, or had Alistar made up the story? She needed to get into the house to find out. "Do you have an angle in mind? Specific dirt you want me to find?"

"Anything to get him discredited." Alistar crossed his arms, his focus over Carrie's shoulder. "Get close to him. Find out all his little secrets. I need something I can use. Can you do that?"

Carrie allowed a genuine smile this time. She was in. "Absolutely."

"Good. Now we need a place for you to stay."

Before he could suggest something unsavory, Carrie asked, "Is there a female boarding house?"

"No." He wagged a finger at her. "But Martins's grandmother takes in women off the street. If you stay there, you could be my inside woman."

This was even better than expected. "Okay. Who is she?"

"Get friendly with that dame who brought you over. Mindy Zahn. She's as naïve as a child. Win her over and she'll tell you everything you need to know."

Carrie grinned. "Gladly."

"Now, go be a good girl and get me my bridal story." He slapped her hindquarters as he shooed her toward the house. Carrie resisted slapping him across the face. Barely. "And don't forget the scoop on Wilson's health."

Good thing she was watching her step or that last bit would have made her stumble. All the positive feelings of a successful entry into undercover work washed away with that news. Was Buck really having a health crisis? He mentioned nothing of the kind. Not that he should have, or that their relationship warranted it. They were strangers now, not a couple on the way to the altar. He owed her nothing.

As she reached the back steps, she took one last look out over the wedding area to settle her nerves. More guests had swelled the crowd. No wonder the ceremony was outdoors. For the bride and groom's sake, she was glad it had turned out to be an ideal autumn day. Crisp breeze, warm sun, bright blue sky. An article about Adaleigh's wedding day would need to include all those types of details. Roses were interspersed between the red, yellow, and green leaves that covered the wooden trellis, beside which the groom stood in an impeccable black suit.

She recognized David Martins—light brown hair, lithe frame, friendly smile—from the engagement announcement she'd discovered while doing research on Adaleigh Sirland before arriving in Crow's Nest. The woman had inherited wealth that hadn't taken too harsh a hit when the stock market crashed in '29. She disappeared in May of last year after her parents were killed, only to resurface as an heiress. Not much was known about the interval, or where she kept herself. Her lawyer and business manager kept the press and nosy citizens out of her way. Curiosity had Carrie looking forward to meeting the woman.

Lord, please bless this assignment. I seek the truth. Help me shine a light in the darkness.

It was a prayer she prayed at the beginning of any undercover work. Adaleigh and David wouldn't likely learn Carrie's true reason for being in Crow's Nest. Would they welcome a nosy reporter staying in their grandmother's house? Doubtful. So how could Carrie spin her reason for being here without giving away her cover? Or revealing Buck's history? Wait, Detective O'Connor was David's uncle. He would know how to spin the tale. She'd present the problem to him first.

Ready to get to work, Carrie pulled open the back door, prepared to find the older man. After she discovered the truth about whether Buck's heart put his life in danger. Because even though he had left her, she still cared. Much more than she wanted to.

The back screen door slapped shut behind Buck. He tried to dig in his heels, but Nick's grip proved too strong. For a bookish man, the doctor had hidden power and Buck didn't appreciate it turned against him. The house had been designated as a woman-only area for Adaleigh to prepare for her wedding ceremony. He—they—didn't belong here.

Mrs. Martins, David's grandmother, swept into the kitchen. But even as her mouth opened with what was sure to be a reprimand, her blue eyes morphed from perturbed to concerned.

"Is it the heat?" She pressed cool hands to Buck's forehead, then moved his chin to peer into his eyes. Marie Martins might be a short, round, grandmotherly woman, but she had the ability to manage the strongest personalities.

"I need to make sure it's not a myocardial infarction," Nick spoke with cool authority. Cold shivered down Buck's sweating back. David was going to kill Buck for ruining his wedding day. If his heart didn't kill him first.

"Goodness!" Mrs. Martins pressed a weathered hand to her chest. She wore an elegant, dark purple dress with a ribbon around the waist, a ribbon Buck stared at as he attempted to breathe past the band around his chest. "Take him upstairs."

When not used as a wedding venue, the Whittlebush house was the Whittlebush Clinic, with patient rooms located on the second floor.

"What's going on?" Mindy blocked their path to the stairs, her gaze quickly taking in everything. Buck had learned early on never to assume her bubbly innocence didn't mean she was unintelligent. She had a way with people, and now that she had Nick's protective presence in her life, she'd blossomed into someone Buck knew he could trust.

Nick repeated himself as Ali and Mrs. Whittlebush, the widow who had donated her house to be used as a clinic and was now visiting from out west, emerged from the parlor. Mortification burned in Buck's stomach as Ali listened intently to Nick's assessment. What a failure he would appear in her eyes. She'd warn Carrie away. Leave him to the consequences of his choices. Second chances were for good men like Nick and David. Not Buck.

Mindy tucked her arm around his, drawing his attention from the sense of dread that threatened to swamp him to the purple hat she wore. Nick's deep accented tone rumbled, but Buck latched onto Mindy's compassionate smile. Perhaps she spoke, because her lips moved, but the rushing in his ears prevented him from hearing her.

And then Mindy was leading the way upstairs, her skirt swishing, Nick supporting Buck as they climbed. Buck could only hope Adaleigh would stay focused on getting ready for her big day. Not on the disruption he was causing. He shouldn't have let O'Connor commandeer his nephew's big day, even if Adaleigh's heiress status provided the perfect cover for Carrie's arrival.

Divested of his jacket and vest, Buck sat on the edge of the bed in one of the rooms as Nick listened to his heart and lungs, and checked his pulse. Mindy hovered nearby, ready to be a nurse should Nick need her, even dressed as a bridesmaid. Ali delivered a bucket of water, then stayed near the door. For such a small woman, she packed a powerful presence. He wished she would leave. No doubt she'd report to Carrie how pitiful Buck had become, how grateful she should be to have escaped a man such as him.

Finally, Nick wrapped his stethoscope around his neck and stepped back. "Not your heart."

"And that's my cue." Adaleigh swept into the room, holding up the train of her swishing white dress, her brown hair a halo of curls. What was she doing here?

"Not your cue." Mindy blocked her. "You need your veil. The wedding begins in half an hour."

"And I can help." Adaleigh twisted around her friend and sat beside Buck on the bed. Closer than she should. Nor should she put her hand on his shoulder as she did. Embarrassment washed through him.

"You shouldn't be here." Buck dropped his chin to his chest. David would be livid when he learned of this. He already hated Buck. If Buck delayed his bride ...

"When did the anxiety start?" Adaleigh's question was quiet.

"That's what this is?" Buck rubbed his sore chest.

Detective O'Connor stepped into the room, one bushy eyebrow raised as he took in the scene. The undercover plan that started out so well was disintegrating before Buck's eyes. Because of him. All his work over the past two years. The sacrifices.

He met Ali's dark gaze. "Carrie lucked out."

"I did?" The woman herself hurried into the room, concern lining her beautiful face. A face he'd seen in his dreams over and over since he'd left. "Is it your heart?"

"It's an anxiety attack, right, Dr. Matrone?" Adaleigh answered Carrie's question.

Anxiety? He was disrupting Adaleigh's wedding because of a little worry? Shame had him pressing his palms onto the mattress on either side of his hips. His left fingers snagged on the silk of Adaleigh's gown. Before he could snatch his hand away, Adaleigh covered his hand with her own.

"You've been having these attacks for a while, haven't you?" Nick crossed his arms. Buck had first told Nick about his lack of sleep, and Nick warned things would get worse if he didn't rest. Well ... apparently they had. At the worst possible time.

"I told you. This is what happens when—" Carrie bit off her words, thankfully reining in her frustration at him before revealing their undercover operation. He'd been under too long. He knew. She knew. And his health showed it. Did anyone else guess? Was he on the verge of blowing his cover?

"It doesn't matter." Buck stood, shrugging on his vest and doing up the buttons, needing to get away from all the prying eyes. "It's Adaleigh's wedding, and I won't disrupt it."

He reached for his jacket, and Adaleigh planted a hand on the fabric. "You didn't purposefully have the attack, Buck."

"It's over now. I'm fine." He tugged on his jacket. Adaleigh didn't budge, even when he looked at her with exasperation.

"You're not fine, Buck. I should know."

Surprised not to see pity or annoyance, but empathy in her eyes, he stammered. "What ... what do you mean?"

Adaleigh stood, clasping her hands at her waist. "When I first arrived in Crow's Nest, I had horrible anxiety. One night, I woke David with a scream he thought meant I'd been harmed. I hadn't been, not in reality, but in my memories. They were so real." She shook her head.

"I don't have that." Buck shoved his hands into his pockets, needing some control over this conversation. There were too many people listening.

"But that heart-racing band that wrapped around you here?" Adaleigh patted his chest as if it were perfectly acceptable for a bride to do so to a man who was not her groom. "I studied psychology, Buck, but I've also felt it. Why do you think it took David and me this long to reach the point of marriage when our friendship turned romantic so quickly? I wasn't ready because I needed to heal inside first."

Buck scuffed his shoe on the rug, not sure what to say. He dared not look at Carrie. Or Ali. Or anyone else in the room. What must they be thinking right now?

"I know you like to appear unaffected, but ..." Adaleigh's tone changed to one of calculation. "But you've been holding this town together even while fending off an overzealous detective. And now you experience an attack of anxiety on the very day two newspaper women appear in town and have a verbal battle with a certain unscrupulous journalist. I'm not blind, Mr. Wilson. Of course, it's all connected."

"You're too observant," Buck muttered.

Adaleigh laughed. "So, who are these two lovely ladies to you? Because I don't buy for a minute they're journalists here just for my wedding."

"They are journalists." Buck waved Carrie and Ali forward. Might as well be honest since Adaleigh had figured it out thus far. "Meet Ali Di Stasio, founder of the Di Stasio Giornaliste Agency. And one of her journalists, Caroline Wagoneer."

Adaleigh's eyes widened and she eagerly shook their hands, lingering with Ali, excitement quickening her words. "Miss Di Stasio, I have to tell you, you're one of my heroes. Your work in helping women ... I have such respect for your search for the truth."

Buck couldn't help a glance at Carrie. Adaleigh knew Ali? Or only her byline? Never had he heard her gush like this before. Carrie gave a little shrug, like maybe she saw this often.

"A few years ago," Adaleigh continued, "you uncovered a corruption scandal involving an acquaintance of my father's. I'd been home from university at the time and remember vividly how triumphantly my father handed me the newspaper. He'd been trying to expose the man for years and was so proud that a female news agency finally revealed the truth."

Ali sandwiched Adaleigh's hands in her dark ones. "Then you don't mind so terribly that Carrie and I are here for a reason other than your wedding?"

Adaleigh glanced at Buck, then her groom's uncle, and finally to

Carrie. "I can see I know the least of anyone in the room. However, if it means revealing hidden crimes, then I want to help."

"It's your wedding, Leigh," Mindy hissed, using the name Adaleigh had first gone by when she arrived in Crow's Nest.

Adaleigh merely placed her hands on her hips, the cut of her dress accentuating her narrow waist, and pinned Buck with a look that said he wasn't getting out of this. "Talk. Fast."

Buck nodded for Detective O'Connor to close the bedroom door. Adaleigh was supposed to walk down the aisle in—Buck checked his pocket watch—seventeen minutes. But maybe, just maybe, revealing his story is what he needed to bring the truth to light.

If his boss learned he broke cover, he'd be fired. Telling Detective O'Connor had been dangerous enough. Then Carrie and Ali. The dam of his secrets had a crack, widening as his very health crumbled around him.

"Buck?" Carrie's voice called to him like a lighthouse in a storm.

He sought her eyes, hated the worry there. He reached a hand out to her, cleared his throat. "Carrie isn't just a journalist."

"Buck, don't." She shook her head, rooted to her spot across from him.

"I have to, Carrie." He rubbed his chest again, nausea bubbling. "I can't do this alone."

In two steps, she was at his side. "That's why you asked for my help. We can do this."

He shook his head. "You, Ali, and O'Connor already know everything. Nick and Mindy know you're my former fiancée. Now Adaleigh does as well."

Carrie gripped his hands. "But the rest. It's too dangerous."

"I tried to do this alone when I left you. Years I have wasted. Sacrificed.

What do I have to show for it?" His heart physically hurt, but perhaps by telling his story, this ridiculous anxiety would release the claws it had dug into his chest. "The people in this room are the ones I trust most in my life. It's time to stop the secrets. I need help and you will have my back."

Carrie's eyes glistened. "Alright."

Buck tried to breathe, but his lungs burned. Blowing his cover would mean the end of his career, but if he didn't find proof of his innocence and his uncle's crimes, his career was over anyway. Maybe his life.

CHAPTER FOUR

Carrie couldn't believe Buck exposed their whole operation. Everything. And to whom? Adaleigh Sirland! The woman was getting married in ... well ... the wedding was supposed to have started already?

"All my questions have been answered." Adaleigh smiled at Buck, an odd look in her eye. Carrie couldn't quite name it. It wasn't romantic love, she didn't think, but it definitely held affection. And sorrow. Did she think Buck was the one who got away? Why would she think something like that on her wedding day?

The door bumped open to allow a young woman entrance. "Leigh, they're getting restless out there and you haven't put your veil on yet." The woman, wearing an identical purple dress and hat as Mindy, raised an armful of sheer white fabric.

"Tell David not to worry." But there was a quiver in Adaleigh's voice that hadn't been there before.

Carrie looked first at Buck, then Mindy, then Detective O'Connor, and all of them had the same startled concern. Was Adaleigh getting cold feet?

"Let's leave Adaleigh to get ready." Mindy urged everyone out the door as she took the bundle from the other woman. Carrie drifted into the corner, forgotten for a moment as Mindy shooed the last person into the hall. Forgotten to everyone but Adaleigh.

The bride cocked her head and patted the spot on the bed beside her. "I need to ask you a question."

"Me?" Mindy turned from the door, closed it with her heel.

"Carrie."

Carrie felt as confused as Mindy appeared. Still, they came obediently to Adaleigh after Mindy smoothed the veil out on the bed.

"What if I …" Adaleigh's voice cracked. "What if I asked Buck to walk me down the aisle?"

"Why would you do that?" Mindy gaped at her. Carrie should be offended on Buck's behalf, but she was too fascinated by Adaleigh's question.

"Are you asking my permission?" Carrie asked. She was missing something. Had to be.

"I wasn't about to ask my old lawyer, Mr. Binitari. I was too mad after he refused to extend an invitation to my sister. Her doctors wouldn't allow her to leave the asylum, anyway." Adaleigh's chin quivered. "So we asked David's uncle …"

"But?" Carrie prompted, glossing over all the information in Adaleigh's explanation.

"I miss them so much." Adaleigh covered her face as a sob shook her shoulders.

Who? Carrie mouthed to Mindy, whose searching eyes went wide. Suddenly Carrie gasped. "Your parents!"

The car accident. The reason Adaleigh fled her home. Why she ended up in Crow's Nest. She'd mentioned her father knew of Ali's work, so perhaps having Ali and Carrie here added to Adaleigh's angst. They were a connection to her parents, to her sister, to life … before.

Adaleigh sobbed harder, bent double. Surely tears dripped onto her dress. Mindy stared in frozen bewilderment. Time for Carrie to take charge. Carrie knew all about what it meant not to have a living father when planning one's wedding day. Even though Carrie had never actually made it down the aisle, she had asked Ali's husband to give her away.

Carrie rested a hand on Adaleigh's silk-covered shoulder but put her attention on Mindy. "Go find David. If they don't want to see each other before the wedding, he can at least stand on the other side of the door so they can talk."

Mindy agreed and swept from the room. Low voices rumbled from outside, but no one came in. Good. Adaleigh didn't need an audience. This wasn't cold feet. In fact, it was the opposite. Today was the most important day of her life, and two of the people she loved most in the world wouldn't be here. Carrie's presence hadn't helped, and as she considered it, Buck's anxiety attack and subsequent story had been a way for Adaleigh to push away the emotion instead of dealing with it. It may have worked if Ali hadn't been here, bringing to life the most painful part of today.

Carrie shifted to rub gentle circles over Adaleigh's back, the fabric cool beneath her palm. Keeping her voice gentle, she asked, "Tell me why you want Buck and not Detective O'Connor to give you away?"

Adaleigh sniffed, tracing one of the lace flowers on her dress. "He reminds me of them. My parents."

Carrie removed her handkerchief from her satchel and passed it to Adaleigh. "Buck? How so?" The Buck she knew had nothing to do with wealthy citizens unless he was arresting them for a financial crime.

"He's so ... suave." Adaleigh chuckled as she blotted her cheeks. "Cultured. Put together. My father would have liked him."

Carrie swallowed. "Do you like him?" Though the *him* Adaleigh described was more the undercover Buck than the one Carrie was supposed to marry over two years ago.

"Oh, goodness!" Adaleigh grabbed Carrie's wrist and laughed. "Not that way. He's all yours, Carrie. And always has been, I might add."

Carrie frowned. "What do you mean?"

"He's a flirt, sure, but in the time I've known him, he's never once taken a girl on a date. And now that I know your story, the shadows I've seen in his eyes stand explained."

"I don't know that we can ever go back." Why was she talking about her wedding and not Adaleigh's? Where was the groom, anyway?

"No, you can't go back." Adaleigh sighed. "I can't go back either. My parents are gone. The couple you were before he left is gone, too."

"Adaleigh?" a male voice came through the door. "Sweetheart? Should I come in?"

Adaleigh chewed her lip. "I don't believe in superstitions, but I always dreamed of him first seeing me walking toward him down the aisle."

Carrie understood. "I have an idea. Because I think you could use one of his hugs. And then tell him how you feel. He'll have an answer for you."

Adaleigh nodded, and Carrie slipped into the hall. David, dressed in a tailored suit, so opposite the intensity in his eyes. His weathered face was scrubbed to a clean-shaven shine, and his brown hair was held in place with pomade. Beside him stood Detective O'Connor, another older man who had the look of a lawyer, Mindy, and the young woman with the black bob who had first brought the veil. Buck and Nick were gone.

Carrie looked at the person she thought would be most accommodating. "Mindy, can you get me a handkerchief, a cloth, something to blindfold our brave groom?"

"Why?" David shoved out a hand to keep Mindy from leaving. "Sam said Adaleigh was crying? And who are you?"

"Sam?" Carrie's gaze snagged on the two unknown persons.

"I'm Mr. Binitari," the lawyer-looking man said, stepping forward to shake hands. "Adaleigh Sirland's lawyer. And you are?"

David interrupted, waving at the young woman. "I meant my little sister, Samantha. Now, who are you and why is my bride crying?"

"David." Adaleigh's voice came through the door. "I'm okay. Please listen to her."

David put his hand on the closed door. "What's going on, sweetheart? Talk to me."

"I will." Adaleigh sounded better, stronger. "Listen to Carrie."

David sighed and looked over at her. "You're Carrie, I presume?"

Carrie nodded, shoving away the jealousy that sprouted at David's concern over his bride. Buck used to— "The handkerchief is to cover your eyes so you can give your bride a hug. She needs one."

He lowered his voice and inclined his head toward her. "Why?"

Carrie followed suit, unable to keep the pain out of her voice. "It's her wedding day and her mother isn't helping her get ready and her father isn't here to walk her down the aisle."

As the words registered, David closed his eyes, and a tear escaped, running all the way down his jaw. Detective O'Connor rested a hand on David's shoulder. Mr. Binitari and Sam both glared at Carrie. Tears pricked Carrie's eyes. Once upon a time, Buck had loved her like David loved Adaleigh. And Carrie had leaned on Buck's strength when the cruel world threatened to overwhelm her. Together, they were an unstoppable team. Putting criminals behind bars and uncovering the truth.

Then he left her to go it alone.

"Wait." Binitari edged closer to her, a protective tone in his voice. "Are you that reporter who—"

"She's all right," Detective O'Connor interrupted. Binitari blustered, but Detective O'Connor shut down any other questions the lawyer could have.

Grateful, Carrie blinked her emotion away, then waved for Mindy and Samantha to help David be with his bride while Detective O'Connor and Mr. Binitari played chaperone just outside the door, bickering all the while. Carrie used the distraction to escape downstairs.

This was why she'd avoided weddings over the past two years. They brought back too many memories. Wonderful memories. Yet because of their sweetness, they were painful, too.

A quick look around and she discovered the parlor was empty. She slipped inside and tucked herself into a corner where no one would notice her if they came to the door. She needed a moment alone. To think. To feel. It made no sense, this heartache mixed with such an intense desire to help Buck. She should hate him, run the other way, protect herself. But she couldn't. Hadn't been able to give up her search for the truth since she forgave him over a year ago.

Then why did it still have to hurt so much?

Buck sat at the kitchen table, drinking a hot cup of coffee. The band around his chest had eased after telling his story. He never should have gone undercover alone. Usually, he had the support of his Treasury contact, perhaps even a team to keep him grounded. This had been an off-the-books assignment. No, not an assignment. A gauntlet. He'd been tossed to the wolves, and if he returned with the expected trophy, he'd have proven his innocence.

Two years of his life he'd forfeited to have a future. At what cost?

His grip tightened around his cup, his heart rate increasing. The same symptoms that had been dogging him more and more frequently these past few months. He hated the weakness. It fed the part of him that wondered whether his colleagues had been right. He was a blood relative of a criminal—two criminals if one counted his step-brother—that blood could make him one, too. Just look at Joe.

"I'm surprised Dr. Matrone left you alone." Ali's accent wrapped around Nick's name, the only indication they shared a heritage.

"You're probably why I get along with the doc so well." He used the toe of his shoe to push out a chair for the sprite of a woman.

Her eyes danced at his lack of chivalry, or his silent welcome. Probably both. She'd once berated him for wasting time on holding a door for her when they were chasing down a street thief and then thanked him for doing the actual takedown so she didn't get her dress dirty. That was Ali Di Stasio. A conundrum wrapped in Italian fervor.

"Wedding still going to happen?" he asked. If he destroyed another wedding, another couple, he would never forgive himself.

"Turns out Adaleigh's situation is not about you, Signore Wilson." Ali rested an elbow on the table, her chin in her hand. "That poor girl was missing her mother and father. Signoras Martins and Whittlebush went outside to assure the guests the wedding would proceed shortly."

"And without scandal?" Buck raised a brow at the journalist. "You know full well Alistar will spin this for his own purposes."

She laughed. "Don't you worry about that. Carrie will give that snake a line that will satisfy him and keep Adaleigh's privacy."

Buck nodded. Of course, Ali would be on top of things. He took a sip. "Why don't you say what you came to say, Ali?"

"What is it you think I'm going to say?"

Buck rolled his eyes. They'd played this game too often for him to have forgotten it. He waited her out.

Ali rested her small hand on his forearm. "She doesn't blame you, Buck. Or hate you."

"She should."

"You would think." Ali patted his sleeve. "But this is Carrie. She has no time for anything but the truth."

Buck jerked out of his chair. "You know that's not true. She feels. Deeply. She cares. That's why she digs for the truth. And I hurt her."

"And you wonder how she could still care about you."

Buck turned his back on Ali, hating the way his vision blurred. "I love her, Ali. I never stopped. And yet I walked away."

"A per carità! Sit down. Now."

He hardened his heart, stuffed his emotions, and returned to his seat. One didn't disobey when Ali Di Stasio used such a tone.

"This pity is unbecoming." Fire flashed in her eyes. "You made a choice, yes. That was then. This is now."

"I brought her to a wedding, Ali." Why couldn't she understand this? "What was I thinking? How cruel could I be?"

More Italian muttering accompanied Ali's gestures. Finally, she huffed. "You are not Catholic, so perhaps you may not know this word."

Buck's brows shot up. He'd never heard her English cushioned with such a strong Italian accent.

She pinned him again with her intensity, banishing any other thought than to pay close attention. "Self-flagellation. Some religious orders believe it is a way of penance, discipline, even devotion. You are doing this to yourself—not with an actual whip, of course—but with your words. It is binding you up. Beating you down."

"I deserve it, Ali."

She clutched his arm. "Did Jesus not take such punishment on Himself? Was he not flogged, crucified, for our sin?"

"Yes." Buck believed that. It was one of the foundational ties he and Carrie had between them. A conviction he'd had to hide to go undercover.

"Then why do you think you must help Jesus save you?"

Buck sat back. "What?"

"Esattamente!" She waved a hand to punctuate her exclamation. "It is ridiculous to consider that we must do something to help Jesus save us. He has paid the entire punishment. You, Buck Wilson, are forgiven. You are redeemed. Why must you wallow in pity? Step into the light, giovanotto. Keep your eyes on the truth."

A verse he'd forgotten sprang to his lips. "Jesus is the way, the truth, and the life."

Ali nodded. "No one comes to the Father, except through Him."

Like an elastic band, the remaining anxiety around his chest snapped. "Thank you, Ali. I needed this."

"I know. I could see it the moment you walked into the Agency weeks ago. You've been doing this alone for too long. It is time to rejoin a team. Telling your trusted group upstairs was wise. After the wedding—"

"Buck?" David appeared in the doorway. The telltale puffiness under his eyes and a tightness to his jaw betrayed his emotions.

Buck leapt to his feet. "I'm sorry, Martins. David. I ..."

David held up a hand, then looked past him to Ali. "You're Miss Di Stasio?"

She stood and extended a hand, not in the business-like way she usually did, but in a feminine, gentile way. "Missus, actually, but yes, that will do fine."

"Adaleigh has great respect for you, thus it extends to me." David took her hand, glanced at Buck, then back to Ali. "You can vouch for him?"

"Did your bride fill you in?" Ali asked.

David shook his head. "She said she will. Later. Much later." His neck reddened.

Ali chuckled. "Good. You need not fret about Crow's Nest. The town is in excellent hands. Isn't that right, Carrie?"

"Absolutely." Carrie smoothed her skirt as she entered the room, exuding the quiet confidence that had drawn Buck to her during the undercover assignment during which they first met. "I am going outside now to send Alistar on a scent of our choosing."

"Blame the delay on me," Buck interjected, ignoring David's surprised expression. "It's my fault. Throw me at him. It's the least I can do."

Ali cleared her throat, giving Buck a look that asked whether he'd paid any attention at all to what she'd just said. He had, but he had to make this right. David and Adaleigh didn't deserve to be caught in the middle of Buck's mess.

"Before you fall on your sword like a beaten soldier—" Carrie rolled her eyes— "David, who's walking Adaleigh down the aisle?"

David shuffled, and understanding struck. Buck slashed a hand through the air. "No. No, no, no. She is not asking me to walk her down the aisle. Your uncle is doing that. Not me. I can't."

"It's what she wants."

"You can't want it." Buck stared at Martins. They'd been enemies since Buck arrived. The local good man and the upstart bad boy. Light and dark. Law-abiding hero and—

"If Adaleigh wants you to escort her, then so do I." David stopped Buck's thoughts. "You represent her past. It's a connection you share. I don't understand it, but there it is. And she wants to begin something new today. Having you give her away is a symbol of that. So, Wilson, it's not about you or me. It's about Adaleigh. Will you do it?"

Buck rubbed his jaw, trying to ease the ache from clenching it so tightly. "Are you sure? You have to know I have never seen her as anything more than a friend."

David chuckled. "I wondered at one time, perhaps, but not anymore." His gaze cut to Carrie.

Buck's neck heated. "We were engaged. Once."

David nodded, and a gleam lit in his eye. "Sure. Once. Now, will you do my bride and me the honor of walking her down the aisle?"

Buck held out his hand to shake on it. No other choice but to accept. "Yes. It would be my pleasure."

Ali clapped. "Good. Now that the young stallions here have worked out their male bonding, Carrie, your mind has been working on the other problem. Out with it."

"This was the missing piece." Carrie acknowledged Buck and David. "Buck, I'm going to take you up on your offer of self-sacrifice. We need Alistar pointed your direction, and your health will be the chink in your armor that we need. Obviously David and Adaleigh delayed their wedding because of your health, and then to assure you they held no hard feelings, invited you to walk Adaleigh down the aisle. As you hand Adaleigh off, you will need to manage a stumble. Clutch your chest. Don't oversell it. And Nick will leap to your side to return you to the house."

"I approve." Ali gave a brisk nod. "And will alert those who need to know."

"It is a good plan." David sighed. "But if you have trouble with Alistar, let Binitari know. He's handled the man before."

"Binitari?" Ali perked at the name. "Lawyer."

Buck exchanged a glance with Carrie. Was there anyone Ali didn't know?

"Adaleigh's lawyer, yes," David said.

"I shall go make his acquaintance." Ali skirted around them to reach the hall. "I wasn't able to do so during that case Adaleigh referenced upstairs, but Binitari unwittingly distracted the other attorney so the agency could access the information we needed to expose a criminal. And I never turn down such a gifted opportunity as this."

Carrie chuckled as Ali disappeared. "I say, she collects informants like bees collect nectar. I once wondered how she could know so much about what happens around Chicago. Not anymore. But that is beside the point. Buck and David, you know your marching orders? Any last questions? Buck, I will repeat: do not oversell your illness. David, focus on your bride. That's an order, sir."

"Yes ma'am," David laughed. "I can see why she's your match, Wilson."

"Get yourself outside, Mr. Martins." Pink dotted Carrie's cheeks. "We have a wedding to get underway."

Before either man could say another word, Carrie spun for the door. Buck wanted to go after her, make sure she was truly all right, helping another wedding go off without a hitch as she was, but David clapped Buck on the shoulder.

"If I were a betting man, I'd lay even odds whether you or Matrone would make it down the aisle next." David hesitated, then added, "I might have misjudged you and I'm sorry."

"As I intended." Buck ignored Martins's matrimonial ideas, planting his hands on his belt. "No apology necessary."

David folded his arms, stretching the shoulder seams of his suit coat as he studied Buck. "Wait ... you're a cop, aren't you? The stance. The authority. You look like my uncle right now."

Buck slammed his hands into his pockets. "Keep it to yourself, would you?"

David shook his head. "It all makes sense now. Wow. Okay."

"And not all cops are aboveboard," Buck muttered.

David acknowledged that with a tilt of his head. "Will you be here when Adaleigh and I return from our honeymoon in two weeks?"

Buck gave David a dubious look. Even a month before his wedding, Buck didn't care what happened after his and Carrie's honeymoon. He had planned to take her on a quiet getaway to a friend's cottage along the Mississippi River.

"She's taking me to see her old house, show me the neighborhood." A ridiculous grin wrinkled David's weathered mug.

Buck shoved David toward the door. "If you give even a thought to anything other than your bride, I swear I will haunt your dreams. Is that clear?"

David twisted, met Buck's eye. "You're one of the good cops, then?"

One of the good ones? No one else thought so, and Buck wasn't even sure himself any more. "Go. Get married. One of us deserves a happily ever after."

CHAPTER FIVE

Carrie paused a step behind Greg Alistar in order to purge her mind of Carrie Wagoneer and embrace the persona of Miss Carrie Neary before interacting with the man.

"What did you find out?" Alistar kept his roving gaze pointed at the crowd, forcing her to engage before she was fully prepared.

Carrie eased beside him. "Quite a bit, actually. My boss is still inside. She won't like it if I'm caught talking with you."

He glanced down at her, but instead of the leer she expected, his eyes held a calculating gleam. "If that makes you nervous, then maybe you aren't cut out to be a journalist."

Interesting. The opposite sentiment was how he'd lured her away from Ali, so what was his game this time? She raised her chin. "Fine. What do you want to know?" She filed his reaction away to make sense of later.

The man shrugged, but there was nothing casual about the motion. "I don't know what I want to know until you tell me everything."

Carrie inclined her head in just that angle to tell him she wasn't cowed by him. A little backbone would garner respect, especially when she deferred to his masculinity. As a female journalist, she'd become adept at ... handling ... men. Except Buck. She never had to do that with him.

Alistar huffed, the exact reaction she wanted. Give the appearance of him driving this arrangement while she remained behind the wheel. She refused to smile at her victory. He removed a small notebook from the inside pocket of his suit coat and she made a mental note not to underestimate him. Just because he was an unethical journalist didn't mean he wasn't a good one.

She would need to think several moves ahead of him if she didn't want to get caught under the wheels of this assignment. Like when she and Buck first met. Before they each realized they were on the same side. She'd thought she was a goner until Buck—

"Start with why the wedding has been delayed." Alistar jerked her attention to the current investigation.

"Buck Wilson." Carrie leaned closer to Alistar to hide the way his name emerged with a breathy sound. "Turns out he has a heart condition."

Alistar's pen froze on the paper. "Oh?"

Yeah, she had a heart condition, too. Broken, shattered, and still in love with the man who'd devastated it. She emitted a non-committal hum to hide her pause. If she didn't get a grip on herself, she'd blow her cover before the wedding even started. "So, is the groom some sort of pious former reverend or something?"

Alistar snorted. "What's that got to do with anything? But yes, he's priggish. Doesn't drink. Doesn't smoke. Doesn't swear. The man might have been a monk for all I knew. Before his dame showed up. That got a rise out of him. Still. I don't trust a man who abstains from vices."

He might have said man or woman, and she made a mental note to choose a vice that wouldn't compromise her Christian beliefs. A hard one, that.

"Well, that explains it, then." She rocked on her heels, carefully reeling Alistar back from the disdain that laced his tone. "They called the groom inside so as not to disturb the bride. Apparently this Wilson person had a heart episode. That dark-haired doctor took care of him, so he didn't need to go to the hospital. But the pious part? Wilson apologized and Martins insisted it wasn't his fault. Took the whole disruption rather well, I think. They must be friends because the groom asked Wilson to walk the bride down the aisle, to prove there were no hard feelings. Who does something like that?"

Alistar gaped at Carrie.

She stepped back. "What? I know it makes no sense, but you look like I just said Wilson and the groom are going to the moon. Like in *From the Earth to the Moon* by Mr. Verne."

"Earth to what? Mister who?" Alistar waved that question away. "What you said makes no sense. Martins's uncle would never let Wilson take his place at the bride's side. He's been trying to arrest Wilson."

"Arrest?" Carrie made sure her eyes were as large as teacup saucers. "Wilson is a criminal?"

Alistar gave the subtlest of pauses, then nodded. "Which is why Martins and Wilson hate each other. Mr. Pious can't stand Wilson's reprobate ways. Thus, what you said makes no sense."

"Huh. Then it makes even less sense than I thought it did. But you said the groom was pious, so it may just be that. I've seen religious types do some pretty crazy things." Like hand over every coin in his pocket to a couple street children. Buck thought no one had followed him that day, but she had because she knew he suspected her. How could his fellow officers turn on such a good man? She tried to shove the thought aside, but didn't manage to eliminate the irritation from her words. "Well, my boss took that story, so I kept an eye on Wilson. Like you asked."

"I wanted a bridal story." Alistar slammed his notebook against his thigh.

Carrie jumped. She needed to redirect this situation. Choosing to help Buck was a bad idea. Too much baggage between them. It distracted her, which would surely blow her cover. She sighed. If she didn't help Buck, he'd lose his freedom. While she risked nothing. Except failing the man she loved. "Mr. Alistar, if this arrangement is not to your liking, then I'll go find my own scoop."

"Just wait." Alistar snagged her arm before she could get away. Carrie stifled a smile. The best way to snag a man like Alistar was to make them think they were in control. "Back to Wilson and Martins. Did they appear friendly?"

Carrie kept her gaze downcast, submissive, giving Alistar's manhood a boost. "Considering Wilson appeared about to pass out? I couldn't say. Martins was all compassion, though. Is that normal for him?"

Alistar grumbled something unsavory. She spent enough time around men who used such language, but she'd yet to grow immune to the way it made her skin crawl, like she wanted to scrub clean.

Giving Alistar the lead, she waited demurely beside him for his instructions. Outwardly, at least. From the vantage point Alistar had chosen, she had a wonderful view of the wedding venue.

She'd never attended an outdoor ceremony before. Most of Ali's Italian connections attended St. Mark's, the Catholic church across the street from Agency headquarters. Ali, however, attended a large protestant church with her husband and his family. Carrie preferred something in between, but with how often she had to slip undercover, she missed more weeks than she attended. Still. Most every Christian she knew married in a church. Hearing how pious the groom was viewed, it surprised her they let something like too many guests move them from a church to the out-of-doors.

"Miss Neary?" The familiar Italian accent came from a male voice, causing her to turn. Ah, Dr. Matrone. He cast a suspicious glance at Alistar, who returned the look with a glare.

"Can I help you?" she asked to sever the intensity between the two men.

Dr. Matrone blinked, then focused on her with a gentle smile. "My fiancée sent me to look for you. She was worried." The implied *with good reason* was left unsaid.

What the man obviously didn't understand was that putting herself near a suspected criminal would get her close to the truth. Not all the women at the Di Stasio Giornaliste Agency could manage undercover work. In fact, most of them couldn't. But Carrie felt the danger was worth the result. She had nothing to lose—especially after Buck had left her—except her life, and that was in God's hands.

"I'm perfectly fine, Dr. Matrone." She edged closer to Alistar to give the journalist the idea she trusted him more than the doctor.

"Nick. Call me Nick." He shoved his hands into his pockets and rocked on his heels.

"What do you want, Mat-ron?" Alistar butchered the doctor's name. On purpose, if she wasn't mistaken.

"This seems as good a vantage point as any." He shrugged, turned toward the arched trellis that would be the altar. "My girl is in the wedding party so I might as well stand here with you."

Carrie narrowed her eyes at the doctor. Nick. "Why?" If he blew her cover because of an overdeveloped sense of male protection ...

"My fiancée said to keep an eye on you." He shrugged. "My sister and Mindy's sister are flitting around like gadflies. Where else shall I go?"

"Let him stay," Alistar whispered in her ear, sending an uncomfortable shiver down her back. "Press him for more information about Wilson's health. I'll wander so you can work your feminine wiles."

Carrie clenched her jaw, not sure which man she wanted to be angry with first, but since Alistar drifted out of earshot, Nick would get the force of her muted irritation. "What do you think you're doing? You made Alistar leave."

Nick snorted. "That doesn't sound like feminine wiles."

Carrie huffed. "You're interfering."

"Mindy wasn't the one who sent me." He glanced down. "Buck was worried."

"Why!" The word jumped out too loudly. She tempered her response. "He is used to me going undercover. I'm perfectly safe. There is nothing to get all worried about."

"How often did you go undercover after he asked you to marry him?"

"Plenty."

"Alone?"

The word *yes* died on her tongue as she realized the truth. "Never. We always went together."

"Had each other's back, sí?"

"Sí." The Italian assent came easily, having heard it from Ali all these years.

"He doesn't doubt your abilities, Carrie." He kept his gaze on the door where Mindy would soon emerge ahead of Adaleigh. "He's ... bruised. And clinging tightly to what he can control because everything is spiraling out of hand. I'll be honest with you, because I can see you still care for him. Buck is succumbing to the stress he's under. Physically. Emotionally. And perhaps spiritually—he hasn't talked about God with me, even when I press. If he loses you because he brought you here, it might destroy him."

Carrie crossed her arms to ward off the discomfort Nick's words caused. "His emotional well-being isn't my responsibility. Not any more.

I'm not his nursemaid."

"No. You're his ex-fiancée who dropped everything to go undercover for him."

Carrie refused to agree, though it was the black-and-white truth.

"And." Nick leaned closer as the back door opened. "You still love him like he still loves you."

Cold washed through Carrie, followed by embarrassing heat. How did Nick know all of that? She wasn't sure of it, but the giddy, school girl joy at the thought of Buck still loving her told her the doctor had the correct diagnosis.

"I've been looking forward to this." Nick rubbed his hands together as David exited the house. "Plus it gives me an excuse to dance with Mindy later."

Carrie forced her churning emotions aside to focus on what Alistar would want from her. "Why is the wedding out of doors?"

"For space." Nick waved a hand at the large number of people standing on either side the makeshift aisle Adaleigh would walk down to greet her groom.

"Any interesting guests to note?" Might as well get the information she'd need for the article her cover persona would have to write.

Nick pointed out various friends and family of the bride and groom, names she filed away for later. Then he moved onto business owners, not bothering to hide whether he approved of them or not. For example, Willie Clifford, owner of the Wharfside, was a negative. But Mrs. Collins, owner of the bakery, was a positive. He also pointed out the chief of police, explaining that Albert Sebastian was a pompous fool who hated the Martins, but they had to invite the balding man because etiquette demanded it. Same with Alistar.

Such drama in a small town.

"Do you know who designed the dresses?" Carrie shifted the conversation. She'd get Buck's take on the local residents later. "Adaleigh Sirland is a socialite, so I'd imagine hers came from Paris."

"Mrs. Whittlebush. She's a seamstress, but also the widow who used to live here. Adaleigh purchased the house and property from her, then turned it into a clinic. Mrs. Whittlebush moved west to be close to her niece. That's Mrs. Whittlebush sitting behind Mrs. Martins, David's grandmother, and Detective O'Connor, and ... wait. That's David's father."

"Why is that so surprising?" Carrie took in the back of the middle-aged man. Couldn't tell much other than that his shoulders stooped in his tan suit coat.

"They're somewhat estranged." Nick's attention returned to the door, obviously watching for Mindy. "And the elder Mr. Martins is rarely around. Don't know where he goes. Don't know if David ..."

Nick trailed off as Mindy stepped into the doorway. The blonde's gaze swept the crowd until it landed on Nick, and then she beamed. Carrie's heart twisted. Did she used to look at Buck like that?

"I can't believe she agreed to marry me." Nick sighed. "I will never fail to thank God for her."

Carrie pulled out her notebook, needing to ignore Nick's sappy love-sickness. Such sweetness set her teeth on edge and making notes would keep her focus where it must be. On staying in Alistar's good graces until she could get Buck clear of this undercover assignment.

Although most of the women at the agency couldn't manage working undercover, detailing an event like this came second nature to them. Not so much for Carrie. She copied down what Nick told her about Mrs. Whittlebush, but her own descriptions tended toward the drab or the suspicious. Not the beautiful.

She noted the way David and his brother whispered together and wanted to ask more questions, but Nick was thoroughly distracted now. Carrie turned to find Alistar smirking at her from twenty feet away. She stalked over to him. "Didn't get much from him," she said.

Alistar laughed. "I figured, but you did good. He did most of the talking, I could tell. Anything of note?"

Carrie hadn't noticed Alistar watching. She always noticed. "Something is going on with that Buck Wilson person. Being a physician, Dr. Matrone was tightlipped about it. He preferred to wax poetic about his girl."

"Do you think the man is handsome?"

"Dr. Matrone?" Carrie whipped to face the journalist. "He's another woman's man. I'm not commenting."

Alistar rolled his eyes. "Wilson, you empty-headed female. Do you think Wilson is handsome?"

Carrie hid her unease behind a scowl. "The man was having a heart episode. Not exactly hero material." But he'd never looked more vulnerable, and she'd wanted to wrap him in her arms and assure him all would be well.

"That's Martins's sister." Alistar pointed at the young woman now exiting the house. A bittersweet smile settled on Samantha Martins's face as she walked toward her brother, the purple bridesmaid dress swishing about her legs. What was her story?

"Dr. Matrone mentioned dancing. What do you know about the reception?"

"Looking for a dance partner?" Alistar waggled his eyebrows.

"No. Looking for information. I'm doing my job." She pressed her pencil to her notebook to emphasize the point.

"I'll get you to loosen up." Alistar draped an arm over her shoulder.

"The fishermen provided the fish for the wedding feast. Mrs. Collins, the owner of the local bakery—called The Barn of all things—baked the wedding cake."

"Good to know." Carrie eased away from Alistar, but not before Adaleigh emerged on Buck's arm.

Alistar tightened his hold before she escaped. Buck's expression turned stoney. The infuriating man was going to ruin Carrie's cover story! Carrie tore her gaze away from Buck to look at David. Love shone in his eyes so brightly, it was clear even at this distance. A string quartet played the wedding march, and Carrie struggled to contain the emotion that threatened to swamp her.

She and Buck should have had this moment. He would have gazed adoringly at her. She would have beamed her way toward him. Just as David and Adaleigh were doing. She bit her lip to keep it from quivering. Two years she and Buck had lost to this stupid assignment. To men who blamed Buck for criminal dealings and sent him undercover to prove his innocence. It wasn't right. It wasn't fair. It wasn't just.

"I think Wilson has a thing for you." Alistar's whisper in her ear had her jerking away from the journalist.

"Maybe he just doesn't like you." Carrie gave an exaggerated shiver. "Don't put your arm on me again."

"I thought you liked it."

"I don't. Now watch the wedding." Carrie waved toward where Buck and Adaleigh were making their way up to David.

She couldn't hear them from here, but David took Adaleigh's hands as Buck stepped aside. No, staggered to the side. His hand went to his chest. Carrie couldn't help the cry that slipped past her lips at the agonized expression on Buck's face. His gaze pinned to hers over the crowd. Nick was running forward. David caught Buck's arm as the man's knees buckled.

This was an act, wasn't it? It had to be. But she'd instructed him not to oversell it. This threatened to ruin David and Adaleigh's wedding day. She couldn't do that to them.

"Go find out what's wrong with him." Alistar nudged her back. "He is obviously taken with you. Use it to get the story we need."

"I was wrong." Nick wrapped his stethoscope around his neck as Buck re-buttoned his white shirt. On this side of the clinic, the sounds of David and Adaleigh's wedding faded to a muted, happy rumble. "It is your heart."

Buck rubbed his chest where that organ pounded a rapid, irregular beat. "What does that mean?"

Nick moved a chair closer to the bed and clasped his hands between his knees as he rested his elbows on his legs. "It isn't presenting typically. It's subtle, but I can detect a difference in the way your heart sounds."

"What does that mean?" Buck repeated more forcefully, then pressed fingers to his head. The lightheadedness that nearly had him collapsing made the room spin.

"Your heart isn't performing the way it should. I'm not prepared to say it's failing, but if you do not rest and allow yourself to recover, it will. Do you understand what that means?"

Fear made Buck shudder.

"It means you could die." Carrie spoke softly from the partially open door. "May I come in?"

Buck held out a hand, needing her beside him, but unable to say so. She clasped his fingers as she sat beside him on the bed. He hadn't the energy to point out the impropriety of her closeness. Nick was here. It would have to be enough. He closed his eyes and leaned back against the mound of pillows behind him.

"What does recovery look like, Dr. Matrone?" Carrie took over the conversation, saving him from having to interact.

Mortality stared him in the face. Not that it hadn't before. Being undercover with mafioso types meant having a gun pointed in his face on a relatively frequent basis. But this? He couldn't knock it away. Outsmart. Dodge. This he couldn't see.

"I've heard this type of heartbeat most often in a widow, usually within days or weeks after her husband passes away after a long, horrible illness. The grief and exhaustion takes its toll."

"Buck isn't a widow," Carrie spoke the obvious question.

Nick chuckled. "No, but he's been under intense emotional exhaustion. And then he reconnected with you. All he lost stared him in the face and at the very type of event he sacrificed."

"So this is my fault?" Carrie said.

"Not in the way you make it sound." Nick adjusted his spectacles. "I won't mince words here. Buck realized how much he lost when he left you. And, frankly, I watched the moment the episode took over. Alistar was flirting with you and your former fiancè couldn't handle it."

Buck groaned. Nick was right, and he hated it.

"Then how do I fix him?" Carrie said.

"He needs to rest without worry." Nick nodded toward their clasped hands. "We need to find a way to maintain your cover while having you visit every day."

"No." Buck shook his head. "I won't trap Carrie here."

"What if it's my choice, you stubborn man?" Carrie shot back. "You didn't give me a chance to go undercover with you last time. You left without a word. So, this time, you don't get a choice. This is my decision. Get that in your thick head."

"How could you want to stay?" Buck rolled his head to see this woman he never stopped loving. "I'm weak. I'm broken. I can't even find proof that my uncle is using the Conglomerate to fund his illegal activities. I've hired an accountant. I watched my brother. I—"

"Hush." Carrie leaned closer. "You're working yourself up again. Let me dig. You rest. We can't take down your uncle together unless you get better."

Buck turned away, not wanting her to see the tear that escaped down his cheek. Except, she pressed a kiss to his temple.

"We will exonerate you, Buck Wilson. And then we'll talk about what comes next."

CHAPTER SIX

Three weeks later ...
Monday, October 26

Buck was sick and tired of being sick and tired. He wanted out of this bed and out of the clinic. But Nick was as good as a jailer.

"Your heart sounds stronger." Nick wrapped his stethoscope around his neck. "Your color has improved. I don't like the smudges you still have under your eyes."

Buck glared at the man as he buttoned his shirt. "I'll sleep when this is over."

"You mean when Carrie is out of danger?" Nick crossed his arms. "Or when you've reconciled?"

Buck clenched his jaw. This wasn't a conversation he wanted to have stuck in this bed. Weak. Fragile. But he had to get better. Worse was the look of disappointment on Carrie's face when she caught him moving around too much last week.

Nick pulled a chair close to the side of the bed and sat, bringing him down to Buck's level. Buck hated that the action lowered the tension. His body was still coiled too tightly, something that wouldn't change until this was over.

"I'm your physician, but I'd also like to think of us as friends." Nick rested his forearms on his thighs and clasped his hands. "I'm worried for you."

Buck shifted. "As a doctor?"

"No, *stupido*. As your friend." Nick's serious expression silenced the tease that jumped to Buck's tongue. "You've side-stepped my questions every time I've asked you about God. I'm not backing down this time. Where do you stand with the Almighty, Buck?"

Buck ran his gaze over the piles of papers he had stacked across the quilt. For three weeks, he'd poured over every note he'd made since going undercover. All for what?

"Why did you join the Treasury Department?" Nick's change in question brought Buck's attention back to the man.

"I have an eye for detail." He traced the blanket's stitching. "I barely remember my father, but he was a deputy. Killed in a bank robbery when I was seven. Unable to support us, my mom remarried a year later, but my step-father was a friend of her brother's—my uncle Perry—and turned out to be a dirty cop."

"I'm sorry," Nick murmured.

"I idolized my father and mistrusted my step-father. Didn't earn me any favors. He'd bring all sorts to dinner."

"You became a quick judge of character."

Buck inclined his head in a nod. "I'd been doing odd jobs around town since I was old enough to wield a broom. One day, when I was sixteen, a shopkeeper paid me with a funny bill. I couldn't say why it looked funny, but I knew something was wrong with it."

The empathy in Nick's eyes urged Buck to continue.

"At the time, I mistrusted my step-father, but I didn't understand that some cops were on criminals' payrolls. Did I mention I was sixteen?"

Nick cracked a grin. "Impetuous and headstrong, I'd imagine."

"And lacking in tact. I asked him about it in front of the two friends he'd brought for supper. I was too big and strong for him to give me a whipping, but the tongue-lashing left welts. The next day, I discovered why."

"One of the friends was an undercover agent."

"Secret Service. Tracking the counterfeit operation." Buck scratched his cheek, unable to contain a smile. "I helped him bring it down."

"And he got you a job."

"Eventually. Yeah." Buck leaned back against the cushions. "You asked about God."

Nick went still.

"Going undercover is hard on a man's faith. You take on a persona that, more often than not, is one of a criminal. You have to hide your faith, even if it was the very motivation for becoming a seeker of justice. I'll be honest, Matrone, the past two years have shaken me." Buck blinked back the moisture that stung his eyes and stared at the whitewashed ceiling.

"God hasn't abandoned you." Nick's words were quiet, but sure.

"I began to believe He did. He took everything."

"But?"

Buck rubbed his face. "But Carrie agreed to help me. If that woman can show compassion to the likes of me, then surely God can, too."

Carrie approached the small building on the edge of Crow's Nest Creek. The splashing of a water wheel out back competed with the clacking from the press machine inside. Stepping out of the brisk wind and into the noisy interior, Carrie prepared her speech.

The past three weeks had been a monotonous litany of assuring Buck he could rest and not worry for her, proving to Alistar she was malleable and willing to do the grunt research he requested, and navigating the multitude of new acquaintances who wanted to hear all about her career, and, discreetly, her relationship with her former fiancé.

Over the weekend, when Alistar had her chasing a lead on whether the new school teacher had a beau who was seeing someone else, she decided to move this investigation along on her own terms. Hence her visit to the tiny building that produced the *Crow's Nest Gazette*.

She let her eyes adjust as she fought the desire to rub her nose against the smell of ink and machinery grease. For all the information Alistar had her chasing, never once had he invited her here. That ended today.

"May I help you?" The woman behind the lone desk in the windowless room looked up from the typewriter. A telegraph receiver sat on one side and a candlestick telephone on the other. The woman herself had blonde, coiffed hair and a neckline too low for what Carrie considered a professional standard.

Reserving judgment, Carrie stepped forward, slipping her clutch under her arm and clasping her hands together, the picture of prim and proper in her serviceable black skirt and white shirtwaist. "I'm here to see the editor-in-chief. Mr. Richard Tinnel, I believe."

Somehow, the woman managed to look down her perfect little nose while looking up at Carrie. "Do you have an appointment?"

"No, ma'am. However, I've been working with Mr. Alistar these past few weeks."

"Let me stop you there." The woman held up an elegant finger. "Neither Mr. Tinnel, nor Mr. Alistar, are in the office at this time."

Carrie frowned. "When are they expected to return?"

"Not that it is any of your business, but Mr. Tinnel rarely works from this office."

An editor-in-chief who doesn't actually oversee operations? "How does he fact-check articles or decide when to include a syndicated column?"

The woman managed to give the impression of rolling her eyes without actually moving the hazel orbs. "The telegraph and telephone work perfectly well. Again, not that it is any of your concern."

Something wasn't right here. Too bad Ali had gone home after Adaleigh and David's wedding. What Carrie wouldn't give to talk over this intuitive discomfort with her mentor. Yes, they had a code for her to communicate with Agency headquarters while undercover, but it wasn't the same as slipping in the servants' entrance of Ali's Gold Coast house in the wee hours to speak face-to-face.

Fortunately, Alistar encouraged her daily visits to the clinic to see Buck. It helped that she always returned with a juicy tidbit for Alistar to include in the paper. She and Buck had decided it wise to allow his enemies to think they were getting the upper hand by painting his convalescence as due to a damaged heart condition, as opposed to a stress reaction that would eventually heal, if he was careful. She'd pay her daily afternoon call on Buck to ask him about the *Gazette*.

"Thank you for your time." Carrie gave a polite smile to the impolite secretary. Was she truly a secretary, though? The woman offered her a blink, then returned to her paperwork. Not the most gracious of welcomes, that was for sure.

Carrie allowed her thoughts to take their own course as she walked back toward Lake Michigan. Crow's Nest was not large, but walking from the water to the creek took a good half hour. She was used to walking everywhere, or at least from tram to tram. Cabbies were expensive. Though Ali gave her journalists a liberal salary. Carrie couldn't shake her frugal roots. She'd gone to bed hungry too many times as a youth.

Her single mother had worked long shifts in a foundry to provide for her. Then Carrie worked alongside her until the winter after her sixteenth birthday, when her mother caught a fever and never recovered.

Carrie wrote an anonymous opinion letter to the paper shortly after burying her mother, decrying the injustice of a woman succumbing to a fever because, without work, she couldn't heat her home. Where was the compassion? Where were the wealthy citizens? The churches?

She got her answer when Ali found her two days after the letter was published and offered her a job with her Giornaliste Agency.

Ever since, Carrie had been determined to ferret out the injustices, the corruption, the lack of compassion, especially among the wealthy businessmen in Chicago. And Ali cheered her on, having done the same type of reporting in her younger years. Perhaps she still did, though no one knew for sure. Even her girls.

Carrie reached Lake Michigan a block from the Whittlebush Clinic and paused to look out over the water. Somehow, the same lake looked different here than in Chicago. More blue and expansive. In Chicago, so much waste combined with the constant flow of shipping boats turned the water darker, almost green or brown. Here, the crisp air held the scent of burning leaves, not factory smoke. One could fill their lungs without coughing on fumes.

Having been born in Chicago, she figured she'd die there one day. Yet, standing here on this cliff, staring at the blue horizon, other possibilities entered her mind. Did she and Buck have a chance at renewing their relationship? Could they make their home here instead of in Chicago?

Was she willing to give up her work with Ali and the Agency to live here? Would Buck officially leave the Treasury Department once they proved his innocence and put his uncle behind bars?

She sighed and turned away. Hope was as fragile as a leaf. One day green and bright, the next it died, fell, and curled to a brittle paper to be crunched under a shoe. She picked up a red leaf, still fresh from a nearby tree, and spun it between her fingers. The best way to preserve such a beautiful part of God's creation was to dry it purposefully, pressed between the pages of a thick tome.

And wasn't that just like God? To preserve his children's faith in Him, He pressed them through trials, knowing that, as the first chapter of James said, *the trying of their faith worketh patience. But let patience have her perfect work, that ye may be perfect and entire, wanting nothing.*

Carrie tucked the leaf into her notebook, planning to find a heavier book to dry it in later so that she might have the reminder of God's work in her.

Sunlight glared over the papers still stacked across the quilt. Both Nick and Mindy suggested Buck close the drapes to rest, but he simply opened them after they left. He needed the sunshine, the reminder of the outdoors, of living, of freedom.

Still battling the churning Nick's questions had caused, Buck was ill-prepared for Detective O'Connor's visit. An anonymous wire had arrived at the station hinting that someone was embezzling from the Conglomerate. O'Connor had intercepted the news and saw no need to inform the pompous chief of police since the Conglomerate was his own beat.

Buck could only think that his uncle was planting rumors, which meant they had to be getting close. Finally. But close to what? And why hadn't Buck's superior, Rick Jennings, a highly respected supervisor within the Treasury Department, warned Buck? He was the only one who knew Buck was on this off-books assignment undercover. Until Buck spilled the truth to people he trusted. What if one of them had betrayed him?

His heart hiccuped, and he tossed a stack of letters on top of one of the ledgers Gilbert Cox had gone over earlier this year. The man had found nothing. Everything appeared to be in order. O'Connor had no cause to arrest Buck.

Had the wire originated with his uncle? That's how Perry Baxter had sidelined Buck two years ago. And Buck had no doubt his uncle would find a way to manufacture proof of Buck's misdeeds, this time to send Buck to jail for good. Unless Buck could prove the man was the one behind the scheme.

"That is quite the scowl." Carrie's tease came from the doorway, bringing his gaze to her compassionate smile.

He swiped his hands through his hair and did up the top button of his shirt. He wasn't properly dressed, but he could at least look less like a hobo. Even add a bit of respectability to the fact that she was alone in his room with him. His insides washed hot, then cold.

"Good—good to see you," he stammered. Why did his words dry up around her? They never used to.

She left the door open as she always did, and sat primly in the seat beside his bed. "What can you tell me about Richard Tinnel?"

Buck blinked, surprised at her leap into business matters.

She waved a hand. "Sorry. How are you today?"

"Who cares?" He hated answering the same old question with the same old answer. And he needed a lead. "Why Tinnel?"

"Don't you find it odd that he doesn't work at the press building? According to the secretary there, Alistar is rarely at his desk, too. What really goes on in that building? Have you been inside to find out? What—"

"Carrie." Buck stopped her questions as irritation spiked. This wasn't a lead, this was a rabbit trail. "Don't you think I would have looked into Tinnel already? Adaleigh and I have been trying to get Alistar reassigned or fired for over a year."

"Yes, but have you—"

"Dug for as much dirt as I could find? Of course, I have!" He flung his arms wide. Creating a breeze that sent a few papers to the floor. "Just because it's taken me two years to find absolutely nothing doesn't mean I'm a greenhorn at this job, Carrie. I'm good at it. I know how to dig. There is nothing to find on Tinnel. I promise you that."

"Buck."

"Do you not believe in me anymore? Think I'm so weak I missed something so obvious? You can't simply walk in here and accomplish what I've been trying to do in two years with a snap of your pretty fingers." Buck clenched his hand, willing his mouth to stop moving, but his heart poured out like a flash flood. "I have been over the books, hired an accountant, dug into my step-brother's affairs, taken down a counterfeiting ring with no obvious ties to my uncle, and so much more. And I can find nothing—nothing!—to link the Conglomerate to anything illegal."

"Are you quite done?" Carrie raised a black brow.

"No." Buck flopped back against his pillows, his heart aching and more disgruntled than ever, yet strangely lighter. As if his chest had emptied of the pain that he'd harbored for months. "Maybe."

A second brow joined the first near her hairline.

"Okay, yes." Buck looked up at the ceiling, then back to her. "I'm sorry, Carrie. You didn't deserve me lashing out at you."

"Good, because you're the one who asked me here to help you. Something you should have done from the very start."

Properly chastised, Buck dropped his chin. "I'm sorry. Truly."

Carrie pursed her lips, making him think of all the kisses they'd once shared. "I don't think you are. Not yet."

His turn to hike a brow. "Calling me a liar?"

"Buck." She captured his hand with hers and squeezed. "You're apologizing like a recalcitrant little boy, not like my fiancé, the man who planned to pledge his life and love to me for the rest of our days."

She'd said fiancé. Not *former* fiancé.

"You're not listening." She gave his arm a shake. "I'm not your mother to straighten you out when you go awry. I wanted to be your partner."

"Wanted?" Not want. The heaviness in his chest was back.

Carrie sighed. "You're missing the point."

"I don't think I am." He leaned forward. "Do we have any chance?"

Her hesitation broke his heart.

"Never mind. I shouldn't have asked." *Asked you to help me, to come to Crow's Nest, to—*

"It's been over two years," she whispered. "I thought you left me. You did leave me."

Something in her tone had him sitting up. "Whereas I kept you close to my heart, the thought of returning to you was what kept me going."

She nodded.

"Carrie. I still love you." He reached for her. "I never stopped."

"I can see that now." She pulled away from him, leaving him bereft. "Do you remember how we met?"

Of course he did, but he waited her out, sensing she was going somewhere with this line of thought. He rubbed his bruised breast bone.

"It was your first day undercover." Carrie paced to the window. "I was already working as a hostess for Frank's. I'll never forget when you showed up at the back door. Frank sent me to let you in, just in case you were out to get him. He hoped you would be distracted by a pretty face until he could take your measure."

Buck had been distracted all right. "All I could do was stare at you, and I barely remembered my undercover name. Thankfully, you got me moving again."

Carrie turned and grinned. "Get your posteriore in here—"

"And shut the door," Buck said along with her, making them both laugh.

"Your jaw was hanging three inches off the ground." Carrie wiped at her eyes as she returned to her chair. "I had to get you moving somehow."

Buck was sure he'd fallen for her in that moment. A challenging situation since, at the time, he'd thought she was caught up in Frank's criminal enterprises. Turning her into an informant had crossed his mind, but he quickly erased the thought. As he'd followed her through the kitchen that night nearly five years ago, he couldn't bring himself to use her. He was too smitten, and from that attraction, respect had welled up. He was more likely to protect her than turn her.

Carrie traced the quilted pattern of the blanket that lay over the bed. "That was the first moment I began to trust you. It was a flash. An instant. But your unguarded expression gave you away. You didn't look at me like most of the men in Frank's employ did. Yes, you offered appreciation, but you didn't make me feel less by your stare."

"You know you still make me stare right?" His battered heart thumped against his ribs.

"Now you're going to make me blush." Carrie covered her pinking cheeks with her palms.

Buck offered a roguish grin to hide his seriousness. "It is one of my favorite pastimes."

Her color deepened. Mercy, how he adored this woman. He knew he'd left to protect her, but how had he survived his long without her? What chance did he have of recovery if there was no hope?

"Carrie," he choked out. "Where do we go from here? Do I have a chance to win you back?"

She slid her chair closer to the side of the bed, reaching a hand out to him. "I want to say a resounding yes."

"But?" He couldn't touch her or he'd crack in two.

"I can't set us up for heartbreak."

Emotion pricked at his eyes. His stomach roiled. What had he done? In his effort to protect the woman he loved, had he truly lost her? He turned his face away, unwilling for her to see his pain.

Except she tossed propriety aside and sat facing him on the side of the bed, clutching his hand in both of hers, drawing him back to her. To those eyes that revealed a soul he loved more than his own.

"I have never stopped caring about you, Buck Wilson. Sure those first months, anger blinded me, but that is because of how much I loved you."

Loved? He tucked his chin against the knifing pain. She didn't love him anymore.

CHAPTER SEVEN

As soon as the words left her mouth, the moment she saw the pain in his eyes, she realized what she'd said. A cauldron of unnamable emotions seethed within her. But right now, Buck needed her.

Only once before had she seen him this vulnerable, the week before he left.

Carrie trailed icy fingers along the scruff of his jaw, gently drawing his gaze back to hers. She steeled herself against the pain reflected in his brown eyes. "I'm a writer, Buck. Grammatically speaking, *loved* is the proper tense. Do you think I would be here right now if I didn't still love you?"

He froze, fear sparking in his eyes, his chest failing to rise. If she offered him this hope and stole it away, he'd never recover. Such power had her sitting back, though she kept hold of his hand as much for herself as for him.

"You and I are different people, Buck, than the two who planned to marry. You must get to know the new me—and I, the new you—before you leap in with both feet. You understand what I'm saying, don't you?" Her words tumbled over one another as reality caved in. "Alistar wants me to fall for you. Every time I give him my update and ask whether I have to keep visiting you. He tells me I must keep visiting."

Buck squinted at her, his vulnerability vanishing at the recognition that *he* needed to be strong for *her*. "This is a good thing, right? Don't you think he is playing right into our plans?"

"What if he uses me against you? That's why you left." She realized that now. Saw it in his raw expression. In her mind, she knew he'd been protecting her, but now she felt the reason. "Your uncle threatened me."

Buck swallowed, then cupped her shoulders. "That path failed, which is why my uncle is seeking to discredit me. Causing harm to you will only send me after him. He needs to put me behind bars to keep me out of his way."

"We've never lied to one another. Never placated." She tried to pull away, but he held her fast. She squeezed her eyes closed. "If you and I get distracted by renewing our relationship, Alistar will use that against you, and I'm afraid everything will fall apart. You and me ... we are on shaky ground. We are partners who can't quite trust one another yet."

"I trust you, Carrie." Buck's voice was rough with emotion. "With every piece of my worthless heart."

A tear dripped down her cheek. "But you don't trust that I will survive this. You've lost me once because of this situation, and you are afraid you will lose me again."

Silence hung between them. Weighted. Painful. As stark as black and white newsprint.

Buck coughed. "You always did read me too well."

That lifted the corners of her lips, and her gaze. "I think that while we can explore whether you and I have a hope of a future together, we also must be careful not to allow the cracks in our foundation to destroy this case. If we do not work together, like partners, the way we used to, this will fail. I don't think ... I can't watch you leave again."

Her whispered last words barely left her lips before Buck swung his legs out from under the quilt opposite her, toppling piles of notes. His shirt was untucked from his trousers, his feet bare, but he rounded the bed frame in an instant, and pulled her into his arms.

She tucked herself against his chest the way she used to, and he tightened his hold. *Please, Lord* ... the prayer faded into an incoherent cry from her heart. They had much to heal between them, but she did not wish this moment to end.

"I can't lose you either," Buck whispered into her hair. "You were right. I left you in Chicago because I was protecting you. And because I've brought you here ... it will be my fault if something happens to you. I can't ... Carrie, I—"

Sweet man. Propriety be hanged, as he would say, and she pulled him to sit on the bed beside her and wrapped her arms around him, urging his head to rest under her chin as he barely suppressed a sob.

"What have I done?"

Her heart broke for him, and her resolve hardened to steel. "Buck, darling, you must trust the mind the Good Lord gave me. I can handle Alistar. You know this. Let me dig. Let me loose. I will find out whether he is connected to your uncle. I'll determine whether he is an unwitting accomplice or whether he is a mastermind behind any of this. And I will re-investigate his boss. You know I can find things that the police have been unable to find before. Let me be your partner. Buck. Please don't shut me out this time."

He pushed to his feet, paced. "How have I gone two years without your encouragement to bolster me? How can I risk your life? Carrie, I'm a weak, selfish man." He stopped, stared at the ceiling, then muttered so low she barely heard the words, "I wish we were married so I would never have to let you go."

The gentle sound of a song carried from down the hall, reminding Carrie she and Buck flirted with a dangerous game. Yes, Mindy was nearby, Nick was downstairs, but she and Buck had been weeks from being married. They'd been determined not to take their relationship into a too-physical place before being married—though many of their acquaintances had no such desire—and this emotional conversation left the door wide for temptation to toss those convictions aside.

Carrie rose, but before she gathered her belongings, she needed Buck to hear one last thing. She gripped his arms, urging him to face her. "Listen to me, my dear. You must trust me. You must trust that God will protect me. And if He does not, if I do not make it, then He will be there to catch you."

"How can you say that, Care?" He searched her face. "How can you still believe that?"

"Because it is the lesson I learned when you left." She didn't flinch, but he did, though she hadn't meant the words to hurt him. "It brought me out of my anger and my pain. And ever since, I have been searching for answers for you. Before you ever begged for my help, I've been in this with you, and I'm not leaving now."

He leaned toward her, a flash of love, desire, and fear swirling in his eyes. Then he jerked away and shoved his hands through his hair. "You should go. We have stretched the bounds of propriety, though I know Nick and Mindy give us more leeway than they should. We cannot risk ..." His voice faltered.

Carrie collected her purse, unable to look at him as she said, "Alistar told me two days ago that I should stay just a little bit longer each visit. That I should stretch that boundary."

"Carrie," he growled.

She glanced at him, her spirits lifting when she spotted the familiar protective glare in his eye. She offered him a coy little smile she knew would only irritate him further. "Did I tell you that I decided that my vice is my desire to please? Some prefer drinking, some prefer gambling. Some have a love of money or a love of women. But the vice that I am showing to Alistar is my desire to please."

"Oh?" His glare took on a flirty twinkle.

"So I will be a dutiful little apprentice to him and do as he suggests." She winked. "And stay just a few minutes longer each day."

He snagged her around the waist before she could escape and she squealed. "You, my troublesome woman, must be careful. Promise me."

She raised her chin, bringing her lips within a kissable distance. "Let's bring this to a close so we can figure things out for the future, shall we?"

He didn't respond and she, not quite ready for the kiss she'd put herself in a position to receive, put a hand against his chest.

"Tomorrow I will be back and we will set a plan for where to go from here. I hear you should be close to being released from the clinic."

"Thank heavens." He relaxed his hold on her. "I am tired of this room. The only time I have no interest in leaving is when you are here."

"Hold on to that feeling, Buck. When this is over, we'll have that talk."

He touched her cheek. "I'm holding you to that, Carrie. It means you have to survive this."

"And so do you."

Unfortunately, that might be easier said than done.

"How was our patient this morning?" Alistar greeted Carrie with a practiced smile as she joined him at a rear table in the Wharfside Cafe later that afternoon. The dim interior was a contrast to the bright afternoon sun that belied the chill autumn air.

"He's improving." Carrie sat across from Alistar and, unbidden, a mental image of her former fiancé appeared in her mind's eye.

"Are you winning him over as well as he is winning you?"

Her cheeks warmed, and she tucked her chin. She never had this much trouble hiding her emotions while undercover. There was something about Buck that got past her defenses. Just like the first time they were undercover, and she fell in love with him.

"This is good. This is very good." Alistar unfolded his napkin to rest it in his lap, but she could imagine him rubbing his hands together in glee. "We can use this."

Carrie sighed. Time to stop mooning and put on her battle armor. She could use her conflicted emotions just as well as Alistar. She looked through demurely lowered lashes. "What do you want me to do? I don't wish to hurt him. He has been very kind to me."

Alistar tapped the table. "You, my dear, have too soft of a heart. It is going to get you in trouble someday."

She ducked her head again. Having Alistar eating out of her hand when he thought she was eating out of his gave her a decidedly giddy feeling inside. She mentally conjured up an image of Buck again and allowed the resulting smile to soften her features.

Alistar groaned.

Yes, it was best for Alistar to think Buck turned her head because, well, he had. Years ago. And he still had the capability, even after their separation. Would they have a future together once this was over? Could she truly move past his leaving? They would most assuredly need to revisit the possibility later, after they brought his dastardly uncle in.

She battled back the anger that flared at Baxter, an emotion she wouldn't dare show Alistar. However, her heart ached for missing Buck. Yes, she would need to learn to trust Buck again, too. Trust went both ways, and trusting him not to leave again nearly stole her breath.

"My dear, you disappeared." Alistar jerked her back to the present with a clammy hand on hers.

She flinched and extracted her fingers.

"Where did you go in that pretty little head of yours? Thinking of Mr. Wilson again, are you?"

A blush once again warmed her entire face and spread down her neck. If she did not get a handle on her thoughts of Buck, she was going to blow her cover.

She smiled through the embarrassment. "How can I not? The man is a charmer, and I have spent entirely too much time with him. There must be something more important you can have me do for you. I don't see how spending time with an ill man will help me be a better journalist."

"So you keep saying," the newspaperman chuckled. "However, you are doing exactly as I need you to do. Wilson keeps his guard up around me, but you will be able to get information from him by batting those pretty lashes of yours."

Carrie made a show of looking disgruntled. "We are barely chaperoned in the clinic. If I ruin my reputation—"

"You're a journalist, doll, That means doing whatever—and I mean whatever—it takes to get your story. Do you want to stay in your boss's shadow or be a real journalist?"

Carrie huffed. She knew female journalists who got leads by doing exactly as Alistar suggested. Not Ali's girls. Their boss paid well to remove the need to use such means. She also had the clout to protect them from those who expected such favors. If Buck wasn't ... Buck ... this assignment would be over.

"I heard you paid my office a visit this morning."

"I was looking for you and your boss." Carrie folded her hands in her lap. "Mr. Alistar, I am used to working for an agency. I wanted to see where everything came together. How the office worked. I did not realize the editor-in-chief does not work here in Crow's Nest."

Alistar leaned forward, forearms on the table, an icy glint in his eye. "Do not visit the office again, am I clear? You work for me off the books and we do not want the paper to know."

Did that mean Buck was right, that the editor-in-chief was likely clean? "I don't understand. You said you were working on getting me a job as a journalist. How can I have a job with you if I'm not working for the paper?"

"Because the *Gazette* is not the job I have in mind for you."

Carrie blinked, forcing confusion into her eyes while internally she danced the Charleston.

"You have shown great promise in your ability to listen and obey, and use your feminine wiles for our purposes. I think it is time to see whether we can take our collaboration further."

"I'm sorry, Mr. Alistar, I am befuddled." Carrie forced words from her lips. She had to maintain her innocent cover, which meant she had to tread extremely carefully. This was a step forward, but her persona, Carrie Neary, couldn't want it too much.

"What confuses you, my dear?" He gave her a patronizing smile that threatened to raise her hackles. She pressed her fingers into her thigh to keep from reacting.

"If I'm working for you, but not the *Gazette*, then what am I doing?" Carrie frowned. "I thought you were helping me gain experience so that I could become a better journalist."

"Of course you are." Alistar might as well have patted her on the head like a child. "And we'll show that boss of yours that you can hold your own and rise through the ranks without her stifling you."

Carrie resisted rolling her eyes. Instead of answering her question, he'd appealed to her ego and tried to placate her so that she wouldn't worry about the answer she didn't get.

Slimy weasel.

"Then if I'm not helping you with the *Gazette,* what am I doing?"

"I need you to encourage Buck to have you help him get home."

"Sir!" Back to Buck again? What was Alistar up to? "I have my reputation to consider. I know visiting him at the clinic stretches the bounds of propriety. But the doctor and the nurse have always been in the building when I've been there. But to follow him home? I don't think I can."

A light lit Alistar's eyes, there and gone in a flash. What had she said that triggered something in his mind? She resisted holding her breath in anticipation of what he would reveal next. She knew she was on the cusp of something big, and she had to play her cards right or risk blowing everything to bits.

When Alistar remained quiet, Carrie sighed. She'd have to give a little nudge. "Mr. Alistar, please stop talking in riddles. I don't understand what you're expecting of me. I have done everything you have asked so far, and I don't understand how following a man home is going to help me. Maybe I should return to Chicago. My boss is exacting, but at least I understand what she expects from me. She left me here to follow up on the wedding drama, which I completed. She will fire me if I don't keep feeding her stories." She pursed her lips into a pout.

"Don't you worry that pretty head of yours." Alistar's eyes dipped below her chin and she dug her nails into her leg to keep from leveling the smarmy man. "I will make it very plain when the time is right. For now, I need you to take one task at a time. I'm working on the details behind the scenes. Your task is to make sure Buck invites you to help him get home from the clinic. That is your task. Do you think you can handle that much?"

Oh, she wanted to throttle him! The challenge mixed with doubt was Alistar's attempt at goading her. It did that, and more. But knowing Carrie Wagoneer's reaction and Carrie Neary's reaction would be different, she forced herself to stay in character. Alistar expected her to rise to the occasion, and she did so.

She squared her shoulders, raised her chin, and leaned forward just that little bit. "All right, Mr. Alistar. I will get an invitation to help Mr. Wilson when he returns to his home. However, I expect you to tell me why you need me to be so cozy with the man. Otherwise, I'm returning home and you'll have to find someone else to seduce him."

It was a bluff that she wouldn't actually fulfill, and bluffing this early could force her out of the game before it even started. However, she sensed rolling over too easily wouldn't earn her what she actually wanted: knowledge of Alistar's end purpose.

Rising, Carrie gathered her things. Alistar grabbed her wrist. "We've come too far for you to back out. Sit down."

Carrie blinked, hiding a thrill of jubilation.

"Sit." Threat laced his tone and Carrie plopped into her chair. "I need you to get into his house so that you can search it."

"Why?"

"Because Spelding failed. I have tried while Wilson has been laid up in the clinic. Now it's your turn."

Interesting. Buck suspected his step-brother had been searching for something, but the fact was, this was the first proof that Joe had been working with Alistar. "What are you looking for?"

Alistar's patronizing smile returned. "I'm sorry to dethrone your handsome knight, but there's a rumor that Wilson is taking kickbacks within the Conglomerate. I want proof. And I want proof before that detective finds it."

Old news, but also the whole reason Carrie was here. "I don't understand why you wouldn't want the detective to find it. If Mr. Wilson is a criminal, shouldn't he go to jail?"

"You're a naïve little girl, Miss Neary, if you believe that." He shook his head. "I'll spell it out for you. If the detective gets it first, then it is evidence and Wilson will have to pay for those crimes. However, if we, as journalists, get the proof first, then I can use it."

Carrie sucked in a little breath. "Do you mean ... blackmail?" she whispered the word.

"I said nothing of the kind." But he gave her a wink.

So that was Alistar's game. It explained why he had such free rein at the Gazette. He was probably blackmailing the editor-in-chief.

But it didn't explain a connection to Buck's uncle. Was Alistar working for Baxter? Or was he blackmailing him? It couldn't be both, and it made no sense for him to be blackmailing Baxter because the man was powerful enough to just have Alistar killed.

No, Alistar was at Baxter's mercy, or the two were altogether unrelated. However, that didn't make sense, either. Alistar was too connected, too observant, had been in Crow's Nest for too long not to know the truth behind Baxter. Plus, he knew Joe had searched Buck's house.

Too many threads to untangle under the eye of Greg Alistar. If he suspected she wasn't all she seemed, she had no doubt he'd ruin her reputation, which he likely considered a side-benefit to encouraging her to spend time with Buck.

No wonder Buck's health had been compromised. The web that had forced him out of the Treasury Department, to leave Chicago, had chased him here to Crow's Nest. That could only mean he had been getting close to the truth once again.

CHAPTER EIGHT

Two days later…
Wednesday, October 28

Buck rubbed his sweaty palms over his trousers, observing the increase in Halloween decorations since he'd last been home. While some of his neighbors had begun celebrating in August, with only three days until a cop's most dreaded night, it had taken over the town.

He glanced at Carrie, who now sat in the back seat of the car. Quiet, too quiet. Today she would see the house he'd been living in since he left her. Would she like it? Be disgusted? Understand?

The Carrie he knew from two years ago was confident, opinionated, able to hold her own in a conversation. The Carrie in the car today was subdued, too much in her head. She always thought out loud with him, or at least they'd compared notes, assessed damages. They were partners. But today it felt as if she was boxing him out.

Or maybe she was just as nervous as him.

Nick drove them to Buck's house in the black Ford Mrs. Whittlebush had sold to the clinic. The older widow had returned to Montana a few days after David and Adaleigh's wedding, leaving Samantha Martins behind. He'd overheard Sam and Bella Matrone talking as they worked together in the seamstress area of the clinic—the room across the parlor Nick kept for his sister to ply her trade. Apparently, Bella was ready to be out from under the scrutiny of her older brother, while Sam was just grateful to be home.

Nick parked along the curb, tires crunching leaves, and glanced at Buck. The doctor knew that this ruse of Alistar's design held too much truth, and having Carrie see this house held too many emotions.

However, this house had not been a home to Buck. It had not been a place of shelter and did not give him rest, which was likely half the reason for his recent heart trouble. He ate at this house, tried to sleep, but frankly, he hated the fact that Carrie was not there with him every night. As he went to bed, he thought of her only to wake in the wee hours, unable to return to sleep at the pain of not waking beside her as husband and wife.

Each day that had passed, putting more and more distance between them, he was reminded that he could have woken to her smiles, her kisses, her compassion. By now, they might have even had children running around their house. He would have been a father, a husband.

Instead, people thought him a criminal, someone to be mistrusted, arrested. Why would Carrie even consider a second chance with him?

"Mamma mia," Nick muttered. "The air in this car is thicker than my mamma's lasagna. You two need to hash out whatever it is that has got you all tangled up because this is pitiful. I'm about to strand the two of you here by yourselves, propriety be hanged."

Buck rolled his eyes, though he agreed with his friend. Since his and Carrie's conversation the other day, they hadn't been able to converse in any coherent manner.

Carrie leaned over the front seat. "Nick, you have to come inside with us, otherwise the pastor will have to officiate another wedding."

Have to? Buck's heart gave a painful thump, but Carrie was right. Ever since Mrs. Whittlebush returned out west, Mrs. Martins had taken over chaperone duties for all the single women in town. Samantha, Bella, Mindy, even Carrie. She housed them all at her home and reminded all the gentlemen, including Nick, that they must be gentlemen.

"For Carrie's sake, I will make everybody a cup of tea the way Mindy taught me, and then you two leave me alone. Understand?" Nick glared at Buck. "Oh, one more stipulation."

"What?" Buck stared back.

"Talk, and not about the case. Am I clear?"

"Nick, we need to talk about the case," Carrie said from the back seat. "We haven't made our plan yet, and we need to be ready."

Nick glanced at her for a moment, but kept his attention pinned on Buck. "Exactly my point. You two need to be ready, and if you are at odds with one another, neither of you will make it out of this alive. Alistar, your uncle, they are coming, and they will find the cracks to exploit them."

Buck ground his teeth. "Why do you two have to say the same thing? It's like an echo."

"Maybe you should listen to one of us for once." Nick opened his car door, but didn't get out. "Maybe mend the relationship between the two of you, because, as both your friend and your physician, you are not going to make it out of this situation unless you end this tension between you."

Carrie patted Nick on the arm. "We are well aware of the situation, Nick. I know you mean well and I know you are looking out for both of us, and I appreciate that. But let us work things out, okay?"

"Debatable," Nick muttered as he climbed out of the car. He opened the back door and helped Carrie to her feet, then leaned inside, lowering his voice. "You need her, Buck. Time to stop pushing her away."

Buck's response was to exit the car and slam the door. He knew that, but he wasn't pushing her away. She didn't trust him. How could he overcome that?

As they made their way up to the house, Carrie hesitated on the doorstep. Taking in her surroundings or looking for an escape?

Buck tried to look at the house from her perspective, to see it through her eyes. It was a two story building, small and old, tucked against the back of the busier part of town. Half-bare trees lined the street and red, orange, yellow, and brown leaves covered the ground. There were other homes around it, other neighbors, all of whom gave him a wide berth as if his home was a year-round haunted house.

The place was supposed to be his place to recoup, to let down his guard. To not be Buck Wilson, head of the Conglomerate, but Buck Wilson, the man who lost his fiancée, the man who was determined to bring his uncle in for all his crimes. However, it hadn't worked out that way. He didn't want to stay here, didn't want to return. He wanted to go home.

But where was home?

Buck shoved his hands into his pockets as he trailed after Carrie and Nick. Chicago had become inhospitable to him, so where else could he go? What else could he do once this was over? He didn't want to stay with the Treasury Department after this. It had cost him too dearly. He wanted to retire, find a quiet place in a quiet town where no one knew him, and have a family. With Carrie. Have the happily-ever-after that he kept watching his friends discover.

How could a man like him have a future like that?

"Are you two going to stand there staring at this old place?" Nick wiggled his fingers, insisting on the key. "I will at least unlock the door and get the fire started. Then I can make tea and leave the two of you to … Just give me the key."

Buck obliged, then cast a glance at Carrie as soon as Nick left them alone in the entryway. "What do you think?"

Carrie closed the front door. "This is where you have lived these last two years?" Her voice was quiet, unsure.

Buck cleared his throat. "Do you like it?"

"It doesn't suit you." Carrie's gaze traveled from the bare plaster walls to the wood framed doorway to the front room. "It's cold and lacks hominess. Even your Chicago brownstone had more character, more life. This … this is like a … a tomb."

She shivered, and Buck couldn't help settling his arm over her shoulders. She was right. It was where his—their—dreams died.

Carrie pulled away from him, stalked into the front room, which held an old sofa and a single wingback chair. She sneezed. "You need some flowers, Buck. Some hope. No wonder your heart gave out, living in a house like this. You should be ashamed of—"

"Carrie." He stopped a foot from her. "I couldn't make it a happy place without you. This wasn't meant to be a home, merely a short-term stopping point, and the longer it stretched, the less I wanted to make it livable and inhabitable. I hate it here, Carrie. I hate being here without you."

"Well, I'm here now." She turned, arms folded, and he couldn't tell if she appreciated his honesty or was protecting herself against it. "And you're not getting rid of me."

Her face flushed red, and she pushed past him to follow Nick toward the kitchen. However, her words stuck with him. He was reasonably sure she'd spoken as honestly as he had, and that it had scared her.

The other day's conversation had caused a crack in the wall between them. He crossed to the mantle, stared into the blackness of the fireplace at the brick that hid all the evidence he'd collected so far, which wasn't enough to free him.

Yet, Carrie's compassion combined with her honesty fanned the hesitant flame of hope that had been lit. And, for the first time since he left her in Chicago, his heart began to beat again.

Carrie's footsteps echoed in the barren house as she fled the front room for the kitchen, and the hollowness echoed within her heart. Buck had been living like this? No wonder his heart gave out. How could he survive here? There was no sense of rest, and while undercover, a person needed a break. A place to be reminded of one's true identity.

She stopped before she gained the kitchen, where Nick crooned words in the language she connected with Ali. Carrie pressed her back against the wall.

How could she admit that a part of her was grateful this house did not look like a home? How selfish of her to be glad he had not made a home away from her? They'd had such plans to turn his Chicago brownstone into a place for their new family. Then he'd left.

Lord, please help me. She couldn't make Buck feel worse than he already did by pointing out the starkness of his house. He'd hated leaving her, and she'd forgiven him, well over a year ago, in fact. And, seeing this house, she knew without a doubt that forgiveness had taken root. Instead of anger, pain pressed against her ribs. She ached for her former fiancé. He had put himself in a prison of his own making and had not found peace since he left.

Compassion washed over her. She could no more be mad at Buck than she could a stray dog. He'd been kicked, beaten down, and abused. Now he needed somebody to love him, care for him, to show him that there were people around him whom he could trust. That he had people who loved him ... one person in particular who still loved him, even if trusting him scared her silly.

Yet, on the heels of that flood of compassion came an intense urge to fight. For him. For them. She searched for the truth because she needed answers. She agreed to go undercover in Crow's Nest for the same reason. Now, however, her motives shifted. Yes, she wanted to find the truth, seek justice ... but most of all, she would fight for Buck. And she would make sure his uncle paid for the destruction he'd left in his wake. Buck deserved freedom from all of this, and he did not deserve the smudge against his name.

Needing to be near him, Carrie quickened her pace back toward the front room. Just as she reached the doorway, Buck emerged. He grabbed her shoulders as she planted two hands on his chest to keep from crashing into one another. Her palms remembered too well the firm muscles beneath her touch and her heart sped up.

His fingers flexed against her shoulders, his gaze pinned to hers.

"Nick is right," the words came out breathless.

"I heard that," Nick hollered from the kitchen.

Buck covered her hands with his, his heart pounding strong and constant.

"We need to talk out whatever this is between us. I thought we could wait until this was over, but I can't see your house, see the way you've been living ..." Emotion captured her voice.

Buck's Adam's apple bobbed. "What are you saying, Carrie?"

"I'm saying that you should ask me out again."

His eyes darkened. "As Carrie Neary or Caroline Wagoneer?"

"Both."

"Are you sure this won't muddle things? And ... and if we go forward with this ... I can't go back, Carrie. Are you sure?"

Was she? Tears pricked. "I don't know how long it will take to investigate your uncle. I don't know whether this situation will end the way we hope. But I still care about you. I still ... I can't walk away. We're in this together. We are partners. And I want you to win me back."

Buck took a step away, and her heart broke as her hands fell to her side. The prickly tears splashed hot on her cheeks. Buck dashed them away with his thumb, cleared his throat, and she braced for his rejection.

"Miss Caroline Wagoneer." He put a hand on his heart. "Miss Carrie Neary."

Her own heart was about to pound its way right out of her chest.

He caught his bottom lip in his teeth, then exhaled. "Would you do this crusty old bachelor the most incredible honor of allowing him to escort you to the Wharfside for luncheon tomorrow at noon?"

She covered her mouth, tears flowing, and nodded.

A muscle along Buck's jaw jumped.

"I wouldn't say the tension is gone, but it's a start." Nick appeared with two steaming mugs. "Now, what's the plan?"

Buck reeled. Not simply cast adrift without mooring, for that suggested floating. No, the last few moments had buffeted him like a boat in a storm.

Carrie accepted the mug of tea Nick held out to her. His lighthouse. Hope flared like a beam through darkness.

I want you to win me back.

"Tea?" Nick offered the second mug.

Buck gave a single shake of his head and pushed back the edges of his suit coat so his thumbs and first fingers could straddle his waist. The action relaxed his shoulders better than tea could.

Until Carrie's gaze followed his motion, a gleam ignited in her eyes, and he realized what he'd done. He dropped his hands into his pockets, heat prickling his neck.

"He's there." Carrie smiled at him over the lip of her cup. "The old Buck."

"I'm not the same man, you said it yourself." Buck stepped back, searching for the confidence he portrayed as the Conglomerate Head. As the old Treasury Agent, too. Carrie had this ability to strip him of all pretense. To lay bare the man inside.

"No ..." She drew out the word, glanced at Nick, then back at Buck. "The old Buck has been tested by fire and will emerge from this a better man."

Buck turned away, grateful he hadn't taken Nick's proffered mug or he would have dropped it. Fire blazed within his chest. Heat of embarrassment, yes, but something more. Something only Carrie had ever been able to stoke in him. He'd yet to put a name to the feeling, had forgotten the scorch of it. It built like the heat of a hammer striking gunpowder the instant before a bullet left a gun barrel.

He spun back to Carrie and Nick. "We need to end this. No more searching for proof. We draw out my uncle. We make him confess."

Nick raised a brow. Carrie quirked her lip.

Buck pointed at Nick. "You've treated people like my uncle. I need your perspective. Grab whatever refreshment you need and meet me upstairs. We're turning the spare room into a war room. We're taking the fight to Baxter."

"How have you said it?" Nick tipped the mug to Carrie. "I like this version of Buck."

Carrie grinned. "Me, too."

Buck rolled his eyes, but he smiled, genuinely, for what felt like the first time in over two years. The lightness inside had him climbing the steps with a bounce. This fight would be a knock-down-drag-out battle that he still might not win. Then again, perhaps he—no, they—would.

In no time, he and Nick turned the spare bedroom—the room Joe had occupied when he lived there—into a workspace, having moved the furniture to one side. A single window overlooked the street, which Carrie covered with a blanket. The worn floorboards creaked beneath their steps as he and Nick arranged a small table with pins and a pair of scissors. Plaster cracks ran up all four walls, highlighted by the lantern Carrie lit to illuminate the room.

Buck tossed Nick a ball of gray yarn and handed Carrie a notebook and pencil, then rubbed his palms together. "Ready?"

"Start at the beginning." Nick pushed a pin into the center of the back wall and wrapped the end of the yarn around it.

Carrie wrapped her arms around the notebook as she leaned against the side wall, pencil tapping against her lips.

Buck tore his gaze away. Now wasn't the time to be distracted. He planted his hands on his hips and paced as he talked. "It began the year of the Crash when a fellow agent went undercover in Al Capone's organization. Capone managed to get the monopoly on the bootlegged supply so that the other organizations had to buy their liquor from him."

Nick pressed his lips together, a scowl darkening his face. Buck knew the Italian struggled sharing a heritage with the criminal mafia boss.

"I was sent undercover with one of those other organizations. Best way to follow the money is to be the one feeding it." Buck glanced at Carrie, those days before he left still vivid in his mind. "The plan was to stay under until the wedding. What no one realized was the organization I had infiltrated was my uncle's."

"You didn't know he was a criminal?" Nick tossed the yarn ball from one hand to the other.

"No." Buck paused, considered. "I supposed that's not entirely true. I knew he had shady dealings. I knew he bought off cops. So yeah, I knew he was a criminal. I didn't know he was such a powerful one."

"How did you find out?" Carrie's quiet question returned him to the story. She didn't know this next part. The reason he left her.

"Uncle Perry came to town for our wedding." Buck focused on her. "The perfect cover to check on his operation in the city."

Carrie sucked in a breath. "You were made."

"And you're alive." Nick's breath whooshed out.

Buck ducked his head, hands sliding from his waist to his pockets. He and Uncle Perry had physically collided, shifting Buck's world as only an earthquake could.

"This is a thread we need to document." Nick unrolled some of the yarn, cut it, and wrapped it around another pin he pushed into the wall a foot away from the first. "Carrie, label that pin *collision* and this one *Baxter in Chicago*."

"I'll add the date, too." Carrie quickly complied with rapid efficiency.

"What happened next?" Nick prompted.

Buck rubbed his mouth. Pain and anger stole his words.

"He threatened me," Carrie said, no question in her tone.

"Not at first." Buck scuffed his shoe. "First, he tried to find out what I knew."

"Kindly?" Nick's gaze bored into him.

Buck nodded. "And then not."

"He physically harmed you?" Carrie stepped closer, stopped. "How did I not see?"

"I'm an undercover agent, Carrie. I can hide."

Carrie huffed. "And I was your fiancée. You had no need to hide from me."

Nick cleared his throat. "Mistakes were made. Back to the story."

"When Uncle Perry realized he couldn't coerce me into revealing what I knew of his operation, he threatened Carrie. Ali promised she'd keep you safe and I took what I knew to my boss."

"Ali knew?" Carrie whispered.

"Only that you'd been threatened, not by whom." Buck returned to pacing with his hands on his belt. "She assured me you had received plenty of threats in your career, and that protocols were in place to protect you."

"Yeah, well, I could have told you that," Carrie groused.

"I needed to hear it from Ali." Buck met her gaze. "Because I planned to bring in my uncle and couldn't risk you."

"How long before your wedding?" Nick asked.

"About a month. It was perfect timing because of the opportunity to get out of town for a time after arresting my uncle."

"What went wrong?" Carrie hugged her notebook again.

"My uncle discredited me. He planted counterfeit bills, got me blackballed. I could go to jail for a crime I didn't commit or go undercover again to bring him down."

"A cop in jail?" Nick pushed a pin into the wall to add to the timeline. "No wonder you took the other option."

"And your uncle effectively removed your testimony as proof." Carrie added a note to signify the pin Nick had added. "What proof did that leave you?"

"I had to start from scratch." Buck withdrew the package he'd retrieved from the fireplace. "My boss decided the best option was to take the damage my uncle had caused me and use it. He made a big show of believing the proof and dismissing me from the Treasury Department."

"All they would tell me was that you were let go over official misconduct," Carrie said. "I couldn't get any more than that. Everyone wanted to distance themselves from you."

"I went to my uncle and folded." Buck closed his eyes, remembering the humiliating feel of that conversation. "He didn't trust me, of course, so he set me up in Crow's Nest with tasks to prove my willingness to follow orders."

"What did he make you do?" Carrie's quiet words brought up his gaze.

"Run unwilling business owners out of town."

"That's why O'Connor began investigating you," Nick said.

"And why Martins, and everyone else hated me."

"But you wouldn't do that," Carrie said.

Buck warmed at her confidence. "I discerned which ones I could trust, and those I told as much of the truth as I dared. They helped me set my reputation and I set them up elsewhere."

"And no one was the wiser," Nick said.

"That was the goal." Buck shrugged. "I hoped O'Connor would find the threads I needed to bring in my uncle, but obviously he is no closer than I am."

"What proof have you gathered?" Nick asked.

Buck dropped the portfolio on the table. "Only documentation of what I have been required to do."

"Which won't hold up because he's destroyed your integrity," Nick said.

"Exactly. I need proof from an unbiased, incontrovertible source and I haven't been able to find one that links to my uncle."

"And the closer you get, the more rope he's given to hang you." Nick crossed his arms. "And the more innocents get caught in the middle."

Buck nodded. "You see my dilemma."

"Then it's time to change tactics." Carrie laid the notebook on the piddly proof he'd gathered. "You asked for my help and it's time to use what I can do."

"You're digging into Alistar." Buck knew where she was going, but fear tightened his words.

"Buck." She took his hands, forced him to look at her. "I am part of the legacy of a stunt reporter. We don't just print news, we uncover it. Like the legendary Nellie Bly who entered an asylum to prove the horrible conditions. Ali too has brought to light corruption schemes by the bucketful. That is the type of journalist I am."

"I know." The words scraped from Buck's throat.

"Here's the important part." She gave his arms a little shake. "It's not about me going undercover, it's about what I do with the information. You need indisputable proof because your voice has been stolen. So you need mine."

"A jury of the press." He hadn't considered it before. It wasn't the way he functioned, but it might be the only way.

"It's time to bring C. C. Wagner to Crow's Nest." Determination brightened Carrie's expression. This was her life, her passion, her joy.

Nick adjusted his glasses. "Your uncle won't stand for it."

"Criminals usually don't." Carrie released Buck to include Nick. "Which means he'll be after the leak and not knowing if it's Buck or Alistar will draw him here to Crow's Nest."

It was a sound plan, but ... "It won't be that easy, Carrie."

"Of course not, it rarely is. It hinges on the ability to reel him in so that he alone must investigate the leak."

"Like a round of poker." Buck stuffed his hands into his pockets. He didn't gamble, but while undercover he'd been known as a cardsharp. "We draw him in, make him bet, then go all in."

"And pray the cards fall your way," Nick grumbled.

"Not if I have an ace up my sleeve." Buck met Carrie's gaze. She was his ace of spades. His chess queen. He just hoped he wouldn't have to sacrifice her to beat his uncle.

CHAPTER NINE

Thursday, October 29

"Have you decided what you're going to wear?" Mindy peeked her head into the room Mrs. Martins had offered Carrie, then entered and sat on the bed. Carrie stood in front of her wardrobe, wearing a simple morning dress.

Mrs. Martins's home had become a sanctuary, an oasis amid her undercover work. The older woman did not know Carrie's history or connection to Buck, nor did she ask questions or exhibit judgment for all the time Carrie spent with Alistar and Buck. It allowed Carrie to rest, since her emotions were a storm, especially after yesterday.

"Adaleigh is better at choosing an outfit," Mindy was saying. "She understands that clothes say something and what that something is. I don't."

Carrie turned with a smile. "I appreciate your company, though. I don't need advice as much as I need a friend." The admission, meant to set Mindy at ease, revealed too much truth. She spun back to the wardrobe.

Mindy chuckled. "I know this is a double-layered date—I also know how complicated that can be—but if you're going to put on a good show for Mr. Alistar, you need to treat this like your very first date."

"I know, but ..." she was nervous. Very nervous.

Mindy sat on the bed. "Because it's with Buck?"

Carrie nodded. It was why she still stood before her meager choices, unable to settle on which skirt to pick. In her heart, she knew the blue flowered skirt with a white blouse would be a good choice, but the yellow sleeveless dress with a fitted sweater would be better. The problem? Yellow was Buck's favorite color on her, and she wasn't ready for that yet.

"Tell me about the first date you and Buck went on. You know, way back when."

Carrie blushed. "Oh, well, our first official date? Let's see ..."

"Wait. A *first official* date? That means you went on unofficial dates. Do tell."

Carrie laughed to hide her nerves. Of course, Mindy caught her evasive answer. "Well, we worked together at a speakeasy when we met, so we were around each other a lot. We often ate supper together, and we danced together every night."

At first, Buck had been trying to turn her into an informant, which was what piqued her interest in him. Particularly because she saw his protective side when he shielded her from the more drunk patrons by whisking her into a dance.

"Go on." Mindy waved her arm to emphasize her wish.

Carrie settled beside her on the bed. "At the time, I thought he was one of the criminals. You see, I was undercover in the organization. But he has a noble streak he can't quite hide."

"The way he cares for the widows here in Crow's Nest. The children, too." Mindy inclined her head. "Or when he apologized for his brother's behavior toward me."

Carrie nodded, unsurprised. "One day, the boss sent him on an errand, and I thought it was the lead I'd been waiting for. So I followed Buck and saw him give an orphan girl a whole dollar."

"Why did that stand out to you?"

"Because the orphan was a little girl, and at the speakeasy, girls, no matter their age, were seen as items to be used. Not to Buck. He stopped, squatted down, and cared for this little girl. Saw her." Just like when they had danced. "And that single little moment melted my heart."

"I've witnessed that attention." Mindy brushed her skirt. "It never made sense until he helped Nick protect me."

"Buck caught me looking and tossed me a wink."

"Did you think he pretended compassion to fool you?"

Carrie smiled at the memory. "I did at first, and we kept a mutual mistrust for another two months. However, after that day, he convinced the boss that I should keep joining him on these errands, and Buck found ways to make them last longer. The boss thought he was sweet on me and encouraged the situation. I went along with it because I was after the information I could get from him. Then, another day, one of our boss's rivals ambushed us, and Buck protected me. He blew his cover for me."

Mindy's eyes went wide. "Did it ruin the investigation?"

Carrie shook her head. "Fortunately, he was able to arrest the men who ambushed him and was able to concoct a cover story that our boss believed. When I realized the type of man he was, I brought him to meet Ali. We learned we were on the same side, and because we were then working together, it took only two more weeks for the boss to be arrested and for the whole operation to be shut down. The rumor was the ambushers spilled, which kept Buck and me in the clear."

"So, did that lead to the official first date?"

Carrie knotted her fingers together. The memories were too strong to change the course of this conversation. "We were still undercover when we went on our first date. The boss got us reservations at a fancy restaurant. We dressed up and Buck took me out for a delicious steak dinner. I had never eaten so well or been so pampered."

Mindy nudged her shoulder with hers. "Your eyes are glowing right now."

"I think I fell in love with him that night." Carrie's voice dropped to a whisper. "He was so gallant, so protective. I could be myself. He treated me like an equal. Then to be able to work side by side with him to enact justice, to discover the truth, to bring that investigation to fruition ... that would have been our life."

"But he left you behind when he came here."

Again Carrie nodded. "He was protecting me. I see that now, and I see it hurt him as much as it hurt me." She'd hardly slept last night as she replayed all Buck had told her and Nick yesterday.

Mindy lightly touched her shoulder. "The Wharfside is no steakhouse." The comment was just what she needed to break out of the memories.

"No, no I suppose it's not. But it is on the waterfront and it's a beautiful day." She rose and selected the yellow dress. "And the event is kind of real and kind of not, very much like our original first date."

"I hope it is a wonderful time." Mindy made for the door. "Remember to keep your head about you, just like that first time. And I know you are trying to trust Buck, but the two of you need to come to the place where you are willing to work together. Make that your goal today, okay?"

"You are a wise woman, Mindy, and I am grateful to be able to call you a friend. Say a prayer for me, will you?"

Mindy agreed and hurried out the door, leaving Carrie alone.

Buck bristled at the number of curious eyes as he escorted Carrie from Mrs. Martins's house to the Wharfside Cafe.

Some gazes were directed toward him, some toward Carrie, but most held disapproval at best and disdain at worst. A few of the ladies shook their heads, probably dismayed that he was corrupting a young woman, yet nobody seemed to hold too much sympathy for Carrie, since they all knew she also spent time in Alistar's company. She was a reporter, and in some ways, it made sense that she and Buck stepped out together.

A chill settled in the air, but it went so much deeper for him. Winter was coming, the season of death, and he shuddered. This would all be over very soon. It had to be. His health could not take much more, nor could his heart be without Carrie much longer. If only he could abandon it all, but then all he'd sacrificed—that Carrie had sacrificed—would be for naught.

No, he had to stick this out, had to see it through, had to prove his innocence, had to put his uncle behind bars once and for all.

Buck held the door to the Wharfside and allowed her to enter before him. The outdoor seating area was closed due to the bitter wind that blew in from the lake. The boats had been beached and stored. Now, the waterfront was quiet except for the frigid waves as they splashed against the wooden walk.

All very fitting, Buck thought as he led Carrie to a table in a back corner. The two of them sat kitty-corner to one another, each with their back against a wall so they could both observe the entire room. They'd always sat like this whenever they'd gone out, always sought a corner where they could sit close and yet have security at their backs.

He folded and unfolded his napkin, then refolded it again, unsure what to say. Silence stretched until the waitress arrived. The grotesque Halloween masks decorating the wall seemed to mock him. He'd been wearing a mask for so long, he didn't know how to take it off.

"I find myself not quite sure how to act," Buck admitted as the waitress left with their beverage order of coffee for both. "I am more nervous now than I was on our original first date."

Carrie had kept her hands under the table and patted his leg, then retreated. "I know. Tension is flowing off of you like water from a waterfall. Are you nervous because of me?"

He shook his head. He admitted to his nerves because he trusted her, needed her.

"Can you tell me why you're nervous, then?" Carrie's voice gently urged him to speak.

He smoothed the fabric of the napkin, cleared his throat. "I haven't been on a date since our last one."

"That's why you're nervous?" The humor in her tone had him angling away.

"I'm out of practice, Carrie." He despised the defensiveness.

It didn't help that Carrie laughed. Then she leaned close, whispering in his ear, her breath on his cheek, "Darling Buck, 'tis me. There's no need to be nervous."

He looked at her then. Found eyes inches away. Love stared back at him and slowly his shoulders released from around his ears. He laid his napkin in his lap and used the movement to squeeze her fingers under the table. "Why did I ever think—"

The moment was cut off when the waitress returned with a carafe. Awkward silence settled, but the woman took their food order and then disappeared again.

"Mindy used to work here. She always made the experience very pleasant. She would chat and put a customer at ease. Nothing against this woman—I missed the name on her name tag—but she seems as if she's just going to go through the motions."

"Poor woman is probably intimidated by you." Carrie rested her elbow on the table, cheek in her hand. "I've heard of your reputation, you know."

His lips tipped up at her flirty tease. "Or maybe it's because of you. You are the first girl who's actually agreed to go out with me."

Her eyebrow raised. "You've asked others?"

Buck grinned at the spark of jealousy in Carrie's eyes, the feeling freeing something inside of him. He lowered his voice to a conspiratorial whisper, "Nobody else knows that I haven't. They all think I've been turned down over and over."

Carrie rolled her eyes even as her relief washed between them like sea foam. She scooted her chair closer. "Tell me more about the Crow's Nest Buck." He missed having her listen to him with that expression on her face, the one that said anything that came out of his mouth was pure gold.

"What have you observed?"

Her cheeks turned pink. Oh, he loved flirting with her, had from the very moment when he first asked her to dance.

Before either of them could say another word, Greg Alistar entered the cafe. Carrie and Buck both emitted matching groans.

"Is he checking up on us?" Carrie asked under her breath.

"Who knows?" Buck scowled at the man as he met his gaze from across the room.

Alistar simply gave a cocky grin and wandered over. "So I see you have managed to coerce the young lady into a date." Alistar pulled out a chair at their table next to Carrie.

Buck glared. "Yes, I asked the lady on a date, and you're interrupting."

"I've come for business reasons." Alistar ignored Buck's irritation. "I need to make an appointment with you Mr. Wilson, on *Gazette* business. Thing is, I need to do a fact check before I publish this article I am writing. I know what a stickler you are for the truth."

The man's Cheshire grin cast an uneasy shiver down Buck's spine.

"So tomorrow, say 8:00 in the morning?" Before Buck could agree or decline, Alistar rose. He gave Carrie a smarmy smile. "Convince him to meet me."

Then Alistar was gone.

"What is he after?" Buck wasn't sure he actually said the words aloud until he heard Carrie's grunt of agreement.

"He has something on you, that's for sure," Carrie said. "Or at least he thinks he has something."

"I know the power of insinuation." Buck rubbed his face. "The question is ... is he holding pocket aces or is he bluffing?"

"Definitely not bluffing." Carrie took a sip of her coffee. "I have learned that look in the last several weeks. He might only have something as good as queen-jack, maybe a pair of tens, but not aces and not nothing."

"I've forgotten how good you were at cards."

Carrie waved away the compliment. "Working for Franks gave me quite the education, but it was worth bringing truth to light."

"Yeah, that was another benefit of when we became an item. Franks protected you for me."

"That he did, that he did. So now what, Mr. Wilson?"

He covered her hand with his. "Now we pretend we are on a date while we quietly figure out what Alistar thinks he has."

"Perhaps after we eat, you might escort me on a stroll so I can see the town from your perspective?"

The hope in her eyes, the promise that this was more than an undercover date, strengthened him. It was too soon to steal a kiss, but never had he wanted to do so more than right now.

Carrie tucked her arm around Buck's as they strolled south along the boardwalk. Oddly terrifying cut-outs of jack-o'-lanterns and witches seemed to follow them as they passed closed-up shops. An icy wind blew in from the lake, sending a shiver down her spine. She adjusted the collar on her wool coat and snuggled just a little closer to her former fiancé.

The beauty of fall was giving its last gasp. In a few days, Crow's Nest would hunker down for the winter.

Over the last several weeks, Buck had told her much about the case. He built details here and there and she'd avoided jotting those notes down so that no one would find them. Which meant they were all jumbled in her mind. She needed to find a place to store her notes. A safe cubby hole or a loose board that she could slip her notes behind.

Yesterday, they'd begun mapping out the case. Yarn now created a web on the wall of Buck's guest room—currently hidden by a combination of bureau and mirror. She needed a reputation-protecting excuse to visit Buck again so they could continue. So she could free Buck from this prison.

"You're awfully quiet," his voice rumbled.

She rested her head against his biceps, her knit hat snuggly securing her hair. She had her unofficial notebook with her, the one that she allowed Mr. Alastar to get glimpses of here and there as needed. It wasn't enough. She needed time. Time to blend what she'd discovered with the information Buck had gathered.

"Are you cold?" He dislodged his arm from under her in order to wrap it around her shoulder, tugging her even closer.

"I wish you'd taken me with you." The words slipped out before she could stop them.

He rubbed his thumb where he held her.

"We don't need to rehash it." Why hadn't she kept that thought to herself? They needed to move forward, not continually look back.

"I didn't say this yesterday, but my reason was more than just to protect you."

Carrie's feet refused to move, dislodging her from Buck's hold.

His arms seemed to flail, his hands going from inside his pockets, to his waist, to loose at his sides. "I needed you to be able to honestly say you had no idea where I'd gone. I needed your grief to be real."

Her jaw dropped. Not wanting to admit to the pain of that sentiment, she grasped irritation. "That is unflattering, Mr. Wilson. I am quite capable at pretending."

The utter desolation that aged her former beloved's face made her regret the words.

"Buck, I—"

"I didn't want you to have to pretend. Not in this case. The scrutiny would have been too much, too intense. I couldn't. And I thought I would be back within a matter of weeks."

Carrie paced to one of the wood pilings that held up the wharf. "Why didn't you come back, then, and have me go along with you once everything died down?"

She felt him behind her, but he didn't touch her. "The longer I was away, the more fear I had at facing you again. And the longer the fear built, the more cowardly I became."

Carrie closed her eyes, a tear escaping down her cheek.

"It was springtime, the day everything fell apart," Buck spoke in a whisper. "I remember the scent of apple blossoms the day my supervisor turned up at the brownstone. He bought a team of Treasury investigators who claimed I was in league with my uncle."

"I discovered that much." Carrie kept her gaze on the water. "They were sure you were guilty. Tried to show me proof you embezzled funds, but the fact you weren't behind bars told me they didn't have enough. "

"It was circumstantial, so my boss issued an ultimatum. Find proof Baxter was behind everything, that he was the embezzler everyone thought I was, and everything would go back to rights."

She turned then, her back against the post and Buck entirely too close. "He gave you two years?" Unheard of.

Buck shook his head. "He gave me three days, and I found enough proof to convince him I wasn't embezzling from my uncle's company. I certainly had never seen those funds, nor did I know the amount I was accused of stealing. But my word was not good enough. I was guilty by association. Then Uncle Perry threatened you again." He cupped her cheek.

"You offered to go undercover."

His thumb traced her cheekbone. "And you would have been guilty by association, too."

Carrie closed her eyes. "You know that doesn't matter to me. I'm an investigative journalist and I seek the truth. I would have helped you."

"The people in Crow's Nest think Baxter to be generous. He has helped people, but when I came in, he forced me to do his bidding or he would expose me with false evidence. I had to make those people against the Conglomerate lose their jobs. So I did." The words came out a croak and Carrie's heart broke. "What nobody here, or even my uncle, knows is that I paid for their escape from Crow's Nest. I asked them to stay quiet, so I suppose that amounts to a payoff, but I gave them enough money to start over in a different town."

She rested her hands on his chest, the strong beat of his heart under her palm. "So everyone in Crow's Nest thinks you're a bad apple, but if we can find the people you helped again, they will speak to your character."

Buck shook his head. "If my uncle finds out that I did that ..."

"I said yesterday we need to force his hand. We need to bring him here so the townspeople can see him for who he really is." See Buck for the hero he was.

"Carrie." His chin dropped, his shoulders rounded. Defeated.

Fire ignited that sense of justice that drove her. She gripped his lapels. "I am here. I have your back. Now you have friends who know who you are. You have a detective who will not stop until he finds the truth. You are in the best place possible to set yourself up as bait."

His gaze met hers. "Bait?"

The idea took root. "Yes, bait. We use Alistar and whatever he thinks he has on you. It's the perfect opportunity to draw your uncle here and expose him."

His eyelids dipped. "They'll never believe me."

"You were never this cynical." Carrie gave his lapels a little shake. "Did you not hear me? I. Am. Here."

"You saw the people in the Wharfside." The words emerged from his lips, but a spark of hope gave his voice a lilt. "They think I've corrupted you, or they lump you in with Alistar."

"I don't care." She pushed up on her toes, leaning her fists against his chest. "You can count on me to fight for you. Forever."

Then she kissed him.

A desperate kiss.

One infused with all the promise she could muster.

Memory of their many shared kisses swamped her, but Buck stiffened beneath her touch. Her heart sank. He wasn't ready. How could she convince him they were partners, and no matter what pain he'd caused, forgiveness and love could overcome? That such grace was already his?

Just as she relaxed her muscles to drop back to her heels, Buck's arms snaked around her back. And there, on the wharf for all to see, he surrendered to her kiss.

CHAPTER TEN

Two years—more—since he'd held Carrie in his arms. Since he'd kissed her.

He tightened his hold, squeezing her to his chest as he deepened the kiss. Desperation—hers and his—added urgency, drowning out his good sense. He knew he needed to stop this kiss. The threat of ruining Carrie's reputation by kissing her in such a brazen way in such a public place ... but he couldn't stop. Didn't want to stop.

Fortunately, Carrie had better sense than he. She pushed against his chest, breaking their kiss. He closed his eyes, unable to look at her. Completely undone. Emotionally bare before her. Embarrassed over his lack of self-control.

Her fingers trailed along his cheeks. "You're crying."

He turned away from her. What man cried when he kissed a woman?

Look how weak you are, hissed the insidious voice inside his head.

Carrie grabbed his arm, turned him back to her, but he refused to meet her gaze.

"I think everyone needs to know that Perry is your uncle, that you are not here to usurp him, but indict him."

Buck shook his head. "They think he's a hero."

"Do they? I don't get the sense that the conglomerate is so highly prized. And if people realize they have been manipulated, they will lash out at everybody, including your uncle."

"And you."

"No one is going to remember little old me. Anyway, the people who matter to us know the truth."

He wanted to protest, but instead, he dropped his chin into his chest. "Perhaps. I suppose if David willingly allowed me to walk Adaleigh down the aisle, maybe this will work." He doubted it, though. But this had to end. He wanted Carrie back.

Carrie pressed her lips to his, pulled away before he could react. "It will work because you are not alone, Buck Wilson. You asked for my help, so stop being a lone wolf. It is time to be a team again, to be partners, to do this together the way we should have done it from the start."

That brought his head up and he searched her face for any hint of placating. The earnestness he saw infused him with wonder. She still loved him. How? "What did you think of me those first days after I left?" The question bubbled up from his bruised heart.

She cocked her head, hesitated, then tucked herself under his arm, hugging his waist. "The detective that interviewed me was determined to trap me into saying what an awful person you are. But I couldn't do it. I knew that whatever had driven you away was serious and I refused to let him goad me."

He leaned his cheek against her hair.

"My anger stemmed from the fact that you did not trust me enough to bring me into your confidence, and that you didn't take me with you. So I began investigating." She dislodged his chin as she raised hers. "I found your dirty cops, Buck. One in the Treasury Department and the ones on the police force. Ali helped me expose them."

Why hadn't his supervisor told him? "Does that mean I could have come home?" Had he wasted all this time he could have been with

Carrie?

"It means that unless evidence surfaces again, there are no charges against you."

Should he feel elation or despair?

"However, I can't find the source of those false claims." She pulled away to pace the wooden wharf. "The policemen I exposed were patsies. Expendable. I thought I was making headway on the source of those false claims when you showed up. Now I fear that if you were to return to Chicago, your uncle would just dump the so-called proof right into some other bought-off cop's lap."

He rubbed his face as hope sank. "You're right." Of course.

"I also don't think your uncle would waste money just to prove you're embezzling when he could simply have someone eliminate you."

He flinched at the truth she spoke. "Then why am I still alive?"

Carrie drew a one-dollar bill from the bag hanging from her elbow. "Because I suspect he's printing it."

Evidence snapped into place. The counterfeiting ring Nick and Mindy exposed. The reason Gil couldn't find anything wrong in the Conglomerate books. Alistar's unscrupulous reporting. His step-brother's criminal actions.

"Chief Sebastian." The man was an incompetent fool, but somehow he kept his job as police chief. Until this moment, the pompous man seemed more annoying than ill-intentioned. What if he'd been wrong?

"Who?" Carrie asked.

"I've gone into this investigation all wrong." Buck took the dollar bill. "I was looking for criminal evidence, but I should have been looking for this."

"Love, you're not making any sense."

Buck's breath hitched at Carrie's use of her old endearment.

She tucked her arm in his and urged them down the wharf. The movement shook his thoughts loose—she knew him so well. "This dollar bill is merely a test case. My source indicated they plan to work up to the point of adding three zeros."

Buck's brows shot up. "Jackson, Hamilton, or Cleveland?"

"What?"

"The thousand dollar bill has had multiple faces printed on it, depending on when it was issued. Most recent is the blue seal from '18, which has Alexander Hamilton's face on the front. The green seal has Grover Cleveland, and that's been in circulation since '28."

"My source didn't say. Sorry."

"That's okay." Buck eased out a breath. "The counterfeiting ring we broke up here in town had mainly tens and hundreds. No thousands."

"Is Baxter escalating?"

"Why wouldn't he be?" Buck studied the counterfeit bill, letting Carrie guide them down the wharf. It didn't feel like the same rag as an official Federal Reserve Note. If Cora Ward were here, he could have her authenticate it. As an archaeologist, she knew all about the history of paper and watermarks.

"Buck?" Carrie interrupted his thoughts. "Love, can you explain your comment about looking for criminal evidence? Why should you have been looking for a counterfeit bill? Didn't you say you found a counterfeit ring?"

They stopped outside The Barn, the local bakery. Like the Wharfside, the outdoor seating had been packed away for the winter. November first and the town basically closed up, except for a brief flurry at Christmastime, until April or May.

"Buck?" Carrie prompted.

No one loitered outside. "I was looking for something wrong, not something right. Like this bill. It's easy to see this is counterfeit because I instantly know it's not right. I don't need to know what's not right, just that it is not a true bill. I should have trusted my instincts."

She bumped her shoulder to his. "Didn't you, though?"

"I suppose." He shoved his hands into his pockets, Carrie's challenge shoring up his confidence. "You're right. I knew my step-brother was up to something, and we finally figured that out. I've known Alistar was up to something, but have yet to dig up proof. Now my instincts are questioning whether our buffoon of a police chief is another puppet of my uncle's."

"See, you have been doing exactly what you should have been doing." Carrie smiled at him, as if she were proud of him. His chest swelled. "And now that you have a collection of suspicions it's time to send in the investigative journalist."

He couldn't help but laugh. "Well played, Miss Neary." He winked.

She beamed, then sobered. "I will see Alistar for our daily meeting later this afternoon. Do you have a pressure point you want me to press?"

"No." Buck rocked on his heels. "Not yet. I need to call a meeting of our friends. It's time to build a team to bring down my uncle. As you said, no more lone wolf for me."

"I'm glad to hear it, Love." Carrie kissed his cheek. "Now how about you buy me a coffee and muffin from the bakery. I'm cold."

Buck waggled his eyebrows, his mind dashing to ways they could keep warm ... had they married as planned.

Carrie rolled her eyes. "This is supposed to be our first date. That kiss ..."

"Was completely in character for the head of the Crow's Nest Conglomerate." A reputation he'd honed with rumor.

She scrunched her nose.

He laughed. Because Carrie Wagoneer was the only woman he'd ever kissed.

Carrie stifled a grin as she approached the barn-like structure—apparently, this place hosted the community dances—where she met Alistar each day. She felt giddy, like she had after Buck kissed her that very first time.

She touched her lips and circled the barn toward the rear, headed for the river that flowed behind the building. Their first kiss had been ... unexpected. Yet she remembered the moment with a clarity that dimmed even the sound of the gurgling water ahead.

The crowd at Frank's speakeasy had thinned after midnight, but a few drunks remained. The speakeasy wasn't the story she was after anyway. She wanted the source of a certain businessman's ability to always win a bet at the racetrack. It wasn't luck. It was a wire scam, and she aimed to end it. However, it required working at Franks's.

That night, a large, well-dressed man had taken a liking to her. Per her undercover identity's expectation, she flirted and plied him with drinks to keep his tab running. But, as sometimes happened, it backfired.

Usually, Franks had one of his goons step in. For all his criminal enterprises, Franks protected his girls, whether they sold cigarettes, their bodies, or—like her—kept the gentlemen buying his illegal alcohol. When the obnoxious gent decided she offered services she refused to provide, Franks sent Buck. She hadn't known Buck was undercover at the time, but had welcomed the feel of his arm possessively snaking around her waist. The other man did not, and when he declared Buck had stolen "his dame," Buck had kissed her.

Her first kiss.

And it had swept her off her feet with the strength of a roaring river. Buck, too, because when he ended the kiss, his red cheeks blazed in the dim lighting. Franks had praised his quick thinking. Buck's gaze had asked her if an apology was necessary. It wasn't, because from that moment, she had determined to find out whether she could trust him.

The rest ... well, the rest of the story brought them here.

"That kiss." Alistar's laugh raised the hair on the back of her neck, but she refused to allow him to ruin the sweetness of the memory. "From the rumors, it didn't sound like your first kiss."

She glared at him. "I've been kissed before, which is none of your business."

"I guess not. However, Buck Wilson is my business." He raised a brow. "You know he's a flirt, probably figured you were easy since you're a reporter. And you kissed him first. Not to mention you spent all that time alone with him while he recovered."

Heat infused her at Alistar's innuendo. "It's not like that."

His shoulders shook as he laughed. "Oh, that's good. You're in love with him."

No point denying it. She was.

Alistar wiped at his eyes. "This is better than I hoped."

She clasped her hands together at her waist, attempting a prim and proper look while shadows surrounded them. "Mr. Alistar, can we get on with our meeting now?"

"Certainly." He chuckled again. "I need you to convince him to visit me tomorrow. Can you work your wiles on him?"

Carrie gritted her teeth without pretense. "Fine."

"Good girl." Alistar didn't bother hiding his grin. "That's all for tonight. I have another appointment. Go woo your man."

Then Alistar walked away, still laughing to himself.

Carrie blew out a breath. Yes, Greg Alistar gave journalists a bad name, but he gave men a bad name, too. Right now she wanted to slap the entire male species for their lascivious thoughts toward women.

She shook off the irritation as the rest of Alistar's comments sunk in. He had another appointment. An appointment she needed to observe. Which meant she needed to clear her mind of both anger against lecherous men and giddiness over Buck's kiss if she wanted to focus on clearing the name of the man she loved.

Lord, please grant Your grace and favor tonight. Amen.

She pulled her knit cap lower over her ears and wrapped her scarf higher over her nose, actions to both protect her from the dropping temperatures and to keep the early evening moonlight from striking her pale skin. Then she kept to the shadows and followed Alistar along the river.

Even in the cold, Crow's Nest was small enough to walk from one end to the other. She walked everywhere in Chicago, so this was child's play—but it still surprised her that Alistar walked all the way to the *Gazette* headquarters, leaving his car outside the barn where they had met. The clandestine nature of such an action drew her like a moth to light.

She ducked into the shadow of the trees lining the road toward the *Gazette* building as he glanced over his shoulder. Unlocking the door, Alistar slipped inside.

Now what?

Carrie crept closer. The clacking of the press machines, preparing tomorrow's paper, drowned out the chatter of nocturnal wildlife that hadn't yet disappeared into hibernation. Why would Alistar not drive his car here if there were workers inside who could see him?

An alibi?

She quickened her pace. If residents saw his car across town, it would cast doubt on anyone who saw him here. However, if a worker saw him here, no one would think twice about a journalist slipping into his own office. Which meant she needed a way in.

After checking that the front door was indeed locked as she supposed, she dodged around to the back of the building, and grinned. She didn't know a small printer building that didn't have the back door propped open in one way or another. Breathing in ink and grease while carefully placing the backward typeface aggravated the matching pounding in one's head as the presses stamped the day's news on the newsprint.

Her senses screamed as the sights, smells, and sounds accosted her when she slipped inside. Yet, awe also swarmed her, as it did every time she witnessed words being printed—potentially *her* words—there on the newsprint for anyone to read.

She shook off the wonder and hurried toward the quiet front room. The secretary, whose name she never did discover, had left for the night. Behind her desk was the stairwell that led to the offices on the second floor.

The presses made too much racket to hear voices, so she turned to her other senses to warn her of danger. All seemed quiet, and the noise covered any floorboard creaks as she climbed the steps.

Breathing out as she reached the top, she assessed the narrow hall. Two doors on the left, one at the end. All dark. Keeping to the wall, she stopped at the first door and listened. Nothing. At the second door, she hesitated. Alistar's name was painted on the glass. She held her breath, pressing her ear to the hinge side of the door. Nothing?

Then she heard the barest thump, a sound not made by the presses below. She froze. Her heart hammered, but she strained her ears. Voices, speaking low and earnestly. Like a ballerina, she scurried down the hall on her toes, then she dropped to a crouch. The scent of cigar smoke mingled with the usual newspaper smells, and a small, flickering light, like that of a kerosene lamp, danced from inside.

Two glasses clinked and Carrie pressed her ear to the wooden door.

"Since Capone's indictment, the boss has been able to open his third speakeasy selling his own alcohol." A bass voice rumbled. "No more having to buy it from Capone's man. No more partial profits as the masses search for places to imbibe. Cheers to open season in Chicago, with Prohibition as our ticket."

A chair creaked and Alistar laughed. "I'll drink to that. Happy boss and all."

The bass voice grunted. "Not so happy, apparently. You haven't done your job."

"How dare—"

"That's why he sent me. So keep quiet and listen."

Carrie willed her heart to quiet. She needed to hear every word. For Buck's sake. For the truth.

"Since his nephew's ridiculous ideals forced him to leave Crow's Nest, he's been trapped in the Northwoods."

Carrie clamped her teeth on her lower lip to hold back a gasp. Perry Baxter was up north.

"What's that got to do with my job?" Alistar growled—or yipped, honestly. Detective O'Connor's dog, and this deep-voiced man, *they* growled.

"He's enjoyed his solitude, but with the snow flying, he's done."

"Then he should go to Florida." A chair scraped and footfalls slapped the ground. "Honestly Douglas, just spit out what you want from me. Haven't I been loyal the last two years? Kept eyes on Wilson. Kept the

Martinses and O'Connor at bay. What part of my job haven't I done?"

Douglas demanded Alistar sit down. A shiver coursed through Carrie. This Douglas person was Baxter's enforcer. A girl didn't live across the street from one of Capone's charity churches and not know one when she heard one.

"You say you have kept eyes on the boss's nephew, but the boss disagrees. Rerouting his business has been laborious, and now his nephew once again threatens to ruin what he's built. So, tell me something helpful." Douglas's threat if Alistar failed made Carrie shudder.

Alistar coughed. "Apparently he is recovering from the heart episode enough to take the girl on a date."

"And what of this dame?"

A chill slipped down her back, reminding her she wore all her winter gear. Only, its warmth did nothing to defend against the tone of Douglas's deep voice. He knew who she was, she'd stake her career on that. And that meant Baxter did, too.

"Oh, working her wiles." Alistar's insinuation didn't even churn her stomach, it made him seem like a boy playing a man's game. He had no idea the web that ensnared him.

Douglas, she guessed, emitted a deep sigh. "Do you not find it too convenient that you have turned her so easily?"

Instinct demanded she get out of there now, but she had to hear the rest, get as much information as she could to pass along to Buck and the detective.

"Do you have no eyes, Douglas? The dame's a looker."

"She's pulled one over on you, Alistar. She's sent two telegrams to Chicago since staying in Crow's Nest."

"So?" Alistar's defense had a petulant edge. "That's where she's from."

Douglas swore. "She's Wilson's former flame, idiot."

"What!" Alistar shouted, not that his apparent indignation would do him any good. "How did you find out?"

Carrie would like to know the same thing. She and Ali had a sophisticated setup to avoid anyone making such a connection.

"Because I know how to do my job. The dame sent the telegram on quite the circuitous route, but we followed it to the cousin of her boss's scullery maid."

Carrie dropped her chin. Such a tenuous connection, how did they find it?

"What's she after?" Alistar asked. "Woman scorned, and all that. You sure she doesn't have it out for Wilson?"

Carrie's ears perked. *Please, please let that be the angle Douglas sees.*

"That is the only grace you have, Alistar. We don't know whether she's for or against Wilson. My contact here isn't in a position to find out details."

Another contact? Who?

Alistar echoed her question, which meant he didn't know either.

"No one to concern yourself with. I need you to find out if she's on Wilson's side or ours."

"And then what?"

Carrie rose, sensing the end of the conversation and her need to get out of the hallway before the door opened.

"And we use her one way or another," Douglas said. "The boss has demanded the end of his nephew's interference, which means, familial connection or not, he goes to prison or in the ground."

Carrie clapped a hand over her mouth and dashed down the hall. *Thank you, Lord, thank you.* This was the break they needed. She only had to get out of here unseen.

Down the stairs she flew as the door opened and footsteps echoed behind her.

Into the office area she ran, only for her gaze to land on the telegraph machine.

Heavy steps descended the steps.

She had to get word to Ali. Buck's life depended on it.

CHAPTER ELEVEN

That night, as they sat around the kitchen table in the Martins house, Buck scanned each face—Detective O'Connor. Mrs. Martins. Nick and Mindy—and marveled at how Carrie had changed everything for him.

A year ago, he never would have been invited to this table. When the house had been damaged by the tornado, he hadn't been asked to help fix it. Instead, he'd been at odds with David, even while delivering news that the man's boat had gone missing.

Yet, now he found himself wishing that David was there. And Adaleigh. They knew this town and were well-respected. If they had his back, he was confident this investigation would succeed. Without them here, doubts crept in.

Once again he glanced down the hall. Carrie was late. Very late.

"I'm sure she's fine." Mrs. Martins placed a cup of coffee on the table in front of him, navigating around Samson, O'Connor's gigantic mastiff, who was sprawled out on the floor under his master's chair.

Mrs. Martins stepped back just as Samson scrambled to his feet with a howl and the older woman clutched Buck's shoulder to catch her balance. He reached to steady her before turning his attention back toward the hall.

Relief relaxed him as Carrie's cheery greeting to Samson drifted toward them, along with an icy wind. The first snow of winter was likely in the next few days, if the temperatures held. Not that snow would dampen the shenanigans that always happened on Halloween. Those had been growing worse over the years.

"I'm sorry I'm late." Carrie unwound her scarf as she hurried into the kitchen. My, she was beautiful, even with her hair pressed around her face by the stocking cap she wore. "Everyone is already here?"

"Yes, dear." Mrs. Martins poured another steaming cup of coffee and handed it to her while Samson returned to his spot under O'Connor's chair. "Samantha, Bella, and Mabel went over to Patrick and Meri's house to see baby Samuel, and so that the rest of the adults could speak honestly and openly."

"Good idea." Carrie took a sip, sighed, then glanced at the others around the table. "Alistar met with someone tonight. I'll describe him later, see if he's someone you all might know, but I haven't seen him before. Neither here nor in Chicago."

Buck stood, pulled out the chair beside him, and waved Carrie to a seat. "Let's deal with this lead first, then go into the plan."

"Wise." She met his gaze, worry churning in her eyes. His gut twisted as he took his seat beside her. Whatever she'd discovered was bad. It might also be the break they needed.

Detective O'Connor removed a notebook from his pocket. "Allow me to ask the questions?" It wasn't a request.

Carrie smiled, seemingly unruffled by the lawman's gruff demeanor, though she leaned toward Buck. Nick had the audacity to wink. Buck wove his fingers between Carrie's under the table, needing the connection. Carrie squeezed. Maybe she did, too.

"I understand you meet with Greg Alistar every evening?" Detective O'Connor tapped the pad of paper with his pen.

Carrie nodded. "He has decided it's better to keep my help off-book, so we meet by the river."

"And you let her?" Mrs. Martins huffed as she slapped a plate of cookies on the table and glared at Buck. He felt himself redden, especially because Nick and Mindy sent him a scowl from across the table.

Carrie rolled her eyes. "I take it none of you have been to Chicago? If you think meeting by the river is dangerous, then you won't want to know where I often meet my other sources."

Buck rubbed his thumb over the back of her hand. He never liked when she traversed the seedier side of the city, but until he'd left, it hadn't caused him indigestion. Now? He forced a calm breath for her sake.

"I can commiserate, having done something similar back in New York." Nick scratched his temple. "But it doesn't sit right that a lady—"

"And that's where you're wrong." Carrie leaned forward, electricity zinging from her body. "I'm not just a lady, I'm a journalist. An undercover, investigative journalist. Criminals, by their very nature, are not upstanding citizens. They lie, cheat, and meet where it is deemed inappropriate for a lady to go."

"Even the wealthy ones?" Mindy's eyes had grown round. While most people considered her naive, Buck knew it only stemmed from her sunny personality. However, she had never left this area, and though she'd experienced plenty, she would be lost in a large city.

"Especially the wealthy ones." Carrie rolled her shoulders. "The last one I exposed, I followed into a drug den. The unemployment rate is reaching forty percent, and if these men don't jump off a bridge when they lose their bank accounts, they drown their misfortunes in other, illegal ways. Of course, that often costs their families what little they have left."

Silence descended, broken only by a rumbling snore from Samson.

What could a person say? Buck feared things would worsen before they got better. But next year was an election year, so maybe there would be hope?

Carrie released Buck's hand to rub her eyes. "I'm sorry. That was off topic."

"It's obvious you're passionate about it." Mrs. Martins patted her shoulder, then joined them at the table. "We simply care about you, and don't wish to see you hurt."

"I appreciate that, however, my ... enthusiasm was likely fueled by reminders of unsavory men and the thought that women shouldn't be journalists." *Only mothers.*

The unspoken statement hung between them, whether the others recognized it or not. His and Carrie's only disagreement about life after they married revolved around the topic of her career. He didn't want her to give up being a journalist, but worried how to protect a pregnant wife, should the Lord bless them with children. She couldn't imagine not uncovering the truth, no matter where it took her.

Buck clenched his jaw. He'd do anything to have had to face that dilemma these past two years. "Carrie is an excellent undercover journalist. May we move on to what she has discovered rather than critiquing her activities?"

Detective O'Connor let loose that ridiculously free-sounding laugh of his. "You sound like my nephew."

Buck figured the statement to be a compliment, but wasn't entirely sure.

"Please." Carrie drew out her own notebook. "I didn't have time to make notes, so if you will permit me, I will simply tell you all that occurred since my meeting with Mr. Alistar."

"Proceed." O'Connor waved a hand.

Carrie told her story. Buck shoved his hands through his hair, tried to stay in his seat ... couldn't. He paced as she talked. Samson watched him, the rest ignored him. Good. He felt raw. Exposed. What kind of family had he come from that his uncle would have no problem murdering his nephew?

"When I got back to the office, I ducked under the desk," Carrie was saying.

It brought him up short. "You didn't immediately run out of the building?"

"I wasn't sure who the other informant was, and needed to alert Ali that our line of communication had been compromised." She raised her chin as she dared him to find her actions faulty. "I waited until they left, then sent the code via telegraph."

"You know how to operate a telegraph machine?" Mindy stared at her.

"Enough." Carrie brushed off the question with another sip of coffee. "Ali will investigate the Chicago end, and will return to Crow's Nest as soon as possible. Or send a co-worker if she can't get here as quickly as she thinks necessary."

"She replied to your telegram?" Detective O'Connor sounded impressed.

"No. We have set plans in place for just such situations." Carrie looked at each person in turn. "This is not my first time undercover, nor my first time having that cover revealed prematurely. The concern here is not about me. Buck is the one in danger."

Buck collapsed into a chair, rubbing his chest with a grimace. Nick eyed him and Buck gave a subtle shake of his head. Later.

"I do believe this conversation has advanced past my capabilities." Mrs. Martins rose, gathering empty cups, which clattered on their saucers in her shaky hands.

"Let me help, Mrs. Martins." Mindy carried the dishes to the kitchen, but Nick's furrowed brow as he watched her indicated he sensed she was also distressed.

"Perhaps we should adjourn until tomorrow," Buck offered.

"No." Carrie's response was immediate. "We don't have time to put this off."

"I agree." Detective O'Connor leaned his chair back to avoid bumping into Samson. "Em, why don't you go lie down. Perhaps Mindy can see after you?"

In other words, the ladies should exit the conversation. The ladies except for Carrie.

"That is a wise plan, Detective O'Connor." Mindy wrapped her arm around Mrs. Martins's waist. "Come with me. I'll keep you company."

By silent agreement, no one spoke as the duo walked down the hall. Samson raised his massive head to observe the situation, then let it drop with a huff. Buck took the moment to appreciate the three people left at the table with him.

Detective O'Connor, the man who had been determined to ferret out the corruption within the Conglomerate. He'd been right, just focused on the wrong individual. A mismatched pair if he'd ever seen one—the respected small town detective and the undercover, unjustly disgraced Treasury agent—but now that they pulled together, perhaps they'd get somewhere.

Then there was Nick, Buck's first true friend in Crow's Nest. The Italian managed to see past what everyone *said* about Buck to the character beneath his undercover persona. With a history that included performing life-saving surgery at gunpoint, there was no one Buck wanted in his corner more than his sparring partner.

And, of course, Carrie. What possessed him to leave her behind when he first went undercover, he'd never know. But looking back at regrets wouldn't give them a future. He had to rein in his fear of losing her because he needed her to be at her best. Her story of the evening proved it.

He also had to shove down the longing to rekindle their love. This wasn't the time for romance. If they succeeded, he and Carrie could explore a second chance. For now, they were colleagues again. And he aimed to make her proud of him.

"I take it you have a plan?" O'Connor lowered his voice.

Buck filled his lungs, then let the air out slowly. "I think it's time to tell everyone the truth and use Alistar to do so." As the words left his mouth, the surety that it was the correct course of action settled in his bones.

"You want to reveal your identity?" O'Connor stared at him. "After all this time, now is when you want to show your true colors?"

Buck couldn't tell if the man approved or not.

"What do you think that weasel wants out of his meeting tomorrow?" Carrie folded her arms.

"Do you think you should find out before you give him the truth?" Nick asked.

"That is a wise idea." O'Connor made a note on his paper. "How do you plan to draw your uncle here?"

"Easy." Buck shrugged, answering the simple question first. "As soon as he finds out that I plan to reveal the truth, he is going to come after me. Carrie's news tonight proves that."

O'Connor met his eye. "And then what?"

Buck scrubbed his face, weariness dragging him down. "Part of that will depend on whether he takes a covert or an overt approach to destroying me."

"His methods have been very covert thus far," Carrie offered.

"Yes." How could his late mother have had the same parents as Perry Baxter? "He's managed to manipulate and buy off the people he needed to put me in a position where I could not find the truth. And he kept things at the Conglomerate completely aboveboard so that I couldn't find evidence."

"Do you think he will attempt to get at you that way again?" Nick asked.

"After what Carrie overheard, I think he will come to Crow's Nest." Conviction had Buck balling his fist. "He knows the conglomerate is legitimate. He knows that the townspeople don't like me. That means he will seek to win their favor and get them on his side so that they stay against me. If the people turn against me, O'Connor may have no choice but to arrest me with the false proof my uncle will provide. I have been risking prison since the day I decided to investigate him. I lost Carrie to this investigation. It is time to go all in."

"This isn't a poker game, Wilson," the detective muttered.

"With my uncle, it is, which means we have to think like that, too. Bluffs and counter bluffs. What to wager. I want to show my cards to everyone, laying it all out there. We'll see what he brings, and either it's the end of me or the end of him."

"Carrie," Nick reached halfway across the table. "Are you alright with that plan?"

"It was my idea." She shrugged with a glance at Buck. "I want my fiancé back. I want us to have a chance to see if we have a future. And we can't do that with this hanging over our heads. My job, my passion, is to find the truth. That is why Buck found me again. It is time to shine a great big spotlight at this. And we are going to use that slimy weasel of a journalist to do it."

"Okay." O'Connor gave a nod.

"Then what do you need from us?" Nick asked.

Buck captured Carrie's hand, needing the connection after her declaration. "I want you all to know the truth so that when the lies and manipulations begin, and a pall is cast over my character worse than it has been before, when the mud starts flying ... I need to know I have people cheering for me. And that if things go poorly you will look out for Carrie."

"Hey now. That last bit was not part of our agreement." Carrie scowled at him and he tightened his grip.

"It is now. I cannot go into this if I'm worried about you. That is exactly what caused my heart condition. I need to know that you are safe." He pinned O'Connor and Nick with a glare. "Do I have your word?"

Nick was nodding before he even finished talking.

Detective O'Connor smoothed his mustache with his finger and thumb. "If this goes sideways, I think we should fully expect Carrie to get caught up in the wave of your uncle's displeasure. He knows who she is, and I have no doubt he will set his sights on destroying her. Are you prepared for that?"

Buck lifted the back of Carrie's hand to his lips. He couldn't answer because the answer was no. But if he wanted this to end, he had to say yes.

Carrie used her free palm to turn him toward her. "It's what you said, Love. We have friends who know the truth, who have my back and yours. I am not from Crow's Nest. I have no reputation to lose. My boss knows who I am. I am here to find the truth for you. I am not at risk."

He leaned into her touch. "He will go after you in Chicago."

"Let him." Carrie shrugged. "I can write under different names. All my identities are separate. There is no risk to me."

"Professionally, perhaps not," O'Connor interrupted. "But physically, emotionally. Are you prepared?"

"What do you mean physically?" Nick asked, a protective tone to his words. "You think he will hurt her?"

Buck put space between himself and Carrie to include the two men. "He doesn't do his own dirty work, so he will not lay a hand on her. He prefers to bribe and manipulate and be a puppet master. The man Carrie saw meeting with Alistar is likely his preferred weapon. However, if he is backed into a corner, I am not sure what he will do."

"I think we know what he will do," Carrie said earnestly. "He will fight back. And he will fight dirty. He will try to destroy you by destroying me. I don't think the question is whether I am prepared to face this. I am. It is whether you can hold up when he comes after me."

Buck shook his head. "I can't."

"Then this is over before it starts." Carrie freed her hand to grip his lapels. "You have to trust me. You have to trust me to God. It is the only way this will succeed."

"How can you have such faith?" He stared at her, wishing they could simply run away together and forget all of this. Except, that wasn't who they were. Neither of them.

"I told you, Love." Carrie smiled at him. "When you left, I could not follow you, I could not find you. So I had to leave you in God's hands. It was a day-by-day struggle. But I prayed for you, and I searched for the truth for you. Will you do me the courtesy of doing the same? Are we partners in this or not?"

He felt the scrutiny of two other sets of eyes on him, but he could not tear his gaze away from Carrie. The fierceness of her expression. This was his warrior journalist. The one who fought for the truth. The woman he fell in love with.

He kissed her lightly on the lips. "I cannot promise that I won't fail, but I promise I will try."

Nick cleared his throat. "Have you prayed about this plan of yours?"

"Honestly?" Buck stalled, putting an uncomfortable distance between himself and Carrie. He hadn't asked the Lord that direct question. Frankly, his prayers had grown less and less frequent the past few years. The more alone he felt, the less he saw God's hand in his situation.

"I believe that answers my question." Nick offered a compassionate smile.

"And?" Buck searched for the condemnation he expected, the demand they stop and bow their heads this moment.

"And nothing." Nick shook his head as if bewildered, but the twinkle in his eye betrayed him. He knew what Buck wanted from him.

O'Connor raised a bushy brow. "Care to elaborate?"

Carrie bumped Buck's shoulder. "Faith is hard to keep when undercover. Since we play the parts of criminals, we're used to cloaking our belief in God. It's a habit that is hard to break when undercover for so long."

"It's hard as a doctor, too." Nick sipped his coffee. "Seeing so much pain and suffering, being unable to save a child from death."

O'Connor shook his head. "How do you think I've been a detective for so long? Yes, darkness surrounds us. And in our professions, we see the worst. But then there's the times when justice prevails, when lives are saved, when the criminal is put behind bars and the innocent are freed."

The words sank into Buck's soul.

"Long ago I memorized a passage from the sixty-first chapter of Isaiah. I think you three need to hear it, so sit up and listen." O'Connor leaned back in his chair and closed his eyes. "The Lord hath anointed me to preach good tidings unto the meek; he hath sent me to bind up the brokenhearted, to proclaim liberty to the captives, and the opening of the prison to them that are bound; to proclaim the acceptable year of the Lord, and the day of vengeance of our God; to comfort all that mourn; to appoint unto them that mourn in Zion, to give unto them beauty for ashes, the oil of joy for mourning, the garment of praise for the spirit of heaviness; that they might be called trees of righteousness, the planting of the Lord, that he might be glorified."

"The garment of praise." The corner of Nick's mouth tipped into a smile.

"Beauty for ashes." Carrie rested her head on Buck's shoulder.

"To the glory of God." For the first time since this whole situation began, peace filled Buck's heart and confidence settled his mind. *Thank you, Lord. Be with us. Protect us.* "Tomorrow. Tomorrow, I tell Alistar the truth."

CHAPTER TWELVE

Friday, October 30

The next morning, when Alistar walked into the Conglomerate headquarters, Buck sent everyone away so they could speak alone. The plain interior of the building no longer reflected the saloon it used to be. The tornado last spring had accomplished that, and Buck had rebuilt the bare minimum.

He wiped his palms along his trousers, stuffed his hands into his pockets, and leaned on the corner of his desk. This conversation was best done standing up. Alastair did not have the same conviction. He took a seat in front of Buck's desk.

"Now, Mr. Wilson." Alistar looked like a cat about to eat the canary. "I have come across some evidence that I need to run past you. Then we can decide what I should do with it."

Buck saw a blackmail scheme coming his way. For now, however, he wanted to find out what type of information the man had on him. "What so-called evidence do you have?"

Alistar didn't blink. "It has come to my attention that you have more funds in your account than you have led us all to believe."

Ah, so the embezzlement charges. "I feel like banking information is private."

"There is an account with your name on it." Alistar glanced at his notebook. "Apparently, it seems to be growing with funds provided through the Conglomerate."

Buck held back the sarcasm that jumped to his tongue. "The audit of our books revealed no such information."

"A cover story, obviously." Alistar rolled his eyes. "We all know these kinds of things are done off book. Which is why I went searching. And, lo! I found one."

"Went searching, did you? And where did you find such a book?"

"That doesn't matter." Alistar laid the ledger on the table and between them. "The fact is, I have proof right here. You are embezzling funds from the Conglomerate."

The man thought it a trump card, but Buck held a better poker hand. "And if I said I'm not?"

"The proof is right here, Mr. Wilson." Alistar thumped the ledger. "What we do with this proof is our conversation. Do I print the story in tomorrow's paper? Or will you make it worth my while to keep this ledger out of sight?"

He couldn't show emotion, had to call Alistar's bluff. "There's no discussion about whether the ledger is actually mine?"

"No. It was discovered in your house. It matches your handwriting." Alistar's voice rose. "I even found the matching account."

Buck's hands shook and he shoved them into his pockets. Planted evidence, just like before. Unless the ledger was hand-delivered to Alistar and he just made up being in his house. Except for the fact that he admitted to Carrie that he had been inside.

The account Alistar mentioned was no doubt the one that got him in trouble in Chicago. His uncle was nothing if not predictable. This was exactly how things began in Chicago. Except, instead of a blackmailing journalist, Uncle Perry had bought off cops to get Buck arrested. Now he was going after his character again, but in a different way. It felt like a distraction for something much worse.

"I'm afraid neither option works for me." He strengthened his tone so Alistar knew he meant business. "I have a different story I want you to run tomorrow. It is an exclusive. And it will shock your readers."

Hooked, a gleam lit Alistar's eye as he readied his pen. "Please, Mr. Wilson, go on."

Buck allowed himself to take pleasure in the moment of suspense. Then he took a deep breath and put their plan in motion. "I, Buck Wilson, am an undercover US Treasury agent, here in Crow's Nest to investigate Mr. Perry Baxter, my uncle."

Alistar dropped his pen, then scrambled to pick it up from the floor. "You know... you know I will need to check these, these facts."

"Of course." Now the man had scruples? Buck again resisted the less-than-helpful reply. "I encourage you to speak to Detective O'Connor. You may also speak to the journalist aiding you. She is a journalist from Chicago of close acquaintance."

Like a fox on a hunt, Alistar chased the offered information. "Is that why you fell for her so quickly? You kissed her quite publicly. Do you plan to make an honest woman of her?"

How honest should he be? It didn't matter. His uncle knew the truth, so best tell everything. "We were almost married. Once."

"You still love her," Alistar spoke like he'd struck gold.

Buck couldn't stop a smile. "I do. I never stopped, even when I had to leave her."

Alistar paused. "Strangely, I believe that is the most truthful statement out of everything you have told me."

"Perhaps it is." Buck relaxed his shoulders.

If Buck hadn't fed Alistar the information on purpose, he'd be disconcerted by the gleam in the newspaperman's eye. The obvious excitement the man attempted to tamp down by leisurely leaning back in his chair was revealing enough. Buck had—from Alistar's point of view—given him proof for what Douglas had said the night before. More, even. And to a man like Alistar, the upper hand was a prize.

Buck moved behind his desk, casual as a confident Conglomerate head ought to be. "Will there be anything else, Mr. Alistar?"

"No."

Buck didn't believe that for a moment.

Alistar rose, putting his notebook and pen away. Then walked toward the door.

Buck pretended to busy himself with paperwork, as if he'd forgotten Alistar's presence. Waited for him to reach the door and ...

"Why tell me all of this?" Alistar spun toward him, advancing to the desk in three strides. "Why distract me from your embezzling by this obnoxious tale of being an undercover agent? I'm not an imbecile, Wilson."

Interesting. Buck sat back in his chair, hands folded across his middle. Did Alistar actually believe Baxter's man over Buck? Or was he attempting to trip Buck into giving up more dirt on himself?

"Maybe I'll go ask Carrie." Alistar turned on his heel.

"Leave her alone, Alistar." Buck infused the demand with steel, knowing full well it would drive Alistar straight to Carrie.

Alistar laughed. "Do you think she'll lie for you? The dame has strung you along this whole time. She's not in love with you."

Buck flinched. While he knew the truth, the last two years had left him with enough doubt for Alistar's barb to hurt as the man intended.

"Letting a dame pull one. Honestly, Wilson. I expected better from a man like you."

Buck closed his eyes and clenched his jaw. Alistar wanted to goad him into saying something emotional, something unscripted. He wouldn't, and hiding behind his pain provided a realistic story.

Trouble was ... He trusted Carrie, but she was a good enough undercover journalist that Alistar could be more right than even he knew.

Carrie rubbed her mittened hands together and bounced on her toes. The air smelled like snow and wind cut through her coat. And people called Chicago the Windy City. Sure, the wind barreled between the buildings like the Encierro—the running of the bulls in Spain—but here? The wind pecked and cawed like the seagulls that still hung about.

She blew into her hands. Where was Alistar?

Buck told her how the appointment with the reporter had gone, but instinct said he hadn't explained everything. Curiosity and worry pulsed through her numbing limbs. Waiting for informants was the worst part of this job sometimes. Especially in the cold. It made her look as jittery as she felt.

She paced to the edge of the river. Icy and sluggish, it meandered around rocks and branches. In the spring, she had no doubt it rushed over the bumpy bed in frothy glory. But winter had a way of deadening even Lake Michigan itself.

Thou hast set all the borders of the earth: thou hast made summer and winter.

The Psalm danced through her mind and she breathed out a prayer in response. "Lord, thou hast made all things. Seedtime and harvest. I pray now that the sowing we have done will come forth in bountiful blessing. Especially for ..."

Quiet steps behind her had the words dying away.

"Waiting long?" Alistar had sing-song quality in his tone, as if he took pleasure in having the upper-hand, which he probably did.

Please Lord. Then she turned, careful to keep a meek expression. "I am grateful you take the time to meet with me."

Alistar wore a dark wool coat, matching scarf, and black hat, making him appear like a dark hole in the night. "Your work has paid off." He hooked her arm and led her away from the river.

"What's happened? Where are we going?" She had to trot to keep up. The nervous energy radiating from him told her this was the break they needed in the case. "Mr. Alistar?"

He remained silent until they reached the shadow of the large barn that Caroline learned served as an assembly hall, when, as she said his name, he stumbled. Instincts built from years as an undercover journalist in the heart of Chicago flared to life. This wasn't just a lead or a break, this was the same tingling sensation she got at the back of her neck when her undercover persona was about to be exposed. The moment before those she sought to reveal turned against her.

In all likelihood, her life—and maybe Buck's—balanced on the edge of a knife. She drew in the subtlest of breaths, then controlled the quiver in her voice to match that of a naïve young woman. "You're making me nervous, Mr. Alistar. Is something wrong? Where are we going?"

Alistar paced away from her, then back again, jaw tight. "I have someone I want you to meet."

Instinct turned to certainty, and the danger ahead caused a shiver to race through her body. "Am I finally going to meet the editor-in-chief?"

Alistar groaned. "Stop the act, Neary, or whatever your name is. Buck gave you up."

"What?" Carrie feigned astonishment, but her heart raced of its own accord. First, Buck wouldn't do that; second, Alistar was usually a better liar than this.

"Yeah." Alistar shoved her against the social barn hard enough to knock something from the wall. "You thought you were winning him with those feminine wiles of yours, but you're as gullible as every other woman. He used you."

Carrie bit her lip, her gaze pinned to the flat, wooden pumpkin face that lay at her feet. She wanted to fight back, yell at Alistar that Buck was an honorable man, but she couldn't. Not if she wanted to succeed. And Alistar's anger told her something big: he was in over his head. And that would make him either more dangerous or offer the opportunity to turn him for good.

Alistar slapped her. "Nothing to say?"

"I love him," she whispered. She knew Buck had declared his love for her to Alistar. What would her fellow journalist do with her admission? It would show her the way forward.

He bent so his nose was an inch from hers. His breath had a tinge of alcohol, as if he'd had a shot to control his nerves. "Even though he left you at the altar?"

She forced herself to scowl. Yes, the gig was up. However, she'd never met Perry Baxter. He didn't know which of her undercover personalities was the real one. And neither did Alistar. If she wanted to get out of this alive, she needed Alistar on her side. Did he have a noble streak she could appeal to as a damsel in distress? Or was he more likely to side with a fellow, hard-nosed journalist?

"What I want to know ..." he leaned in to hiss in her ear.

She clenched her fists to keep from reacting. Buck had taught her a move that would have Alistar on his back in a blink, but doing so would not get her what she wanted. Alistar prized his manhood, which meant she needed to act like a killdeer, a bird that feigned injury to protect its nest. Only once she'd effectively lured the predator away from Buck would she fly away to safety.

Another whisper of alcohol—and not cheap moonshine—she'd been around Chicago speakeasies enough to recognize the good stuff. "Are you here to help him ... or do you want revenge?"

Relief cascaded through her. This was her answer, her way forward. *Oh my love, I'm sorry for what I must do.* Carrie clenched her jaw, forcing anger and hurt into her eyes. "I'm here to expose him for the fraud he is."

Alistar held her gaze, testing. Then he grinned. "Good. Consider yourself hired."

"Excuse me?" She crossed her arms, the only way to keep the elation from betraying her lie.

"You're hired." Alistar waved her toward his car as if he hadn't just pinned her to a wall. "Time for you to meet the boss."

Baxter? Her heart thumped, and she couldn't have moved if she'd wanted to.

"Okay, not the boss exactly. My boss." Alistar's shoulders relaxed. Whatever he'd been commanded to do had been done. "And yes, he's the editor-in-chief."

Carrie didn't pretend surprise. "Richard Tinnel?" Alistar had scolded her for wanting to meet him.

"Please stop asking questions." Alistar caught her arm, a note of fear shaking his voice. "Richard Tinnel exists in name only. It's time you learn how the *Gazette* is really run."

She allowed Alistar to help her into his car, as the news sunk in. The *Gazette* was a front. No wonder Buck hadn't been able to find any proof. It wasn't in the Conglomerate, it was in the newspaper.

Alistar slipped into the driver's seat and unbuttoned his coat with a sigh. That's when she spotted the gleam of perspiration on his temple, and the gun holstered under his arm. If she hadn't played her hand just right, was Alistar under order to kill her? Likely. And Alistar might be a sleazy, crooked journalist, but Carrie didn't think he'd ever killed before.

His fingers trembled as he worked to get the key into place. Alistar's boss had leverage over the man, and Carrie suspected whatever it was would be strong enough to keep Alistar soundly on the bad guy's side.

She settled into the seat. Yes, she was on her own, but most importantly, tonight she'd gain entrance into the world that had destroyed her marriage before it had the chance to begin.

Nick snapped his fingers in front of Buck's face. "Your move." They sat in Buck's kitchen, where they'd been since supper.

Buck blinked, refocusing on the chessboard between them, but couldn't make sense of the pieces. He slid a pawn forward a square.

Nick flopped back in his chair. "You just exposed your queen."

"What?" Buck searched for the piece that would capture his queen.

Nick moved his bishop, taking the queen, and there was nothing Buck could do to retaliate. A free piece, and a queen no less.

Buck knocked over his king. "I surrender."

"And I'm out of ways to keep your mind off Carrie's task tonight." Nick replaced the chess pieces in their case. "Food didn't help. Sparring didn't help. A mental game—"

"Didn't help. I know." Buck rubbed the spot on his jaw that Nick had hooked because Buck had been distracted.

"She promised to stop by as soon as she could, or have Mindy ring for me." Nick set the chessboard and cloth bag of pieces aside. "You have to trust her."

"I do." Buck rested his elbows on the table, head in his hands. "I'm not worried, exactly."

"Could have fooled me."

Buck rubbed his chest without looking up. "Something Alistar said got a sliver in my mind and I can't extract it."

"Give me your wrist." Nick lowered Buck's arm down to the table, pressed two fingers to his pulse. "Too high."

"I could have told you that." Buck glared at his friend.

"You should have." Nick rose. "Don't move."

The dame has strung you along this whole time.

No, he asked Carrie for help.

She's not in love with you.

That kiss said otherwise.

Letting a dame pull one. Honestly, Wilson.

And that grain of doubt undid the rest.

"Take this." Nick placed a white tablet on the table in front of him.

"What is it?" Buck downed it with a slug of cold coffee.

"Aspirin. For your heart."

"You think I'm at risk for another ... episode?" Buck leaned his chair on the two back legs to get a good view of Nick's expression. It would tell him more than Nick's words.

"I do." Perfect eye contact emphasized the simple statement.

Buck clamped back a swear word as he let the chair legs crash back to all four. "So this weird feeling I have is probably because of my heart, and not because of my worry for Carrie?"

Nick returned to his seat across from Buck. "The worry causes stress, the stress affects your heart, your heart increases your pulse, an increased pulse ups your worry."

"How can I make it stop?"

"That is Adaleigh's territory more than mine." Nick folded his hands on the table. "Medically, I'd say rest in a quiet retreat. However, I know you well enough now that I would not recommend that."

Buck snorted. "Not if Carrie wasn't there with me."

Nick winked.

Buck groaned. "We need to finish this."

"I agree." Nick removed his glasses to wipe the lenses with his sleeve. "For your health, you either need to bring your uncle to justice within the next week, or give the assignment to someone else and disappear. With Carrie, if she'll go."

"If she'll marry me, you mean."

"That was assumed." Nick replaced his glasses and raised a brow. "I kept an eye on you two when she'd visit the clinic, you know."

"I know you were there to protect her reputation."

Nick crossed his arms. "No. I mean, yes, of course, but not just that. If you had stepped over a line, I would have entered the room."

Buck's turn to shoot his brows upward. "You were watching that closely?"

"And heard quite a bit because of it."

Buck should've been offended, embarrassed even, but he wasn't. Somehow, knowing someone else knew, a trusted someone else, made this easier. "Then you understand."

"What did Alistar say exactly?"

Buck reiterated the hardest part of their conversation.

"*Letting a dame pull one.* And you believed him for even a moment?" Nick sighed. "Tell me what you admire most about Carrie."

"Her strength. Her commitment." Buck's lips turned into a smile of their own accord. "Her determination. Her innocence in the face of men's duplicity."

"Does any of that sound like she'd 'pull one' on you?"

No.

"You know Carrie's character." Nick leaned forward, tapping his fingers on the table for emphasis. "Alistar is a crook and a liar. Carrie is an experienced undercover journalist. You've seen her as herself and as someone pretending to be something else. Trust what you know to be the bedrock of who she is."

"You're right." Buck slapped the table and pushed to his feet. Perhaps the medicine was working. Perhaps Nick's words banished the worry. Either way ... "Sitting around playing chess isn't the way to wait for Carrie. If she didn't wallow when I left her, it'd be disrespectful to do that to her."

Nick grinned.

"Up to the war room. I've spent enough nights staring at it, I need to look at it from my uncle's perspective." Buck pointed at Nick. "You're going to help me."

"Where are we going?" Carrie asked Alistar as he drove them along dark streets. She wasn't familiar enough with Crow's Nest. She knew Chicago so well that she underestimated the amount of reconnaissance she should have done when she first arrived here.

"You'll see." Alistar kept his focus on the road, which suited Carrie just fine. It gave her a chance to study with new eyes. If she could find the root of how the powers that be controlled him, perhaps she could wrestle that leverage away from them. Until then, appealing to Alistar's humanity would be a waste of breath.

If only the night wasn't so black. The clouds obscured the moon and stars. Once snow fell, it would lighten the area. For now, the darkness felt … heavy. Was it the upcoming meeting or did it have something to do with Halloween? Many people thought the veil between the spirit world and physical world was at its thinnest these next few Holy Days, and used jack-o'-lanterns to scare away unwelcome ghosts.

Carrie's journalist mind demanded proof, but her belief in God made her pause. Ephesians even said, *For we wrestle not against flesh and blood, but against … spiritual wickedness.* And what should a person do when faced with such a battle? Pray.

Alistar turned down a residential road, curving back toward the river. Her time was best used preparing herself for what lay ahead than attempting to mine for more information. Was this editor-in-chief someone they had run across in the course of their investigation, like Douglas from last night? Carrie braced herself against the door as Alistar took the next turn too tightly. Was he trying to get a reaction from her? He wouldn't. She would reserve all her energy for facing the link between Alistar and the main boss, whom Carrie believed to be Perry Baxter.

Which means, Lord, I need to pray.

Before she could ask for more of the Almighty, Alistar pulled to the side of the road beside a stand of bare trees. The river ran opposite, and Carrie recognized it as near the *Gazette* building, which didn't surprise her.

They wordlessly exited the car, and Alistar met her at the hood. "I need to blindfold you."

"Uh, no." Though Carrie had agreed to such a thing several times over her career, she always declined first. "I don't reveal my sources. Not even to Buck."

"Admirable of you." Alistar held up a black cloth. "Turn around or I will make you turn around. This is not a request."

Carrie leaned against the car to prevent him from circling behind her. "Why?"

"Boss's orders." Alistar glanced over his shoulder, then ground the next word through his teeth. "Please turn, Carrie."

She cocked her head. "Why? What leverage do they have? I can help you."

He backhanded her across the face and she lost her balance enough for him to spin, then pin her to the car hood. She could hear Buck scolding her in her head. First, that she'd gotten in Alistar's car without telling anyone. Second, she let Alistar get the chance to blindfold her.

"This way." Alistar grabbed her upper arm.

With sight taken away, her other senses took in more. The frosty air in her nose. The dots of moisture dropping onto her cheeks. The clacking of the presses preparing for the morning edition.

They drew near the noisy building, but did not enter it. Instead, Alistar walked them past it. With the blindfold on, Carrie's sense of direction couldn't determine what side of the building they passed—front, side, back—just that the sound grew loud, and then lessened. Their feet crunched frosty grass, and Carrie was grateful she'd worn flats. Pumps or Mary Janes might be fashionable, but a sprained ankle at the expense of beauty wasn't her way. Truth-seeking came first.

A door squeaked open, a heavy one, if Alistar's grunt meant anything, and then it closed behind them with a click that echoed in Carrie's heart.

"Can I remove the blindfold?" Carrie asked, not liking the sense of being a prisoner.

"Yeah." Alistar muttered.

Carrie removed her mittens, stuffing them in her pockets, then carefully untied the bandana. Not that it made a difference. Darkness stretched ahead of them. What building was this?

Alistar struck a match, lit a lamp, and replaced the glass chimney. "Someday this place will get electricity. This way."

Carrie hesitated. She could back out now, run. Nothing stood between her and the door. Except, then she wouldn't meet the editor-in-chief and, potentially, find the information to free Buck of his uncle.

Lord, please keep me safe.

Then she followed Alistar's light into the darkness.

CHAPTER THIRTEEN

In less than ten minutes, Buck and Nick had refilled their coffee mugs, moved the bureau away from the wall, and dragged two chairs into the spare bedroom. On the wall, dozens of yarn strands led from one note to another to create an intricate web of information. How many times had he created one of these, only to tear it down for fear someone would uncover his true purpose here?

"Start from the beginning." Nick leaned his chair back on its hind legs. "When did you first suspect your uncle?"

"I didn't. Not until we ran into each other." Buck crossed his arms, squinting at the wall, then shook his head. "No, the question isn't when I first suspected my uncle, it's when he first suspected me."

"Okay ... when was that?"

Buck traced the yarn from the moment he and his uncle had crossed each other to where he informed his superior. No. That was Buck's story, and the ramifications hit too quickly for his uncle to have been unprepared.

Nick's chair dropped with a thud. "What do you see?"

Buck tapped a paper connected not to Buck's investigation, but to Carrie's from a couple weeks ago. "She met with a source she calls Ploughshare. Carrie is very careful never to reveal her sources, so she gives them names. That way, if anyone confiscates her notes, or they fall into the wrong hands, her source remains anonymous."

"I'm sure someone could figure it out." Nick's skepticism made Buck smile.

"Her notes are in code. The code is a mix of Morse, English, and Italian, with a cipher thrown in for her high-profile cases. I'm honestly not sure Ali could figure it out." He never had, and Carrie took great pride in her journalistic ethics. *Trust what you know to be the bedrock of who Carrie is.*

"What did this Ploughshare person say?" Nick nudged Buck from his thoughts.

"His boss is printing money. Started with ones, then moved to tens and hundreds, like we found when you helped shut down that counterfeiting ring a few weeks ago. Apparently, two zeros isn't enough. Ploughshare's boss wants to print thousand dollar notes."

Nick stared at him. "There's no way he'll pass those off as counterfeit. I've watched too many people get shot because of phony bills. Patched up a few because they tried to pass them off to the wrong people. But thousands? No one was ... *stupido* to do such a thing."

"I would say that if they wanted to print ten thousand dollar reserve notes. Those are only used in bank transfers and business deals. However, thousands are legal tender for common distribution. Rare, but rare benefits counterfeiting as much as frequency does."

Nick crossed his arms. "How so?" The question was one part disbelief, one part curiosity.

"No one thinks about ones being counterfeit because there's so many, they're worth so little, there is no point. That is why counterfeiters will test their skills on ones." Buck had studied the bill Ploughshare had given Carrie for three hours before he found the mistake. "However, with thousands, no one sees the real ones enough to recognize a fake."

"Can you?"

Buck tried to hide a grin. Of course he could.

Nick rolled his eyes, but quickly sobered. "And you think Ploughshare's boss is your uncle?"

Buck returned to the wall. "Let's assume that for a minute. He wants to print thousands. For the past two years, he has worked up to that denomination. And he could, because I was out of his way."

"Makes sense."

"Killing me outright would bring too much scrutiny, so he hustled me off to little Crow's Nest, which we know has been on a smuggling route."

"What Gil and Marian discovered." Nick shoved his hands in his pockets like Buck usually did. "But that was moonshine, not counterfeit bills."

"Need a product for money to exchange hands." Buck shrugged. "And, with Capone under investigation, it would make sense that my uncle was shoring up his stores for when the feds succeeded. And—Carrie said she found at least one Treasury agent on the take. There's a good chance my uncle would have been privy to investigative details not released to the public."

"Okay, say this is all true ... Why put you here? Why not ship you off to some foreign country?"

"Because he needed to keep his eye on me, make sure I was chasing my tail, not making headway. He thought I couldn't do much harm here, and when the smuggling and counterfeit rings were discovered, what did he do?"

"He's come after you again."

"Exactly." Buck rested his thumbs and forefingers on his belt. "This is all speculation. And one of the reasons I haven't been able to solve anything is because I have no proof."

"You also didn't know about Ploughshare." Nick stepped beside him, also searching the wall. "Your speculation is entirely due to Carrie's investigation."

Buck huffed out a breath. "We should have been working together."

"You've been over that, Wilson." Nick glared at him. "Drop it."

"Keep reminding me." Buck traced the yarn from the smuggling ring to Marian's name, then from the counterfeit ring to Mindy's name. Clenched his jaw. "This is what made me toss my selfishness aside. Nettie and Essie, Marian's little girls. Little Mabel. Children were getting caught in this fight and I won't stand for that."

Nick gripped his shoulder. "What I said about Carrie holds true for you, too. No matter how long you've been undercover, who you are at the bedrock of your soul has never changed. You fight for justice, especially for those too young and too innocent to know the evil that surrounds them."

Light cracked open in his chest. For a moment, Buck closed his eyes, felt its strength, then raised his gaze once again to the wall. To Cora and Adaleigh's names, where so few yarns connected their situation to the rest of the web. Both had been attacked because of situations having nothing to do with the Conglomerate.

But they had something in common.

Two someones.

Buck spun, grabbing Nick's arms, panic spearing through him. "It's Sebastian. He's the link from Alistar to my uncle."

Carrie listened to the dueling church bells strike the hour as she rested her head against the cold brick wall. She was determined to keep calm, even though Alistar had left her barred in this barren room for the past two hours.

Yes, barred. She'd tried to pick the lock after hour one—succeeded—but there was a bar across it that prevented her from getting out. And so she'd returned to her chair to wait.

The room was nicer than a jail cell—she'd been put in one while covering a worker's strike one spring. The lantern light flickered on dark windowless walls. The table and chair suggested this was an interview room. Why had Alistar stuck her in here? Why leave her alone well into the night?

Be with Buck, Lord. Grant him Your peace. Please.

He must be frantic, not having heard from her in hours.

She stood to pace. What was taking Alistar so long? He wanted her to meet his boss. Or were they waiting for Perry Baxter to arrive? Was he the boss Alistar wanted her to meet?

She tapped her fingers on her leg as she walked from one wall to the one opposite. Depending on who walked through the door, the situation would call for different approaches.

For Alistar, she'd play the frightened damsel. It wouldn't be difficult to let fear shake her voice or infuse her tone with anger. She wanted to tell the man what she thought of his manipulative ways. However, she'd need to be careful not to come across as too strong or independent. Alistar needed to think himself better than her if she wished to retain him as a source.

The editor-in-chief—if he wasn't Buck's uncle—was an unknown quantity. Not much she could do to prepare for him. If Alistar accompanied the editor, as would be likely, then she would focus her attention on him while assessing the other man. However, there was a chance the editor was the Douglas person who met with Alistar. In that case ...

Carrie laid her forehead against the cool brick. In that case, would it be better to portray a weak woman or a strong one? Weak could garner protection or allow a man to think he could control her, like with Alistar. But she'd been around too many mafioso types. Showing strength often received a nod of respect. They might still kill the person, but disdain would get her nowhere.

She turned so that her back was against the wall, and she stared at the cobwebbed ceiling. The lantern's light barely reached it, and certainly didn't show the corners. Probably good or she'd see all the spiders that had created the webbing.

A shudder rippled down her spine.

If the reason Alistar had stuck her in here for so long was because he waited for Perry, she should rejoice. Their plan worked. Except for the fact she was locked in this room. She'd never met Perry, which meant she would have to portray the exact type of woman he'd expect his nephew would marry.

Carrie massaged her temples. Lack of sleep was making this difficult to figure out. Buck was much better at improvising an undercover situation. She liked a plan. In and out, get the information, fact check, send it to the printers. It didn't help that Buck's life, and their future, was in the balance. One wrong move and it could get him killed or arrested.

Or her.

She'd kept up denying her own danger for Buck's sake, but she knew the risks. They usually didn't bother her. Tonight? Or rather this morning? They did. She'd declared her love for Buck to Alistar, which made her usable. And left her with a chink in her armor. The bet seemed reasonable at the time. Now?

Where was Alistar?

Carrie returned to the door, pressed her ear against the wood. How had she heard the church bells so well in this enclosed room? It wasn't the *Gazette* building. So where had Alistar taken her?

Carrie huffed as she studied the door. Now what? Waiting around wasn't her way. Leads did not come to her, she sought them out. Time to get herself out of here, too.

She ran her hands along the edges of the door. Why were the hinges on the *outside* of the door? Most doors opened inward. This one opened outward. If she put her shoulder into it, could she jar the bar securing the door loose?

Five minutes later, she discarded that idea. She was good and stuck.

Panic inched its way up her throat as a thought she'd kept at bay rose up with the strength of a tidal wave. What if Alistar never planned on coming back?

"Where is she?" Buck demanded, unable to keep the dread out of his voice as he paced his front room.

No one answered. Because no one had any more answers than they had the last time he asked. All they could offer was their presence. It'd been over an hour since he realized the chief of police was likely connected to his uncle, and no one had been able to find Carrie since.

"Would you please sit down?" Mindy tugged on his arm. "Nick left me strict instructions to watch your heart."

Buck shoved his fingers through his hair. "Why am I not out there looking for her? Why did I agree to stay here?"

"Drink this." Mrs. Martins shoved a hot cup of tea into his hands. She'd left Samantha and Bella with Mabel at the Martins house in case

Carrie went there. "And you know full well why my brother made you stay here."

"So he can find me." Like a prisoner. O'Connor still didn't trust Buck. "I could have gone with him."

"And then he'd be distracted by keeping his eye on you." Mrs. Martins urged the cup to his mouth. "Let my brother do his job and drink."

He tried a sip, and grimaced at the grassy flavor. "What is this?"

"Chamomile." The older woman smiled. "It will calm you."

He set the mug down on the lone side table. "I don't need to be calm. I need to find Carrie."

Buck clasped Mindy's shoulders to move her aside, ignored Mrs. Martins's demand to stay put, and strode for the door.

"Oh!" Meri Martins jumped as he nearly plowed into her, her baby fussing on her shoulder. Terror flashed in her eyes.

Buck wrapped his arm around her shoulder, his other hand supporting the little boy. "I'm sorry."

Meri closed her eyes for a moment, then met his gaze with a smile. "Not your fault."

Something told him there was a story behind that statement, especially since the older Baby Samuel grew, the less like Patrick Martins he looked. Dark hair as opposed to blonde being the most obvious, but Buck had an eye for facial structure. It's what made him good at identifying counterfeit notes. Samuel was Meri's baby, no doubt there, but he was not Patrick's child, though he claimed Samuel as his. That told Buck another man had caused Meri's jumpiness around men.

He tempered his tone, pushed his own fear away for Meri's sake, and stepped back. "It is entirely my fault. I am not thinking clearly."

Compassion replaced the terror from a moment ago. "Of course you're not. You love Carrie and are worried."

Buck bowed his head. He didn't deserve the kindness of these three women. They'd promised to keep him company while O'Connor, Nick, and Patrick went searching for Carrie. He'd warned against alerting Chief Sebastian, and that wasn't a hardship for any of them. No one liked the pompous buffoon. Though Buck wondered if he'd read the man wrong the entire time. Was he really as incapable as he appeared, or was it an act?

"Would you hold Samuel?" Meri's question jerked him back to the present.

"Why?" How could she trust him with her baby? The only reason Patrick was willing to help search for Carrie was because his uncle requested it, and because a woman was in danger. It had nothing to do with Buck.

"Because it will help you." She held the chubby baby so he had no choice but to take him. Samuel's blue eyes stared at Buck, but he neither smiled nor frowned.

"Is he usually awake at this time of night?" Buck asked, not sure what else to say or do.

Meri pressed the baby to his chest, and his heart gave an extra thump. "He's only six months old and has yet to sleep through the night. Perhaps you can get him back to sleep." She sighed that particular sound of a weary mother.

Somehow, it was exactly what he needed. A woman needed his help, a baby needed his comfort. A child who had needed the protection of a man not his father. Buck adjusted his grip on the baby. His left forearm under the baby's bottom, his right hand rubbing circles on the baby's back. Samuel rested his head in the crook of Buck's neck. Surely his unshaven jaw would scratch the child. Or no ... maybe it reminded Samuel of Patrick. The man always had some sort of scruffy beard, like a youth in a man's form.

Meri left him to confer in quiet tones with Mrs. Martins and Mindy. "It's three M names, Sammy. What do you say to that?"

The baby cooed and the sound went straight to Buck's heart.

He closed his eyes and wandered into the hall. The hall where Carrie had invited him to win her back. He couldn't lose her. After all they had sacrificed, couldn't they have a happily ever after like David and Adaleigh, Patrick and Meri, Nick and Mindy? Couldn't they have a baby together like Samuel?

Lord, I have given everything to this. My future, my health, please don't take Carrie away forever. Keep her safe.

All his striving hadn't protected her and now he had to leave her in God's hands.

CHAPTER FOURTEEN

Saturday, October 31
All Hallow's Eve

Voices, then the scrape of wood woke Carrie. She blinked and raised her head from where her arms had created a pillow on the table. Exhaustion had finally won out, so she dimmed the lantern to save light and closed her eyes. What time was it?

"Alistar, you're a hero." A male voice Carrie didn't recognize boomed into the room. Greg Alistar was not a hero, so what had he lied about now? "Have you been in here all night, Miss Neary?"

All night?

"I don't know how the door locked, Sebastian, but I'm glad I noticed." Alistar strode into the room behind the chief of police.

Carrie stood, forced her eyes wide and wrung her hands as if she were nervous. "What happened?"

"This is the warehouse behind the *Gazette*." Alistar cast her a pitying smile. "Were you poking around? It's the only way I can think you got yourself locked in here."

"Females aren't known for their intelligence." Sebastian shook his head as if her half of the population was his burden to bear.

Of all the—Carrie tightened her grip on her fingers, trying not to pretend it was Sebastian's neck.

"Come on, girl, let's get you back to Buck." Sebastian ushered her from the room, turning back to motion to Alistar to grab the lantern. "Not that he's been out looking for you."

She stumbled into the hall, but quickly righted herself and schooled her features, pressing herself against the brick wall beside the door as she absorbed Sebastian's words. There was a reason for that barb. But what?

Icy wind blew down the corridor and she donned the mittens she'd stuffed into her pockets. Sebastian and Alistar spoke in low tones. Instead of eavesdropping, Carrie used the reprieve to gather her wits.

She'd been around enough cops and criminals to recognize when the lines blurred. Attempting to manipulate a person's memory of a situation was one such tell. They wanted her to believe their story so that when they told it to others, no one listened to her side. Unfortunately for these two men, she saw through their attempt, and it made her raise her investigative antenna.

"Miss Neary?" Sebastian emerged from the room. "I need to take your statement down at the office, then you're free to go."

She couldn't prove it, wouldn't voice it unless the proof was indisputable, but intuition said this cop was on the take. But whose payroll?

Carrie uttered a weary sigh and massaged her temple. "I don't feel all that well, sir." She listed sideways, then blinked rapidly as she righted herself.

Sebastian caught her arm. "This ordeal has been too much for you."

Carrie bit her lip, feigning weakness. "Might you take me to see the doctor first? I think I might—" She spun away and pretended to gag.

Sebastian muttered something unsavory about helpless women. Usually she'd take offense. Today, she had to stifle a smile. The ruse worked. She couldn't be sure Nick would be at the clinic—no doubt he was searching for her—but the clinic had a telephone, which she aimed to use.

"Fine. Let's go." Sebastian tightened his hold on her arm, setting a brisk pace toward his police car.

To keep her ruse, she stumbled twice and pressed her fist to her mouth until they exited the building. Then she stopped. Sebastian swore, but Carrie made a big show of gulping the fresh air. Snowflakes fell softly from the pre-dawn sky. She closed her eyes and let their gentle touch cool her face.

For all her acting skills, gratefulness to not be locked in that building was as genuine an emotion as she'd ever felt. It allowed her to admit the fear she hadn't allowed herself to entertain: that she'd be left in that room to die.

"I'll have the doc check your sanity, too." Sebastian muttered as he roughly directed her to his car.

Carrie forced herself not to hesitate when Sebastian helped her into the backseat. She'd be at his mercy, but the fictitious persona she'd portrayed would trust the chief of police who saved her.

Alistar slipped into the front passenger seat as Sebastian started the engine, eliminating any doubt that Sebastian was a crooked cop. Was Sebastian both the chief of police and the editor-in-chief?

She allowed that thought to roll around in her mind as they made their way through town. Would they take her to the clinic? Would they risk Nick being home? Unless they could guarantee he wasn't ...

Speculation, that's all she had.

For now.

Low clouds still dropped white flakes, preventing the sun from showing. She caught a glimpse of a broomstick and witch's hat on someone's porch. Tonight was Halloween … when the sun set, the pranks would begin.

Seemed childish to call them pranks, for she'd seen enough property damage and dangerous situations over the years. Fires in abandoned buildings. Wagons on rooftops. Doors removed from their hinges. In fact, the last few years, these so-called pranks had grown worse.

Young men without work, without money, with nothing to do used the night to get back at the employers and businesses that had laid them off. She understood the emotion, having felt it herself before Ali rescued her. With forty percent of the city's workforce unemployed, Carrie could actually be grateful to not be in Chicago tonight.

Not that her current situation felt much safer.

Sebastian parked in front of the clinic and ushered her inside the unlocked building. He and Alistar didn't bother calling for Nick, which answered one of her questions.

"Go make us coffee." Alistar shoved her toward the kitchen.

"Go with her." Sebastian strode into the parlor on the right as if he owned the building.

She needed Alistar to stay here, and she knew just how.

"Get a move on." Alistar nudged her shoulder.

"Okay." Carrie blinked, sniffed. When Alistar eyed her, she swiped at her eyes and muttered, "I'm fine."

The man rolled his eyes. "I can't be bothered with female hysterics. Get yourself under control, woman."

Carrie nodded rapidly and scurried for the kitchen. She threw open the oven door, tossed in two logs, stirred the coals with a third, and left the door open. Then she glanced down the hall. Assured by the low voices that traveled toward her, she lifted the telephone receiver. Time to call for reinforcements.

"Operator?" She matched her voice to Mindy's. "Can you connect me to the Martins residence?"

"Of course, dear," said the operator, a woman with a kind, middle-aged voice. "One moment."

Lord, please stop up their ears.

"This is Sam," Samantha Martins answered.

"I'm at Nick's. Tell your grandmother." Carrie hung up without waiting for a reply.

Her heart pounded as she quietly closed the oven door. Her fingers shook as she filled the kettle with fresh water and set it on a front burner. Buck would rescue her, but was she drawing him into a trap?

Buck walked the hall with Baby Samuel on his left shoulder and a cup of coffee in his right hand. It increased the longing to be married—to Carrie—to have a family of his own, to be a father. Even though he'd lost him, he still wanted to be the kind of father his had been to him.

Meri had been right. Holding the little one had calmed him, probably because the baby slept instead of fussed. So when the tyke woke around four, he'd insisted Meri go back to sleep after she fed and changed her baby.

Please protect Carrie, Lord. Help someone find her.

The three M ladies, as he'd dubbed them in his whispered conversations with Baby Sammy, dozed in his parlor. What an undeserved blessing to have them here at this time. Their presence reminded him he wasn't alone in this fight. Not any more.

O'Connor, Nick, and Patrick had searched all night, only stopping in briefly to provide an update or catch an hour of sleep. Buck knew Carrie hadn't just disappeared, though it sure felt as if she'd vanished.

Had she been injured or ... kidnapped? But then why hadn't there been a ransom, or a demand that he do as his uncle wanted?

Baby Sammy raised his head, his little eyes still closed, then plopped it back down, turned the other way. Yes, holding him put everything into perspective. Once they finally had enough proof to bring to his superior and clear his name, Buck would beg Carrie to marry him and then they'd ... what? The concept of *after* had been shoved so deeply into the closet of his mind, it felt odd to bring it into the light.

The ringing of the telephone shattered the silence. Baby Samuel shifted on Buck's shoulder again. Buck tightened his grip on him as he ran for the kitchen. Setting his mug on the table, he grabbed the receiver.

"Hello?" *Please be Carrie.*

"It's Sam Martins. Is my grandmother there? Or ... is Mindy still there?"

Buck tried not to reveal his disappointment. "Both are, but they're sleeping." He almost asked for news, but why would Samantha ask for one of the women instead of just telling him, if she had information on Carrie?

"That's odd."

Buck perked up, lightly bouncing Samuel to keep the baby asleep. "What is?"

"I thought Mindy just called me. It sounded just like her, though now that I think about it, she never said her name. I assumed, because who else would ask for Nick? But I know Nick is out looking for Carrie."

Buck sorted through her rambling. "What were this person's words exactly?"

"She said, 'I'm at Nick's. Tell your grandmother.' But if it wasn't Mindy—"

"Carrie." Buck barely had the wherewithal to say thank you before he slammed the receiver down on the hook and raced into the parlor. "I know where she is."

The three women blinked at him. He couldn't wait for them to make sense of his words. He plopped Samuel in his mother's arm, told Mindy to send Nick to the clinic, and ran for his car.

Part of him knew full well this was likely a trap, the part of him that parked the car around the corner from Mrs. Whittlebush's old house. But Carrie hadn't called under duress. They had a code word for that. Nor would she have disguised her voice if she wanted anyone but him to know she was there. But the short, cryptic message also told him she wasn't alone at the clinic.

Buck double-checked the pistol at his back and the knife in his belt buckle. Being undercover meant hiding his weapons, but he never went without them. Then he leaned on his car and prayed.

His heartbeat slowed. He became aware of the snow softly falling around him and the splash of water below the cliff across the street. He opened his eyes, drawn to the horizon where light gray clouds danced with the waves.

Calmer than he'd been in weeks—months—Buck made his way toward the clinic. Whoever had Carrie would keep her alive as long as they could control Buck by using her. Did he present himself to her kidnappers or try to rescue her unseen?

The question stalled his steps. The chime of the church bells beginning their top-of-the-hour song reminded him to pray. Again.

No more hiding. Time to face this situation head-on.

And so he climbed the porch steps, kicked the snow from his shoes, and walked inside.

"Buck Wilson." Chief Sebastian's voice boomed from the parlor as Buck made his entrance.

"I'm looking for Carrie." Buck shoved his hands into his pockets. "Is she here? I can't find her."

"Buck." Carrie emerged from the kitchen, holding a tray with a carafe and two cups, with Alistar a step behind her. She met his gaze with a look of hope. She knew he'd come for her.

He tipped up just the corner of mouth, then turned to Sebastian. "Thank you for finding her."

Something shifted in Sebastian's expression. Buck couldn't say exactly what, only that, in an instant, he knew he'd been right about the man. It all made sense, the web of people Uncle Perry had left behind to run his Crow's Nest operation ... of course the chief-of-police would be one of Uncle Perry's cronies.

"Now what, Sebastian?" Buck rocked on his heels. "Do we fight to the death? Do you haul me in for supposed embezzlement? Lock me in a hole never to be found?"

Sebastian waved toward Carrie and Alistar. "We have two reporters in our midst, so mind what you say."

"I'm not afraid of the truth, Sebastian. I've already told Alistar I worked for the Treasury before your boss took everything from me."

As Buck hoped, the barb turned the man's face purple. "Insolent pup."

"Don't like that I know you work for Perry Baxter?" Buck pushed.

Sebastian fumed, his lips pressed together as if to contain a spew of words.

"I knew it." Carrie shoved the tray into Alistar's hands to stand beside Buck. He wove their fingers together to show he welcomed her help. "Your pompous nature betrayed you, Mr. Sebastian. Trying to manipulate a storyteller will only get you caught."

Alistar laughed. "I told you she was too smart for that ploy. You've no respect for journalists, Sebastian."

Buck kept his mouth closed and let the wordsmiths do the work. A vein bulged in Sebastian's neck.

"We will expose you, Mr. Sebastian." Carrie raised her chin, her words confident but not condescending. "You cannot hide—"

"Enough!" Sebastian shouted.

Carrie flinched but kept her chin high. Buck wrapped his arm around her waist. They'd pushed Sebastian to the point of action. Hopefully, he wouldn't take drastic measures before he cleared the decision with his boss. However, running out the door wouldn't end this dilemma, merely postpone it, which meant they had to stick it out, no matter how dangerous.

Buck pressed his fingers against her hip, a signal that they needed to force this to an end. Together. As they should have done from the beginning.

"To the kitchen." Sebastian cleared his pistol from its holster.

Carrie tucked her hair behind her ear, meaning she'd follow Buck's lead. Even with a gun barrel pointed at his chest, Buck's confidence returned. He'd been held at gunpoint plenty of times. Often with Carrie undercover at his side. This is—she was—what he'd been missing.

"Put it away, Sebastian." The gun at Buck's back called to him, but he couldn't shoot a cop, even a dirty one, unless to save Carrie's life. As much as Buck wanted to bring this stand-off to an end, there was no point. This battle would not decide the war, and Buck had learned long ago to bide his time. "This is between my uncle and me."

"Douglas is chauffeuring him here, so you'll get your wish." Sebastian waved the gun. "Now follow Alistar to the kitchen. I want fresh coffee."

Carrie gave a tiny snort. Buck supposed Sebastian hadn't gained his girth by skipping meals—or coffee.

"I'm not your nursemaid." Alistar shoved the tray back into Carrie's hands. "She gets coffee."

Sebastian narrowed his eyes at Alistar for the briefest moment. "Only if loverboy takes the first sip." Sebastian slapped Buck on the shoulder, propelling him down the hall.

Coffee sounded good right about now, if he were honest.

Sebastian settled him into a kitchen chair, securing his hands in front of him, while Carrie remade coffee under Alistar's supervision. Unfortunately, it also meant Sebastian found his gun. Another reason Buck trained in other forms of self-defense: he could never guarantee that a weapon would be at hand. And, after his heart episode, Nick had made sure Buck could still spar before releasing him from the clinic.

The clinic. The beginning and the end of Carrie's investigation into Alistar would end right here. He only hoped they wouldn't need the surgery on the other side of the far wall. He'd helped Nick build it over the summer. Had Mindy found Nick yet? He and O'Connor would make a plan, but would it keep Uncle Perry away?

"Quite the studious expression, Wilson." Sebastian sat kitty-corner to Buck. "Your dame's got the coffee ready. Drink up."

Buck offered Carrie a smile when she set the cup in his bound hands. The worry in her eyes eased.

"Hello?" A female voice followed the opening of the front door. "Nick? Are you here?"

Carrie gripped his shoulder. What was Adaleigh doing here? Why had she picked today to return from their wedding trip? David was going to kill him if she got hurt.

"Anyone here?" Adaleigh's steps grew closer.

Sebastian swore, whipped out his knife, and cut the ropes around Buck's wrists. He wagged the blade at Carrie. "Behave or I use this on her. Got it?"

"Of course." Buck relaxed in his chair as if this cozy meeting were his idea.

Adaleigh stumbled to a stop as she entered the kitchen. "I'm sorry. It appears I've interrupted."

She looked good. Happy. Buck hated to bring anything negative into her first morning back in Crow's Nest. "Nick isn't here. Welcome back, though."

Her smile broadened and she waved his words away. "We just got in and I hoped he'd know where I can find Mindy. She wasn't at the house. I'll try the bakery next. Carrie, did you want to join us?"

Sebastian emitted a low hum.

"I'll go." Alistar grinned his usually slimy smirk. Buck squeezed a fist to keep from smacking it from the man's face.

Adaleigh glared, then seemed to take in the fact that Buck sat in a room with Alistar and Sebastian. A trio of men who had made her life miserable. Her frown deepened. "This is quite the gathering. Anything I should know?"

Buck shook his head. "Just conducting some business while we wait for Nick. I have a check-up with him for my heart." He tapped his chest.

"Yeah." Adaleigh didn't believe him, which meant he needed to make her leave.

He knew exactly how, too, because he knew how Carrie would respond if he asked her, "Does David have time to meet with me tomorrow?"

"Men." Adaleigh shared a commiserating look with Carrie. "They think all we're good for is getting coffee and making appointments."

"Hey, cooking, too." Buck added to sell his point.

Sebastian slammed his palm on the table with an oath. "Unless you plan on baking us a cake, Miss Sirland, we have a meeting to finish."

Carrie dug her fingers into Buck's shoulder to keep him from reacting. *He* could insult Carrie and Adaleigh in this moment because at least Carrie knew it for the lie it was, but Sebastian meant the belittling words.

"It's Mrs. Martins now, Chief Sebastian. Alistar." Adaleigh's tone shifted to a kinder one as she said Carrie's name. Then she pinned Buck with a look that said he better take care of his girl. "You do know your way around a kitchen, Mr. Wilson. Have a good morning."

How she managed to stomp from the house with lady-like grace, Buck would never understand. But that was Adaleigh. He admired ... wait. What had she said? *You know your way around a ... kitchen.*

He wasn't the only one selling a story. She'd been sent for reconnaissance. Now she could tell O'Connor exactly who was in the house and where they were. What surprised him most was that David let her walk in here, knowing full well the danger she faced. But had one of the men—David, Nick, even Patrick—tried what she did, they may not have walked out alive. But Adaleigh? Not only had she gathered information, she left a message for him. The last time one of their friends had been trapped in a kitchen with a criminal, Buck had led the rescue.

Help was here, but they understood the goal and, since they sent Adaleigh instead of storming the doors, they wouldn't interfere until Buck gave the word.

Carrie breathed deeply as the door closed behind Adaleigh. No civilians need enter this mess. Not that Adaleigh couldn't handle herself. Carrie liked the newlywed, appreciated her intelligence and friendship with Buck. Once this situation ended, perhaps they could be friends. However, she would also hate to see her injured so early in her marriage.

How long would they have to wait for Buck's uncle? The room fairly crackled with tension. Jitters crawled along her skin. She wanted to act, to …

Buck squeezed her hand five times in quick succession. Another squeeze. Again, then longer. Morse. *Peace*. By the last dot, the jitters had settled. His thumb traced hers, further calming her.

Besides, Carrie knew subtext when she saw it—Ali was a master at it—and Adaleigh had just delivered a message to Buck. What, Carrie couldn't guess, of course. However, if she didn't understand it, likely Sebastian and Alistar didn't either. Though they probably saw no farther than Adaleigh's gender, which gave Carrie an idea. She'd get these men their coffee and push a few buttons.

The tense silence deepened as she wrapped a towel around her hand to protect her palm from the hot handle of the coffee carafe. She'd already needled Sebastian, and Alistar backed her. Sort of. Perhaps she would win an ally before pushing Sebastian again.

She handed her fellow journalist a fresh, steaming cup of coffee. "So, how does this end, Alistar?"

"What do you mean?" He took a sip.

Carrie shifted her weight. "We're both journalists, we know how this goes. Do you think everything can go on as it has?"

Alistar bristled. "Of course. Might even bring you on like I said last night."

Interesting.

Sebastian watched them with his cop-stare, following her movement as she refilled his cup, then topped-up Buck's. Buck reached for the cup before she set it back down, and their fingers grazed. Her heart warmed at his intentionality. He supported her plan.

She returned the carafe to the stove and stood beside Alistar, shoulder to shoulder. Colleagues. "How would that look, Mr. Alistar?"

He looked down at her with a look that gave her the creepy crawlies. Did he really think women liked to be looked at that way? "You said you only wanted revenge. Ditch the sap. Work for me."

Carrie closed her eyes. She couldn't respond to the tightening of Buck's shoulders. Couldn't react to the innuendo in Alistar's tone. Whatever she said next would determine much.

"Carrie?" Buck approached, hurt in his voice. He took her hands, and she raised her gaze to his. Love shone back, not pain or betrayal. Then he tapped his forefinger against her wrist, giving her his answer.

"What's it gonna be, huh?" Alistar shoved his face between them. "Lover's quarrel or kiss and make up?"

Carrie dropped Buck's hands, folded her arms. "You're unmarried, aren't you, Alistar?"

He jerked as if she'd slapped him. "Yeah, wife divorced me."

And he wonders why. Instead of the sarcastic thought, she opted for sympathy. "Because you put everything into the job, of course."

Alistar's knuckles turned white.

Carrie let the moment thicken. Having three men's attention on her was rather unnerving, not that she hadn't faced worse before. Still ... "Why do you inflict your anger at her on other women?"

"What is this?" Alistar shouted at her, his spit spraying her cheek. "An interrogation?"

Buck took a ready stance. Sebastian rose.

Carrie allowed a disgusted expression. "You are a disgrace to our profession, Mr. Alistar. Printing stories you're told to print. Hiding the truth or just plain twisting it to your liking. That is not what we do. We tell the truth. We expose people like Chief—"

"I've given everything to working for Baxter." Alistar crowded her against the cupboard as he set his cup beside hers. "I've taken his orders. Pushed his news. It's gotten me nothing but disdain from pretty dames like you."

"Back off." Buck's low words reminded Carrie he was there. He wouldn't step in unless she needed him.

"Alistar." Sebastian commanded.

The journalist pressed closer, his coffee breath turning her stomach. "Maybe it's time I take—"

She pressed her heel on top of his foot, just past the sturdy part of the toe. "What did you want to take?"

He swore, broke away, and backhanded her.

Ouch. She stumbled to her knees. Before she could look up, Buck had Alistar pinned to the ground and Sebastian had his pistol aimed at all of them.

"Wilson, sit down." Sebastian jerked his chin toward the table.

Carrie pulled Buck away from Alistar.

"Nice leash." Alistar stood with a smirk.

Buck gathered Carrie to his chest, his muscles taught beneath her cheek. So much for Buck letting her handle Alistar as a journalist. She had one more threat up her sleeve, but it would keep. "Gentlemen, could we all sit down?"

Sebastian did, keeping his pistol on his knee.

"I'd like her to apologize." Alistar plopped into a chair like a petulant child.

"For what?" Buck put himself between them. "You crowded her, then hit her. She deserves your apology."

"She stomped on my foot." Alistar lifted the offended limb.

"I didn't see any stomping." Buck held her tightly to his side. "You crowding her may have gotten your foot under hers."

Alistar stood abruptly, knocking his chair over. "I've had enough. Tell Baxter he can use the dame as his journalist. I'm through."

Sebastian wrapped his thick fingers around the butt of his pistol. "You stay until Baxter gets here. Sit down. All of you."

"What have I gotten out of all of this? Nothing." Alistar spat at Sebastian's feet and headed down the hall. "No respect. I am walking away, and you can't stop me."

"Buck?" Carrie whispered, leaning into him. This wasn't good. She'd seen this before. Could predict what would happen as it played out in slow motion.

"Alistar." Buck stepped forward, wishing to stop what he surely could see as well.

Sebastian raised his gun. Carrie covered her mouth as his pistol fired, and screamed.

CHAPTER FIFTEEN

Buck gathered Carrie to his chest, hoping to shield her from the man bleeding out in the clinic hall. Sebastian had shot Alistar in the back. The thought had bile burning Buck's throat.

Then the kitchen door flew open and O'Connor stepped inside, his gun leveled at his boss.

"It's not how this looks." Sebastian raised his hands in surrender.

"You shot a man in the back." O'Connor motioned with his revolver. "Put the weapon on the table and back up."

While Sebastian obeyed, he looked neither remorseful nor caught. Of course. Uncle Perry would get him out of jail. Anger mixed with nausea. Their chance to catch his uncle had failed.

"Matrone!" O'Connor called as he handed Sebastian's pistol to Buck. The doctor entered, and Buck was forced to release Carrie so he could cover both O'Connor and Nick.

She put on a brave face until Adaleigh peeked her head inside and beckoned her. Then Buck caught the quiver of Carrie's lip and wished he could comfort her. He caught Adaleigh's eye and gave a nod. She'd look after his girl.

"He's gone." Nick looked up from where he knelt beside Alistar's body.

"Albert Sebastian, you're under arrest." O'Connor secured the chief's hands behind his back.

Buck expected Sebastian to make up a story, maybe blame Buck or Carrie, but the man kept silent.

"How could you shoot him in the back?" The question seeped out of Buck.

Sebastian's lip curled.

"I'm taking him in." O'Connor pushed Sebastian ahead of him. "Matrone, make sure no one touches Alistar and nobody leaves. Got it?"

As soon as O'Connor and Sebastian exited, Buck pulled his chair away from the table where he wouldn't see Alistar and sank onto it. Nick took Sebastian's seat, leaving him with a view of both doors and Buck.

"Say it." Buck hated waiting for what judgment the man would make.

"Say what?" Nick rested his elbows on his knees and folded his hands.

"I failed." Buck shoved his fingers through his hair. He never did that, yet he'd done it how many times in the last twenty-four hours or less? "I failed to trap my uncle. I failed to get proof of his criminal activities."

"Buck."

"I let a man—" his voice cracked.

"You didn't kill him." Nick stared at him. "Do you hear me?"

"I should have stopped him." He'd seen it happening, as if directing a play. "How does a man shoot another in the back?"

Nick shook his head. "We've seen the basest of criminals display honor and some we thought decent, show no decency at all. Who are we to judge a man's heart? Actions are all we can go by, but the Lord knows."

Buck looked at his friend as if the man had a rope to save a drowning man. "What does the Lord see in my heart?"

Nick took a moment. "He sees a sinful man clothed in Jesus' righteousness. A man trying to bring justice to a broken world. A man tormented by the evil he faces. And a man who has a woman who loves him."

"Until death parts us." Carrie stood in the kitchen doorway, tear stairs on her cheeks, but a smile on her lips.

Buck leapt to his feet, knocking over his chair.

"This isn't over, Buck." She walked toward him, but he couldn't move. "We will clear your name."

"And then?" he croaked.

She stopped before him and pulled at a chain around her neck. She lifted it over her head, then gathered his hand in hers. He watched, mesmerized, as the chain pooled in his palm, laying a ring on top. Not just any ring. The engagement ring he'd given her.

"You kept it." His vision turned watery.

"Ali did that first year. I couldn't look at it." She closed his fingers around it. "Then I needed it because I knew you hadn't left me to end our engagement. You left to protect me. I vowed to find you. And now I give this back so you can present it to me again."

Buck pressed his thumb and forefinger into his eyes.

"Now come along. You should kiss me, but not with a dead body in the room. It might be Halloween, but that is much too macabre for me."

Laughter sputtered. "Leave it to my journalist to know the right words to say."

What a day. Carrie wished she could drop into bed and wake in time for Christmas.

"No rest for the weary." Adaleigh wove her arm through Carrie's as they entered Mrs. Martins's home. Buck and David walked behind them, as did Nick and Mindy.

"Does Mrs. Martins know to expect a houseful?" Carrie hated to cause the older woman more work, especially since learning of the dangerous aspects of Carrie's occupation had seemed to tax her the other evening.

"She would have it no other way." Adaleigh patted Carrie's hand.

"What about you?" Carrie stopped them in the hall. "You and David are newlyweds. You don't need our mess tainting your first days together."

"Sorry to disappoint." David shoved a thumb at Buck. "He already added drama to our wedding."

Buck reddened.

Carrie bristled. "It wasn't his fault."

"And that's what friendship and family is all about. Right, darling?" Adaleigh kissed David on the cheek.

He shifted to catch her lips. "Yes, ma'am."

"I can't watch this." Buck started down the hall.

"Ah, il mio amico." The Italian words had Carrie spinning around.

"Ali!" When had she arrived?

Her boss wrapped her in a hug, then cupped her cheeks. "Is he grumpy because he has not yet kissed you?"

Carrie's cheeks heated.

"Mamma mia. He has!" Ali turned to Buck and dragged him to where she could reach a hand to his forehead. "You do not seem sick. Has your heart healed?"

"I'm fine, Ali." Buck kissed her cheek.

"He refuses to accept that David Martins might be happy." Adaleigh grinned, and Carrie marveled at how the woman's happiness had not been dimmed by the morning's events.

Buck muttered and led the way down the hall. The others followed, but Ali held tight Carrie's arm to keep her by the door.

"How are you?" Ali barely came up to Carrie's chin, but she packed a world of Italian Mamma comfort in her petite frame. As if she could read Carrie's thoughts, Ali hummed and wrapped Carrie in another maternal hug. "I'm sorry, la mia stellina."

So many emotions crashed through Carrie, but Ali's embrace seemed to soak them all from her body, like bread did gravy from a plate.

"Carrie?" Buck returned, stopped a respectable distance from them.

How much time had passed? "I'm sorry, I'm keeping everyone."

"It's okay." He stepped closer. "I was worried, is all."

Ali smiled. "I am glad to see this. You two. Together. Ah! But I have a surprise for you, Carrie. First, though, Adaleigh has information you both will want to hear. To the cucina."

Carrie chuckled. Ali used Italian words in the most unusual times. One never knew when one might appear.

Buck wrapped his arm around her shoulders and pressed his lips to her hair. "I'm not keen on letting you out of my sight. Last night about killed me."

She rested her head against his chest. "The people who matter most to us are right here in Crow's Nest."

He bent his head to capture her gaze. "You want me to propose right now? I will."

She kissed him, quick and light. "I don't know."

"Alright." He studied her a moment longer, then kissed her temple. "Alright."

He didn't explain his words, but as he led her toward the kitchen, Carrie felt confident he'd read her answer, one she couldn't even formulate yet, and would act at just the right moment.

Had it only been two nights ago Buck had sat in this same chair, looking around the table at the people gathered to help him? He'd wished for David and Adaleigh, and now not only were they here, Ali and Adaleigh's lawyer were here, too.

From going it alone to having so many people that David and Nick had to stand to allow enough seating.

The front door opened and Samson loped down the hall, followed by his master. "Em said you have news?"

"Sit, Michael." Mrs. Martins jumped from her chair, but her brother waved her off.

"Can't." He rubbed his face, looking as haggard as Buck had ever seen the man. "Can Samson stay with you tonight?"

"Of course," Mrs. Martins fussed. "Now sit before you fall over."

He took the empty seat next to Buck, using Buck's shoulder as a support to ease himself into the chair. It wasn't the time to ask if the man was okay, but he would.

"Who has news?" O'Connor took the mug his sister pressed into his hands.

"We do." Adaleigh shifted to the edge of her seat. "Before we left on our wedding trip, I made sure Mr. Binitari had all the information I knew about ... well ... everything. Ali filled him in on the rest and the two of them have been busy."

"I hope you actually had a *wedding trip*," Nick muttered. Adaleigh and Mindy both blushed.

David grinned. "Binitari was kept busy and left us alone."

"Shut it." Buck glared at the two. It's not that he didn't wish them happiness. He did. He dropped his head back. "Sorry. I'm jealous is all."

Silence.

Buck straightened to find everyone staring at him. "What? I was days from marrying the love of my life, and having this happily ever after stuff shoved in my face while my fiancée is sitting next to me—so close and yet so out of reach ..."

"We can wake up a preacher. A judge ..." How David managed the words with a straight face.

"Sea captain?" Nick slapped David's shoulder. "Got one of those right here."

"As much as I appreciate this male ribbing," O'Connor groaned, "Binitari, speak."

The uptight man preened for a moment, then shared the spotlight with Ali. For twenty minutes they laid out everything Buck had been searching for. Records and paperwork. Transactions and shipments. Names and dates and transcripts of conversations.

"How did you get all of this?" Buck slid the pile of paper closer, sifting through the pages in wonder. "I've searched for two years for this."

"It's because you focused on just the Conglomerate." Ali spoke kindly, without a hint of judgment. "Carrie didn't find it either because she focused on the Chicago angle. When Mr. Biniari and I put our heads together, we combined those angles as well as our own."

"I have court contacts." Binitari acknowledged Ali. "She has a great many wealthy contacts."

"My husband does." Ali inclined her head at the knock coming from the front door. "I also have a secret weapon."

Carrie came to attention. "He found something."

Ali nodded. "And he's here to deliver it in person."

Everyone murmured, and Buck looked to Ali. Should he be worried

Carrie just dashed down the hall to meet a *he*?

"I can't say whether you would have met him before." Ali read his expression. "And since none of us reveal our sources, you wouldn't have heard his name unless you came across him in your own sphere."

"I have met him." Binitari twisted in his chair as footsteps grew closer. "Just once. I didn't realize he was such a prized source for these ladies. The fact he's willing to reveal himself as such speaks to the importance of your case."

"He's right." Ali's serious expression underscored Binitari's words. "He is very careful about remaining neutral so he can help those who need it most."

Carrie had her arm in that of another Italian. Dark features, black hair, and a grin that could cause any woman to swoon. "He's also a helpless flirt and impeccable matchmaker." Carrie's eyes twinkled too much for Buck's way of thinking. "Everyone, this is Gio Vella."

"Ciao." Gio doffed his flat cap with a slight bow, then searched the faces before landing on Buck. "You are Buck. Ah, how do you say? Carrie, uh—never mind. Inglese ... uh, it is my pleasure to meet you."

Buck speechlessly shook Gio's hand. He was used to Ali's occasional stumble into Italian, even Nick's mutterings, and his sister, Bella's constant jabbering in a convolution of languages. But Gio's thick accent was unlike what he'd experienced before.

"Carrie, she has spoken highly of you." Gio was still shaking his hand, his other moving with his words. "I could not leave this information to be delivered. I found the, how do you say? The smoking gun."

Buck shot a look at Carrie, who was nearly bouncing with happiness. She had brought all these people together to help him. Rallied people who once considered him an enemy, a bad person, a criminal.

He broke away from Gio, not caring what proof he'd found, and wrapped his arms around Carrie. Whether other people spoke or whispered or stared, Buck didn't care. This woman had stood beside him, even when he pushed her away. She was—

Buck pulled away. What was he doing *thinking* these things?

Carrie's happiness hiccuped when Buck abruptly released her from his arms. Bereft, she staggered a moment. Until he clasped her hands and dropped to one knee.

Her heart leapt to triple time as she stared into eyes that shimmered.

"My love, you astound me." Buck cleared his throat. "You are loyal and fierce and determined and beautiful and I cannot believe I cut myself off from you for two years. No wonder my heart was broken. It cannot function without you."

She clamped her teeth on her lower lip, willing it not to tremble.

"You have accomplished in weeks what I have strived for years to do, because you know the value of working together. And I want to work together with you for the rest of our lives. Side by side, the way we have faced good times and gun barrels."

A giggle slipped out, freeing a tear to trail down her cheek.

"Marry me, Caroline Wagoneer."

She started to nod, wondering how she could have wondered whether she was ready for a second proposal just an hour ago, but Buck stopped.

"Marry me tomorrow?" Urgency weighed his voice.

"Yes." She bent forward and kissed him. "First thing, we'll wake a preacher. But first, let's handle your uncle."

"No." Buck winked. "First you need your ring."

The moment the simple band with the three tiny onyx stones slipped onto her finger, applause reminded her Buck had proposed—for the second time—in the middle of the Martinses' kitchen in front of all these people. The very people who, as Buck declared, she'd gathered to help him clear his name.

Buck clasped her hand as if he'd never let it go. "All right, Mr. Vella, I'm ready now. Show me the proof."

And what proof it was. Photographs and wiretaps of Perry Baxter organizing his counterfeiting ring. What clinched it was the image of Buck's uncle holding a one-thousand dollar federal reserve note while standing beside the press that had just printed it.

"How did you get this?" Buck stared at the face of his uncle. Carrie leaned over his shoulder, noting the narrow, angled features that matched Buck's. However, instead of giving Baxter an air of authority, as they did Buck, the older man looked aged and hard as steel.

"People owe me favors." Gio shrugged, drawing her attention back to the rest of the evidence he'd gathered. "And I am good at operating the telegraph wires and the radio. Your uncle, this Perry Baxter, he has enemies willing to help—how do you say?—put him out of business."

"How legal is all of this?" O'Connor picked up an inventory list, but looked at Binitari.

"I found a judge willing to help us." Binitari motioned to Ali. "Pardon, Mr. Di Stasio found a judge."

Carrie stifled a grin, as she always did when people referred to Ali's husband in such a way. Di Stasio was not Ali's married name, but they all referred to her husband as *Mr. Di Stasio* since they guarded her undercover reporter work so closely. She glanced at Buck. Perhaps they should do something similar to protect their family.

"A judge in Illinois does us no good here." O'Connor tossed the paper down. "In fact, none of this does us any good. I cannot charge a man based on evidence not in my jurisdiction."

"That is where I come in." Buck set down the photograph and placed his thumbs and forefingers on his belt, transforming into the Treasury man she'd originally fallen in love with.

Carrie's heart melted. Her Buck had returned. Better. Stronger. And somehow, she loved him even more than she had the first time she planned to marry him.

"When this is over, I'm moving out of this house." Buck paced his parlor, hating the room more and more with each step.

Night had fallen, and with it the temperatures. Though it no longer snowed, the chill permeated the air, hissing through the window cracks. Not even the fire crackling in the parlor's fireplace could warm the chill that continued to arch down his back.

"Where will you go?" Carrie sat on the sofa, clasped hands resting primly on her knees as she watched him.

"Where you go." The answer popped out without thought. He didn't care where he went next. As long as it did not include this wretched structure, but did include Carrie.

The afternoon had been a flurry of preparation. He and Detective O'Connor had spent most of it at the station, updating Buck's boss, filing the evidence, and setting the evening's plan into motion. The sacrifices of the last two years would end tonight.

Carrie tilted her head. "How many hours have you walked this room?"

"Since you arrived in Crow's Nest, or since I did?" Buck might have well created a track from the door to the fireplace and back. Surely the wood beneath the area rug showed signs of wear. This house was a jail cell and Buck paced it like a prisoner.

"My point, Love." Carrie shook her head. "Walking won't make your uncle arrive any faster. It will just use up your energy."

"I have too much energy." But Buck understood her point, so he sank onto the sofa beside her. Any other time, he'd worry about her reputation, alone as they were in the house together. But they would marry in the morning—if he survived the night—and Gio Vella had wired the house to transmit next door, where he, Ali, and Binitari waited to record every word.

Something round smacked the window across from them, making both startle. The thing stuck to the window, then slid down, leaving a mess in its wake. Halloween mischief makers.

"Is that a pie?" Carrie rose, her long, flowing skirt—her undercover dress, as she called it—swishing against her legs. Usually she only wore tailored, feminine suits.

Buck caught her wrist, tugging her back to the sofa. Not wanting her far from him, nor close to the window. Just in case. "A pie is tame. Last year, they removed all my shutters. Never found either the culprits or the shutters."

He didn't mention the flaming cow pie someone launched through his broken window last year. A part of him would be sad to leave Crow's Nest when this was all over. It harbored secrets, as any small town did, but it contained good people, too. People Carrie had managed to win over, ones he would be willing to call ... friends.

Carrie rubbed her thighs, the motion causing Buck to sit up. How could he be so focused on himself, he forgot to comfort his fiancée. *His fiancée* ... he'd missed calling her that.

"Hey." He caught her eye. "Are you nervous?"

"No." She offered a brave smile, but Buck knew her too well. She was definitely nervous. "Why would I be? O'Connor is watching from across the street. David and Nick are nearby. So are Ali and Gio. The others, I know, are praying. It's going to be fine."

"My boss sanctioned this sting. He's sending the BOI." The Bureau of Investigation. Buck took her trembling fingers in his and rubbed his thumbs on the back of her palms. "My uncle has nowhere to go. He will be arrested tonight."

"I know." She dropped her chin. "But your boss didn't say whether the evidence will allow you to return to work."

Is that what had her nervous? Buck kissed her, quick and light, on the lips. "I don't care. I'm resigning."

She sucked in a breath. "But you love your job."

He cupped her cheek, loving that her first thought was about him, not about how he would provide for their family. He hadn't told her about his conversation with O'Connor before leaving the police station that afternoon. It would keep until this was over.

Shouting outside drew them to the windows, though Buck tried to keep his body in front of Carrie. One of the neighbors stood in his dressing robe, yelling at miscreants making off with his front door.

Carrie snorted.

"I hate Halloween," Buck muttered.

"What's not to love?" said a voice behind them. "It's a good day for needed distractions."

Buck spun toward the parlor entrance.

Perry Baxter had arrived.

CHAPTER SIXTEEN

Buck stepped forward, putting himself between his uncle and Carrie. He wanted to reach for her hand, or for the gun at his back, but spotting Uncle Perry's bodyguard in the hall, Buck opted to keep his hands where everyone could see them. "You received my invitation."

With O'Connor's help, and his boss's approval, Buck had dangled bait they knew Baxter couldn't resist. The photograph Gio Vella had provided sat on the mantle behind Buck. He'd offered to hand it over, but only to Perry so that "it didn't fall into the wrong hands."

"Nephew." Perry shrugged out of his snow-dusted gray coat and tossed it unceremoniously on the sofa. Buck had forgotten how tall and rail-thin his uncle was. It made him appear frail, but Buck knew the man was anything but. Seeing his uncle now, who shared his mother's eyes, brought memories that clouded Buck's thinking.

The bodyguard, a burly man of solid muscle—very much his uncle's opposite—ducked just inside the door, resharpening Buck's attention. Buck angled himself to keep both men in clear sight. Carrie brushed his arm as she stepped beside him. She was a vital part of this plan, but he wished she were far away from this danger.

Everything he'd sacrificed the last few years came down to this moment. He needed a confession.

"Is this your blushing bride?" Perry asked, and Buck realized he'd let silence go on for too long.

Be civil. Buck coached himself. "Uncle Perry, this is Carrie."

Should he say her full name? Her undercover name? Sweat moistened his palms. He always knew how to respond in a situation like this ... but even with the plan they had in place, all his ideas vanished. He didn't know what to do. How to bring this to an end.

Carrie slipped her arm around Buck's left one, wisely allowing him freedom to go for his pistol with his right, if need be. She offered a welcoming smile. "It's good to meet you, Uncle Perry. Honestly, it's been two years too long. We should have met at the wedding."

The barb snapped the mask from his uncle's face. "No pleasantries, then? Straight to business." Usually, Buck would ease into this type of conversation ... not today. He was done playing nice, dancing to his uncle's game. This needed to end today.

"It's always been business, uncle." Shouts of mischief-making youths echoed outside. How many children had been caught in the middle of his uncle's web? Anger simmered and he held up a finger. "Before I get the rest of the proof you came here to retrieve, tell me why."

"Buck." Carrie whispered the warning. This wasn't part of the plan, but he had to ask.

Mock pity crinkled the lines carved into Uncle Perry's features. "You are too much like your father, Buck. You think the world is broken into right and wrong. Good and bad. When a man is desperate, those lines fade."

Buck opened his mouth to protest, but stopped. The last two years had proved his uncle's words.

"The question is not about which side of the law you're on—you know full well a badge does not equal law-abiding." Uncle Perry crept forward, like a panther stalking his victim. "No, the question is whether you are the beggar or the supplier."

Buck clenched his jaw to keep from closing his eyes. His uncle was right and he hated him for it.

"I had to make you see." Baxter shrugged, as if merely teaching his nephew the proper way to light a fire. "Your sense of duty was misplaced, so I'm happy to discover your years of exile have paid off. You've reunited with your girl. Now you can step into the role of my second in command."

No amount of gritting his teeth could keep his mouth closed. Even Carrie coughed beside him. His uncle was … "You're out of your mind!"

"Am I?" Again he carved that pity smile onto his face. "My contacts here have spoken highly of your work the last two years. You have shown exemplary work. The fact that you are at odds with O'Connor and his nephew proves it."

Buck's stomach churned, though his uncle's words were proof they'd managed to keep Alistar's death and Sebastian's arrest under wraps.

"I say again, Buck, that you are ready to move up in the organization. And you're bringing a reporter with you. This is good, son."

"I am not your son." The words burst from Buck's chest, heedless of his uncle's shocked expression or the way his bodyguard moved into the room. "You are not my father. You have never been my father. My father was a good man. A just man. Whatever you say about it, he was one of the good ones and he died for it."

Carrie wrapped his arm in a hug, tethering him to the task at hand, as she said, "You understand, Uncle Perry, my fiancée has been under quite a bit of stress. Please forgive his outburst."

The bodyguard didn't move, but Baxter relaxed. "You've gotten yourself a good woman, nephew."

"Yes, well." Buck forced himself to calm so he could deliver his lie with conviction. They still needed a confession or every sacrifice would be for naught. "Carrie and I don't plan to stay in Crow's Nest after this. I want my position back, and I want assurance Carrie will be protected."

"That can be arranged." Baxter stepped forward. Did he sense an ally? Buck hoped so, because it was the only plan he had left.

Buck slipped his hands into his pockets, gathering himself as the Buck of the Conglomerate. "I won't be your hired gun either. Seems you have one of those."

Baxter laughed, clapped Buck on the shoulder. "That I do. Douglas here is a wealth of information."

Carrie tensed beside Buck, the warning Buck needed to see through his uncle's words. Douglas knew Carrie was tied to Ali, which meant Buck was being led to the slaughter as his uncle tied a handy noose around his neck.

"You know, uncle," Buck tossed a counter bait, "you say your man here knows plenty, but does he know the types of articles Carrie writes?"

"She works for that Di Stasio woman." Baxter shrugged. "Getting an informant within that organization would be a coup."

"That woman—" Carrie started.

Buck cut her off, needing a confession before they delivered the final blow. "That woman has been a thorn in my side. Carrie's, too. Now tell us what you want from us."

Baxter shook his head and Buck knew he'd pressed too hard.

"I'm sorry." Buck rubbed his temple. "The last two years have cost me my fiancée, my health, and nearly my faith. What do you want from me now?"

He felt Baxter's scrutiny, knew he'd just laid himself bare. This wasn't undercover Buck his uncle saw, but the real one. He could only hope he hadn't made a grave misstep.

"Do you want to see the picture?" Carrie retrieved it from the mantle. "One of my informants took it. It's of you beside a printing press."

While Carrie kept hold of it, she angled it toward Baxter, who swore as soon as he got a glimpse. "Where did you get that?"

"My informant." Carrie snatched the picture back. "Now, Buck convinced me to give you a chance to change my mind. Otherwise, I would have printed it already."

"Printed it?" Baxter's voice rose.

"Yes, sir. As you said, I'm a reporter and my boss doesn't like it when I don't come up with a story." She waved the photograph. "This is a story."

Baxter stepped into her space. "You're a dead man if you print that."

Buck bristled, but Carrie appeared unfazed. "Dead woman, I believe you mean."

"Yes!" Baxter's command was low, and the more deadly for it. "Now give me the photograph or I'll have Douglas take it from your cold, lifeless hands."

Pain shot through Buck's heart. Physical shooting pain. And it took everything in him not to grimace. He blinked his sight clear. His heart couldn't give out on him now.

Carrie cocked her head. "Do you kill every reporter that prints something you don't like?"

Buck didn't see the backhand coming or he would have saved Carrie from it. Instead, the sound twisted in his chest. His heart was failing him. He bent over, hands on his knees, and glanced toward the mantle where Gio had hidden the transmitter. No video would show what was happening, but a single phrase would bring O'Connor, and Nick, running.

Carrie pinned her focus on Baxter. She had to get a confession, and fast, before Buck's heart gave out. From the corner of her eye, she could see the perspiration on Buck's forehead, and the way he wavered on his feet.

God, please help us here.

"I'm not one to smother evidence." She held the photograph on one side, as if to tear it. "But perhaps we could find a compromise."

"Your life for the photo." Baxter shrugged.

"Leave her alone." Buck staggered toward his uncle, but dropped to his knees.

"Are you threatening to kill me if I don't hand over this evidence?" Carrie held her breath. This is what she needed him to say, to admit to premeditated attempted murder. *Hurry up, Buck needs help.*

Baxter leaned in, and she eased back, closer to the mantle and the transmitter. Baxter followed her step for step. "Not only will I kill you, I'll have Douglas kill your beloved Buck, and then I will kill you."

"Like you killed his father?" Carrie knew it was a leap, but the way Baxter's eyes sparked said her intuition had been spot on.

"Yes." Baxter backed her against the fireplace. "I gutted my sister's husband like the rat he was, and I'll do the same to that fiancée of yours. He threatened to undo my operation once and I won't have his sniveling reporter do it to me again."

She had him for murder, and her anger erupted at all this man had cost Buck. "Ever heard of C. C. Wagner?"

The way Baxter paled told her he had.

"I am C. C. Wagner. And this photograph will be printed. I will make sure the entire Chicago area—no, this column will be syndicated across the United States—will all know you framed Buck. You forced him from his federal job by planting evidence. Isn't that right, Perry?"

White gave way to red, then to purple as Baxter matched, then exceeded her own anger. He wrapped a hand around her neck. "You want the truth before I kill you? Yes. I framed Buck. I ordered my men to plant counterfeit bills in his place. And I paid an agent to make sure all his colleagues ostracized him. And I'll do that to you, even if you won't be alive to see it. Your reputation will be destroyed."

Though air barely seeped into her lungs, Carrie didn't struggle. She closed her eyes and tears slipped down her cheeks. They did it. "Bring us into harbor."

Baxter dropped her, pointed to Douglas as he made for the door. "Finish them and meet me at the *Gazette*."

"Carrie!" Buck was on his knees, but as Douglas drew his weapon, Buck pushed her toward the sofa.

The bullet crashed into the brick where she'd been and Buck returned fire. Carrie peered around the sofa in time to see the man crumple.

"Baxter, stop." Detective O'Connor blocked the man's escape.

Buck staggered to his feet, his face ashen. "This ends now, Baxter. You're going to prison for counterfeiting, attempted murder, and for the … murder of my father."

Baxter sneered. "My blood runs through your veins, boy. You think you're so good, but you have a criminal in you."

"Maybe." Buck glanced at Carrie for the briefest moment. "But I don't have to be one. I've been forgiven and no longer have to find justice on my own. A threefold cord, uncle, is not easily broken."

"Then I'll sever it." Baxter yanked a pistol from his waistband and fired it at Carrie.

Carrie's cry as she fell might as well have been a bullet through his own heart. He dropped his gun, confident O'Connor had Baxter in hand, and crawled for his love.

"Carrie? Talk to me, please?" *Please be alive.*

If he'd gotten her killed … His heart twisted, stealing his breath. He cradled his left arm to his chest as he leaned over her. Blood pooled below her right collarbone.

And then, praise be to God, Carrie blinked open her eyes. Pain shimmered, but she lived.

"My love." Buck kissed her.

A harsh Italian phrase Buck didn't understand preceded Nick's appearance. Nick dropped to his knees and dug in his doctor's bag. "You are going to swallow this aspirin, then lay on this sofa. Is that clear?"

"Carrie …" Buck accepted the medicine, swallowed it without water.

"If you don't rest, you won't be alive to take care of her." Nick jabbed his finger at the sofa. "Now lay down."

Buck sat, but he wouldn't lay down until he knew Carrie was out of danger. His attention snagged on the arm of the sofa. He ran his finger through the hole.

"How is she?" Mindy echoed Buck's continual question as she joined them.

"Bullet is near the surface below the clavicle." Nick pressed the area around the wound, causing Carrie to moan. Buck wanted to stop him, but knew Nick wouldn't cause pain unless necessary. "God protected her. The bullet missed her lung and was slow enough it didn't shatter her scapula."

The sofa had slowed the bullet. "Then she'll be okay?" Buck grimaced as another pain arched through his chest.

Nick met his eye in unblinking contact. "Provided the wound doesn't become infected, this should not be a fatal gunshot."

"Thank you, Lord." Buck closed his eyes. Gentle hands—Mindy's—eased him to lie down on the sofa. She even lifted his legs.

"Rest, Buck." She squeezed his hand. "We'll take care of her."

He watched as David helped Nick lift Carrie, and Mindy followed after with Nick's doctor's bag. The room quieted, and while the electric light overhead still illuminated the room, and the fire in the fireplace still danced, everything seemed dimmed.

"Buck?" Adaleigh knelt beside him. "Don't worry about Carrie. Between Nick, Mindy, David, and Ali, she is in good, capable hands."

Buck sighed. "And ... Baxter?" He couldn't call him uncle anymore, knowing without a shadow of a doubt that the man murdered his father.

"Uncle Mike has him in custody." Adaleigh settled on the ground, her back against the sofa, as if she planned to stay awhile. "Mr. Binitari and Gio went along to see after the evidence. You and Carrie did good work. My lawyer thinks this will completely clear your name."

"At what cost?" Buck closed his eyes only to see the bullet screaming toward Carrie again and again.

"Fighting for truth, for justice, for good to prevail always has a cost." Her words were quiet. "How can we expect not to pay a price when we follow a God willing to send His Son to vanquish evil with His life?"

"I'm not worthy to be considered in such a thought."

"None of us are. And you know that. It's the beauty of God. He is rich in mercy."

Buck leaned his head back and the rest of the Ephesians 2 passage whispered through his mind. *For his great love wherewith he loved us, even when we were dead in sins …*

"Is he awake?" O'Connor's question shuttered the moment.

"Be gentle with him, Uncle Mike." Adaleigh rose. "His heart needs rest."

Seemed a double meaning, but O'Connor merely nodded and pulled a chair to Buck's side. "Bureau agents arrived. They'll want to debrief you when you're up for it."

"My … and Baxter?"

O'Connor set his hand where Adaleigh's had been. "It's over, son. You did good."

A sob choked him, then another and another. Buck rolled to his side as the emotion overtook him.

O'Connor stayed, his hand steady, as Buck cried. "Well done."

CHAPTER SEVENTEEN

Sunday, November 1

"You are not well enough for a wedding." Mindy glared at Carrie as sunlight blazed through the bedroom window. Buck's bedroom window.

"It's scandalous that I'm in his bed." Carrie's cheeks heated. "Even if it's temporarily a hospital room, and Nick took him to the clinic last night."

Mindy gave no indication of softening. "And you took a bullet. It could still get infected."

"Then I want Buck here to nurse me back to health. As my husband," Carrie huffed. "Mindy, I've waited two years for him. I don't want to wait until the perfect circumstances."

Mindy sank to the bed. "I understand, I do. But won't you regret having a wedding ceremony ... in bed?"

Carrie smirked. "Who said anything about staying in bed?"

Mindy threw up her hands. "What is the point of arguing with you? You're going to have your way whether it's medically sound or not."

"Please, Mindy." Carrie leaned forward, careful of her right side. "As soon as the preacher has finished with Sunday service, I want to marry Buck."

"Yoohoo!" Mrs. Martins called from downstairs. "I brought breakfast."

Mindy rolled her eyes. "Now you'll get the matchmaker of matchmakers on your side."

Carrie would argue that Gio Vella might have Mrs. Martins beat on that score, but since Gio had already left for Chicago, she'd take advantage of the matchmaker she had left.

"How's our patient this morning?" Mrs. Martins huffed as she reached the top of the stairs. She wore a brown woolen coat buttoned up to her chin, a thick scarf, and a hat that wouldn't keep her ears warm.

"Ornery." Mindy took the basket from where it hung on Mrs. Martins's arm. "Perhaps you can convince her to stay in bed."

Mrs. Martins eyed Carrie with a twinkle that kept Carrie's mouth shut. "Oh, I wouldn't worry about that. But I could use your help downstairs. Just leave the basket on the bedtable here."

"Carrie can't use—"

"It'll be fine." Mrs. Martins hooked her arm through Mindy's. "Come along."

Curiosity had Carrie tapping the fingers of her left hand. Her entire right side ached to distraction, but not enough to keep her from wondering why Mrs. Martins left the door open. Or should she say, whom the older lady had left it open for. Buck perhaps?

Her stomach turned giddy. Mindy declared Buck needed rest, and lots of it, but so far, it appeared he'd come through his heart episode last night. That's all Mindy would tell her, though, and Carrie needed to see him for herself.

Adaleigh peeked in the door. "Mindy's gone?"

"Mrs. Martins dragged her downstairs." Carrie tried to hide her disappointment that it wasn't Buck.

"Good." Adaleigh closed the door and darted to the basket. "She sent jam and bread. Something simple since she figured your stomach may revolt with something too rich, like eggs."

"It might." Carrie rubbed the troublesome spot on her belly. The pain medicine was wearing off, but she didn't want more until she'd spoken to Buck. It made her so drowsy. But the pain made her queasy.

"How is the shoulder?" Adaleigh opened the jar of jam and spread a liberal amount on a slice of bread.

"Nick extracted the bullet and said it hadn't gone in too deep." Carrie would shrug, but didn't dare move her shoulder. Fire still smoldered inside.

"He's seen worse, from what Mindy tells me. Not that it makes your pain any less." Adaleigh plated the bread and set it on Carrie's lap. "If I can spring you from Nurse Mindy, would you like to move downstairs?"

Carrie ignored the bread. Hope turned her stomach to butterflies. "How is Buck? Mindy says he's fine."

Adaleigh sat on the side of her bed with a smile. "He wants to see you, but it's not proper for a groom to see the bride on her wedding day."

Carrie set the plate aside. "Truly? He ... we ..." She smothered a cry with her left hand as her eyes turned watery.

Adaleigh squeezed the fingers of her right, careful so as not to jostle them within the sling. "Nick has threatened to tie him if he so much as puts a toe outside his blankets. For an Italian, he isn't the least bit romantic."

Carrie gave a soggy laugh.

"But my David convinced Nick that marrying you is the best medicine for Buck's heart."

"Is he up for it? It won't set him back? My legs work just fine. I'll go to him."

Adaleigh chuckled. "Let us worry about the details and getting you from here to there, or him there to here."

"As long as you promise to do whatever is best for him, and that ..." Carrie dropped her gaze. "That I can still marry him."

"He said much the same thing, so we'll see it happen before the sun goes down." Adaleigh replaced the plate on Carrie's lap. "Now, you need to keep up your strength. Eat, let Mindy give you pain medicine, and rest."

"But—"

"Not *buts*." Adaleigh pulled the basket to her and lifted out a pale yellow dress covered in auburn embroidery from the basket. "*Then* we get you dressed in your wedding finery."

Carrie gasped and fingered one of the embroidered leaves along the cap sleeve. A fall dress, light and airy like a crisp autumn day. "Is it still snowing?"

Adaleigh shook her head. "Temperature rose into the forties. Plus, Meri had the perfect shawl to match the dress." She pulled out a brown slip of fabric.

At first, Carrie wasn't sure what to make of the color, then Adaleigh unfolded it and draped it across the yellow dress. Yes, the shawl was brown, but not a dull, tired brown. It was a deep, vibrant brown with threads of yellow and red.

"You and Meri?" She touched the fabric again. "For me?"

"And Ali has something else for you, though she wouldn't tell me what." Adaleigh laid the dress and shawl at the foot of the bed. "Whatever it was, it took her to Hawk's Creek."

Carrie leaned back against her pillows, tired, happy, sore, and yet ...

content. Or she would be once she was Mrs. Buck Wilson. "Thank you, Adaleigh. This is more than generous of you."

Adaleigh paused at the side of the bed. "You helped me on my wedding day. This is the least I can do for you, and Buck. It took me over a year to marry the man I love because of the pain I faced. You two helped make it a day of joy."

"Even with Buck's episode and the undercover bit?"

"I entered Crow's Nest using an assumed name." Adaleigh chuckled. "It was the perfect counterpoint."

"Adaleigh." Carrie gathered her courage to ask this one last question. Then she'd eat the bread and rest. She was rather tired after all.

Adaleigh clasped her hands and waited, all her attention on Carrie as if she had all the time in the world.

"Are you glad you left?" It wasn't quite the right question, but pain fogged Carrie's mind.

"Are you asking me because you want to stay in Crow's Nest?" Adaleigh asked, her question gentle.

"I think so." Carrie sighed. "But I don't know what Buck wants, other than not staying in this house. And it would mean leaving Ali and the agency."

"Do you need to think about it today?" Adaleigh adjusted the blankets around her. "Getting married is a big enough decision, and neither of you should travel for a while. You have time."

"I suppose so." Carrie picked up her bread, but didn't yet take a bite. "And no matter where life takes us, I plan to stay at Buck's side."

"What did she say?" Buck sat up in the bed that Nick refused to let him out of as David walked into the room. "Is Adaleigh back yet? Did she talk to Carrie?"

David closed the door as he shook his head. "Last I knew you were saying *I* was a lovesick fool. Or was that Nick? Or Silas? Or … well, I'm pretty sure you've said that to all of us. Now here we are."

"Why'd you close the door?" No point addressing the rest of it.

David took his dear old time pulling a chair to Buck's bedside. "Nick is grousing downstairs about this wedding idea of yours. However I understand, firsthand, that marrying Carrie will do more for your heart than anything Nick can do for you right now."

"That's not why you shut the door, Martins." The man was working up to say something important. Something Buck might not like. At least, it appeared it didn't have anything to do with Carrie, or his health.

"The last few weeks, I got to see Adaleigh's world." David rested his elbows on his knees. "Why she chose me, I'll never know. Why she didn't choose you."

"Is that what this is about?" Buck muttered, not bothering to hide his annoyance. "The woman never loved me, nor I her. There is no point being jealous."

"Thanks for that." David chuckled, so that was a good sign. "She had wealth, Wilson. Has wealth. I took forever proposing because of it, and now …"

"What are you worried about and why are you talking to me, of all people?" Two questions. If he was in his right mind, he'd ask one at a time, like a good investigator.

"I'm worried she'll regret it." David kept his eyes on his clasped hands. "And I want to know if you're planning to take my uncle up on his offer."

Understanding dawned. "You want to know why—after all this, knowing where Carrie is from—I'd choose to stay."

David nodded, still looking anywhere but at Buck.

"First of all, Adaleigh won't regret it. She loves you, Martins. Sure, she might not understand why you struggle with the fact she has more money than you. But you gave her something money can't buy."

That brought David's head up.

"The same thing marrying Carrie will bring me. Peace." Buck leaned forward to emphasize his point. "You, Captain Martins, are her safe harbor. You are her home."

David blinked, then quickly pressed his thumb and forefinger into his eyes. To give him a moment to collect himself, Buck turned toward the window, the same window he'd spent too much time staring out of when Carrie had first arrived in Crow's Nest. Soon she'd be at his side again. He hoped.

Finally, David cleared his throat. "And why would you choose to stay? Carrie's life is in Chicago."

Buck picked at the quilt. If he never spent another night in this bed ... "I'll go wherever Carrie is, you're right about that. I haven't told her about O'Connor's offer. I also haven't told her I resigned last night."

David sat back. "That's a lot you haven't told her seeing that you plan to marry her today."

"Don't I know it." Buck scratched at the scruff he'd need to shave before the ceremony he hoped would happen. "O'Connor thinks it would work, me staying here. Would I have your support?"

"Mine?"

"Martins, if I've learned one thing these past two years, you are the unofficial leader in this town. Mayor, chief of police, head of the Conglomerate ... no one respects any of those positions like they do you."

David reddened. "I don't know about all that."

"I do. And it's why I have an offer for you." He hadn't planned on this until he'd talked with Carrie about O'Connor's offer, but the timing seemed right. "I want you to take over the Conglomerate."

"What?" David straightened. "Explain."

A smile threatened, but Buck tamped it down. "Like I said, you have the people's respect. You also have integrity. You can change the Conglomerate to be what the people need it to be, especially since I suspect the economy is going to get worse before it gets better."

"I don't know …"

"Then talk to Adaleigh."

David glared at him.

"Ah, so you know she'd agree with me." Now Buck grinned. "She'll be your partner in it, David. You two will protect this town. They need you."

David rubbed his thighs, considering Buck. "You called me David."

"So I did. Offended?"

David's jaw ticked. "I'm sorry, Buck. I misjudged you from the moment we met. I'm sorry I left you to fight this battle on your own."

Apologies made him itchy. "I didn't mean for you—"

"Save it. I know you were undercover, but that means nothing. I shouldn't have let my negativity toward you put up a barrier. You needed a friend and it took Nick to do right by you. I'm sorry I wasn't that man."

"Forgiven?" Buck held out his hand, grateful and yet ready to move on.

"Thank you." David shook. Held a moment longer. "If you can convince Carrie to stay, I'd be honored to serve this town alongside you."

"There you two are." O'Connor burst into the room without knocking, a scowl on his weathered face. "Wedding is on and I've been instructed to get your lazy bum out of this bed and help you down to the parlor to await your bride."

Buck had never smiled so big. "Martins, find yourself a suit and be my best man."

David laughed. "Consider it done."

Carrie took one last look in the hand mirror as Patrick and Ali waited by the front door of Buck's house. The wedding had taken everyone's help, but it would begin as soon as she arrived at the clinic.

Her old black Mary Janes clicked on the wood steps as she made her way down the stairs. She lifted the slight veil on the new yellow fascinator—a gift from the Martins clan and made by Samantha—so she could watch her step. The borrowed yellow dress fit perfectly, the sleeve light on her injured shoulder, the skirt flowing over her shins. And the shawl, secured by a blue broach provided by Mindy and Bella, covered the sling that pinned her right arm to her chest.

"Bellissima, la mia stellina." Ali clasped her hands under her chin. "You make a stunning bride."

Carrie felt heat rise in her cheeks, even more so when Patrick met her at the bottom of the stairs and offered his hand. "May I have the honor of escorting you to the ceremony?"

From what she'd heard from Mindy, with Nick and David helping at the clinic, Patrick had offered to be the chauffeur and deliveryman. What that meant, Carrie couldn't imagine, however, the spark in Mindy's eyes said she would be pleased.

The last vestiges of daylight created a hazy glow over the town of Crow's Nest. As they drove by, she noted residents taking down Halloween decorations and cleaning up from last night's mischief makers. Harvest time was nearly done, then would come the long rest of winter.

Patrick parked close to the clinic, then helped Carrie into the house. Ali would walk Carrie down the aisle. Adaleigh and Mindy would stand up for her. Were they already in the clinic's parlor?

"Bella offered to sing." Ali stopped Carrie before she could peek inside. "When you're ready, we'll begin."

"Is everyone ... is Buck ready?" Carrie pressed her good hand to her belly. Mindy had timed the pain medicine so the drowsy effects would have worn off, but she'd still have perhaps an hour before needing a new dose.

"Everyone, including Buck, is ready." Ali reached a hand to Carrie's cheek. "I'm proud of you, Carrie."

Carrie blinked to keep the tears at bay.

Ali grinned. "Let's get you married."

Her boss nodded to Patrick, who swung open the doors. As Bella's beautiful soprano wafted out in a lovely rendition of *Ave Maria,* Ali led Carrie to the entrance. Mrs. Martins, Samantha, Meri with Baby Samuel, and Detective O'Connor sat in chairs that made a short aisle. At the end, Adaleigh and Mindy stood on one side, David and Nick on the other. And in the center, in front of the preacher, stood Buck.

He wore one of his expertly tailored suits, though it hung loosely on his frame. His clean-shaven cheeks were pale, new lines had been carved into his handsome face. But it was his eyes that caused the room to disappear. They shone with such love that they sparkled with tears.

She kept her gaze tangled with his as the preacher said words. What words, Carrie didn't know. She paid attention only long enough to repeat her vows. Through the ceremony, she watched Buck's strength fade. Her own pain was nothing in her desire to hurry the preacher along. Until finally, they were pronounced man and wife.

Instead of a kiss, a chair was pushed under Buck's knees, forcing him to sit. He nearly collapsed into it, but pulled Carrie to his lap. "I want my kiss in case I pass out."

She took his cheeks in her hands and obliged. The applause around her brought the room back into focus. She broke the kiss to take in the friends who had gathered, the happiness and relief on the faces in the room.

And then she was being bundled off to the sewing parlor. She attempted to protest, but the women had her too well in hand. Her shawl was removed, her dressing checked, then she was left alone with Ali and Mindy.

Carrie tried to rise. "Where is Buck?" Why had they hurried her off?

"He's fine." Detective O'Connor entered the room. "Nick is being overprotective because he wants you two to have a long and happy life together."

"Okay, but I want to be there." Again, Carrie tried to rise, only for Ali to press her back on the sofa.

"Just wait, he'll be here in a moment." Ali pressed the inside of her wrist against Carrie's forehead. "You're flushed, but there's no fever. Must be happiness."

Or worry.

Worry that wouldn't abate even when Buck walked over to her, unaided.

"I'm fine, love." Buck eased onto the sofa next to her. "Though I wish all these people would leave so I can kiss you again."

Carrie ducked her chin. *Now* her flushed face had nothing to do with worry.

"You'll get your time alone." Detective O'Connor pulled a chair close. "The four of us need a word with you first."

Buck wrapped his arm around Carrie, tucking her good side close to his. "What's this about?"

"Housing arrangements." Nick smirked.

"And job opportunities." Mindy grinned.

O'Connor rolled his eyes, and Ali laughed.

"We aren't living in my house," Buck muttered. "I'm selling it."

Nick pushed his glasses up on his nose. "You can do whatever you want, after I discharge you. For now, you are a resident of this clinic. Carrie, too."

"That solves temporary housing arrangements." Buck shrugged.

But Carrie narrowed her eyes. "You have something more elaborate in mind. Mindy, what is it?" She knew the weak link, the one least likely to tease Buck with the answer.

"You're right, of course." Mindy clasped her hands, her cheeks pink. "With David and Adaleigh back from their wedding trip, the girls want to move out of the Martinses' home. That's me, Sam, Bella, and Mabel. They need their space, and Mrs. Martins plans to stay with Patrick and Meri through the holidays to give Adaleigh and David that time."

"Where will you go?" Carrie asked, though she figured she and Buck were somehow a part of the answer.

"We can't stay here very well." The pink in her cheeks darkened. "Not until Nick and I get married."

Nick hooked Mindy's waist. "No, which is why I can move out, if you two would consent to being these girls' chaperones."

Before Carrie could express her pleasure, Buck stood. "You want me to look after your fiancée, your sister, and little Mabel? The three women dearest to you?"

Nick gripped Buck's shoulder. "Yes. I trust you."

Buck's breath whooshed out, and he sat again, resting his hand on

Carrie's knee. "Wow. I'm honored. But I take my responsibility seriously, Matrone. No canoodling on my watch."

Carrie playfully slapped Buck's arm. "You're embarrassing Mindy." The poor woman's cheeks were as red as a Christmas ribbon.

"If their version of chaperoning us is any indication, we'll have our hands full." Buck coughed back a laugh. And Nick rolled his eyes, but Carrie didn't miss the respect behind his grin.

"Are you two quite finished?" O'Connor mumbled.

"I hope so." Ali's eyes twinkled. "Because now that housing is settled for the next month, Detective O'Connor and I have two job opportunities to offer the both of you. For after Nick clears you to return to full duties."

"First, though." Buck turned to Carrie. "I didn't tell you before because no one would let me see you. I resigned from Justice. Or the Treasury. Or whatever branch they had me working for. I'm too tired, and I refuse to do undercover work without you."

Carrie's stomach churned. "Do you want me to stop doing undercover work?"

"You two are getting ahead of yourselves." Ali interrupted. "Detective, if you would?"

Buck gripped Carrie's hand as Detective O'Connor explained his offer. "With Sebastian in prison, the job of police chief is open. I am temporarily filling the role, but, frankly, I think I'd like to retire by the end of this year. Like you, Buck, I'm tired. And now that the Conglomerate is back on solid footing, we can close the Special Investigation position. All that to say, I want you to put in for chief."

Carrie tucked in closer to him, pride at her husband welling inside. He glanced at her. "It would mean staying in Crow's Nest."

"You're right." The words slipped out without emotion. She didn't know what emotion applied to them. Was she happy? Sad? She'd asked Adaleigh about staying.

"This brings me to my wedding gift." Ali lifted a piece of paper from the bag at her side. "I spent the morning in Hawk's River tracking down the last connection between Baxter and the trouble here in Crow's Nest. The secretary, it appears, was the one sending information from the *Gazette* offices."

"I'm not surprised," Carrie said, though it seemed an odd wedding present.

"Which is why I purchased the *Gazette* and fired her." Ali handed over the paper, a deed with Carrie's name on it. "I'm gifting you the *Gazette*, Carrie. You will own the building, be editor-in-chief, if you desire, hire the journalists you wish. You're ready for this promotion, Carrie."

"And Crow's Nest needs you both." Detective O'Connor's bushy mustache bobbed with what seemed like a smile. "You will keep truth and justice in this little town, and I can think of no better couple to grant the mantle."

Excitement coursed through Carrie and she turned to Buck, thrilled to see the same emotion in his eyes. They didn't need words, a conversation, to know this was exactly what they wanted.

Buck's forefinger tapped against her wrist. Dash. Dot. Dot. Dash. Dot. A question mark.

Carrie grinned. And tapped twice, and twice again.

Yes, and for always.

Curious about Samantha Martins' happily ever after?

Read on for an excerpt from

His Boss's Little Sister

His Boss's Little Sister

Friday, November 13, 1931
Fox Dune Hollow, Wisconsin

Samantha Martins strategically arranged the plate of scones, dish of butter, and ring of Kringle on the tray meant for customers of Das Teehaus Café, an elegant German tea shop on the outskirts of town.

She'd sworn she'd never be a waitress like her brother's friend Mindy, but her need for independence won out. Especially since both her brothers were now married, and even Mindy was engaged. Sam had needed out of her hometown of Crow's Nest, a small fishing town north of Racine, Wisconsin. And this was the first job that made such an escape possible.

Herr Vogel, the large-waisted baker who made every treat except the famed Kringle, tapped the side of his head with the back of his wrist. The owner of the bakery, Astrid Becker, hated it when one of the waitresses had her blue fedora askew. It was part of the required uniform that offered a nod to Frau Becker's German heritage. Only ten days on the job, and Sam had been scolded thrice. One of these nights, she'd make herself a properly fitting one—once she'd saved enough for the materials, which might not happen for a long time.

Setting the fedora-inspired hat with the black lace firmly on her bobbed hair, Sam gave Herr Vogel a nod of thanks and lifted the tray to her shoulder. She liked the middle-aged baker. He was quiet, but had no time for fussy waitresses. She was glad he'd taken a shine to her. He'd saved her a scolding more than once.

Leaving the bustling kitchen, Sam wove through the tables, each covered in starched white linen with autumn-inspired centerpieces, a reminder that Thanksgiving was merely two weeks away. When David had conceded that Sam needed to get out of Crow's Nest, he'd encouraged her to wait until after the holidays. That hadn't stopped her, though. Her brothers, her friends, they were all so *happy*.

The large picture window allowed bright November sun to filter in, making the ornate chandeliers above sparkle. Even the walls had gorgeous oil paintings commissioned by Frau Becker. It was unlike anything they had in Crow's Nest, and Sam always took a moment to soak it in, especially before greeting these particular customers.

"Here you go, ladies." Sam forced a congenial smile. Smiles were easy when gentlemen joined the usual female customers, but not with these two older ladies. Regulars. Widows. And entirely too full of their own importance. "Scones, butter, Kringle, and a plate for each of you. Do you need another pot of tea?"

Winifred Farncombe sniffed, the feather in her wide-brimmed hat—two decades out of date—bobbing at the movement. "We wouldn't need one if you hadn't taken so long to bring our food. Now it's cold."

Beulah Pritchard eyed the scones through her spectacles, and the tiny fascinator perched on her gray curls looked a breath away from falling into her plate. "These don't look like apple."

Sam eased out a calming breath as she set the teapot on her tray.

Mrs. Farncombe and Pritchard always required another pot of tea when the food arrived, and they always complained about the scone flavors, no matter what they ordered. "They are apple cinnamon, ma'am. Herr Vogel pulled them out of the oven not two minutes ago."

Mrs. Pritchard turned up her nose, which was small, like her eyes, but they fit in her narrow face. "I don't like cinnamon. I asked for apple. Take them back and bring the correct scones."

Continue reading
His Boss's Little Sister
daniellegrandinetti.com/his-bosss-little-sister

FROM THE AUTHOR

Dear Readers,

Thank you for joining me, not only for Buck and Caroline's story, but for the entire Harbored in Crow's Nest series. It's bittersweet bringing this series to an end. I have loved every moment I've spent with these characters as well as the in the town of Crow's Nest. If you watch closely, you'll likely see these characters pop up in future books.

Like Gio, who I couldn't resist bringing into this story. He's a fan favorite who appears in the Unexpected Protectors series, and is the hero in *A Silent as the Night*. You can find out more at daniellegrandinetti.com/unexpected-protectors.

Want more Ali Di Stasio and her female reporters? Check out *Undercover Wish*, the prequel novella of my 1930s historical romantic mystery series, The Di Stasio Giornaliste Agency. I'm also growing a paid dispatch on Substack with Ali's notes, vignettes, and flash fiction stories. Visit daniellegrandinetti.com/wire to learn more.

Finally, don't miss *His Boss's Little Sister*, Sam's story and a Hansel & Gretel retelling. The youngest Martin sibling finally gets a chance at a happily ever after. Find out more at daniellegrandinetti.com/his-bosss-little-sister.

Thank you again for reading *Investigation of a Journalist*. I hope you enjoyed it. If you did, would you consider leaving a spoiler-free review on your preferred retail site? That will help readers decide whether they'd enjoy this series, too.

Happy Reading!

Danielle Grandinetti.

HISTORICAL NOTE

When I began writing this story, I had Thanksgiving as the holiday I'd include. However, with the undercover nature of this story, Halloween proved a much better match. In the 1930s, Halloween pranks reached their worst, partially due to the unemployment rate. The Halloween decorations I included in this story were also based on decorations that would have been hung in the 1930s. If you'd like to learn more about the history of Halloween, visit history.com, "Halloween: Origins, Meaning & Traditions."

The heart condition Buck exhibited in this story is called "Broken Heart Syndrome," or stress-induced cardiomyopathy. While it commonly affects widows after the death of their spouse, it can affect men, especially after extreme emotional and/or physical stress. This syndrome is often mistaken for a heart attack—a term for a myocardial infarction that was used in the 1930s, from what I could find—since the symptoms are similar. However, while it can be fatal, the cause is not due to heart damage or blocked arteries, and the heart can recover with rest. To learn more, visit the American Heart Association's article "Is Broken Heart Syndrome Real?".

The history behind the agents who tracked counterfeiters and the sale of illegal alcohol is fascinating and rather convoluted. First, the Secret Service originally dealt with counterfeit crime (and still does) before also protecting the president. However, prior to 2003, the Secret Service was housed officially under the Department of the Treasury. Similarly, Prohibition Agents were originally part of the Treasury Department's Bureau of Internal Revenue, but in 1927 were moved to the Justice Department. This is why agents such as Elliot Ness, who eventually led the team to arrest Al Capone, worked for Justice, not the Treasury, though Capone was arrested for financial crimes. They also worked closely with the BOI, or Bureau of Investigation, the predecessor of the FBI. However, the Treasury did have undercover agents, such as the one who worked undercover in Capone's outfit. I decided to take all these webs and weave them into a singular character: Buck Wilson.

As for Caroline's undercover journalism ... the history of female undercover journalists goes back to journalists like Nellie Bly, who is perhaps best known for going undercover in an insane asylum in 1887. Bly's story has always intrigued me, so I loved the idea of creating a female character who also worked as an undercover journalist. However, as I researched, I learned that Bly was part of a generation of female reporters known as "stunt reporters," a term that had faded by the time Caroline's story would take place. And so I created Ali Di Stasio, her journalism agency, and a brand-new historical romantic mystery/suspense series coming your way in 2025. Stay tuned to my website for all the latest!

Join my Fireside News

Grab a spot on my virtual hearth and receive a weekly email filled with bookish content. As a thank you for subscribing, you'll receive a digital copy of my historical romance novelette: *Fire and Water*.

Subscribe Here

Fairytale Retellings

Heart of Beauty

stand-alone origin novella

Discover the origin of Crooked Tooth Ranch in this 1870s western retelling of Beauty and the Beast.

daniellegrandinetti.com/heart-of-beauty

His Boss's Little Sister

stand-alone novella in the Apron Strings Tea Tale
multi-author series

A touch of fairy tale, a spoonful of history, and a teacup of hope ... a 1930s historical romance retelling of Hansel and Gretel.

daniellegrandinetti.com/his-bosss-little-sister

UNDERCOVER WISH
stand-alone novella, part of the Di Stasio Giornaliste
Agency series

*A Di Stasio Giornaliste Agency origin story and a retelling of Aladdin
and the Magic Lamp.*

daniellegrandinetti.com/heart-of-beauty

Unexpected Protectors

Visit small-town Wisconsin during the Dairy Strikes of the Great Depression in these three historical romances.

For details, visit:

daniellegrandinetti.com/unexpected-protectors

To Stand in the Breach

Strike to the Heart, #1
She came to America to escape a workhouse prison,
but will the cost of freedom be too high a price to pay?

A Strike to the Heart

Strike to the Heart, #2
She's fiercely independent.
He's determined to protect her.

As Silent as the Night

Strike to the Heart, #3

He can procure anything, except his heart's deepest wish.
She might hold the key, if she's not discovered first.

248

Di Stasio Giornaliste Agency

La Verità con Integrità. Truth with Integrity.
The Legacy of a (Girl) Stunt Reporter.
daniellegrandinetti.com/di-stasio-giornaliste-agency

Undercover Wish

Di Stasio Giornaliste Agency, #0
Alessandra Di Stasio
Chicago World's Fair: World's Columbian Exposition

Eyewitness Sketch

Di Stasio Giornaliste Agency, #1
Gabriella Salatino
Prohibition

Sabotage Games

Di Stasio Giornaliste Agency, #2
Emma Hancock
Summer & Winter Olympics: Lake Placid & L.A.

Shrouded Trail

DI STASIO GIORNALISTE AGENCY, #3
Lena Carney
Presidential Election

Fraudulent Progress

DI STASIO GIORNALISTE AGENCY, #4
Klara James
Chicago World's Fair: A Century Of Progress Exposition

Pursuing Dust

DI STASIO GIORNALISTE AGENCY, #5
Tabitha Jóhannsson
Dust Bowl

Hostile Ally

DI STASIO GIORNALISTE AGENCY, #6
Liesl Kaufman
Berlin Olympics

Christmas Cabin Series

The Sheriff and the Outlaw

Christmas Cabin, prequel
**Discover the beginning of the Christmas Cabin series
in this Christmas suspense short story.**

The Baby and the Guardian

Christmas Cabin, #1
**A baby in danger, a man in turmoil,
and a woman determined to save them both.**

The Neighbor and the Gifts

Christmas Cabin, #2
Twelve days. Twelve gifts.

One unlikely hero.

The Robber and the Witness

CHRISTMAS CABIN, #3
A simple favor, a best friend's promise,
and the end of the line.
Releasing July 2026

OUR HOUSE NOVELLAS

As the world marches toward what will become WWII, visit Our House as we join the resistance.

The Italian Musician's Sanctuary
Romance, history and intrigue at Our House on
Sycamore Street.

Hunted by one man, can she open her heart to another?
Eden Cove, England, 1931—Margherita Vicienzo flees Italy pursued by her former fiancé, a member of Mussolini's Blackshirt. Smuggled illegally into England, Margherita is a foreigner at the mercy of strangers. Her limp from an improperly healed broken leg means she has nothing to offer the Ferryman family, who offer her sanctuary, and nothing to appease their son who resents her presence.

Luke Ferryman needs a wife. He wants to marry for love, but carries the weight of his family's generations-old expectations on his shoulders. Though he inherited the role of both baker and ferryman, he knows he can't fulfill both needs once his aging grandparents retire. A wife would help, but not an illegal one like the refugee his matchmaking grandmother is harboring.

As opposite as night and day, Luke and Margherita forge a tentative friendship that grows despite the constant threat of Margherita's discovery. But when strangers appear in the close-knit seaside town, threatening Luke's livelihood and Margherita's safety, the choice between justice and mercy becomes harder. And sacrifice proves the only answer.

The Recluse's Vindication

Rumors, Monsters, and Second Chances at Our House
on Heather Wynd

The Loch Ness Monster isn't the only recluse seeking a Scottish haven.

Bieldfell, Scotland, 1933—Falsely accused of murder sixteen years ago, American cowboy Benjamin Ford has chosen to hide out in the Scottish Highlands. Reclusive and not afraid to die, he rescues children out of an increasingly dangerous Germany. When his childhood best friend appears at his door, he's not the boy she remembers.

Eleanor Finch's life ended sixteen years ago. In one horrible day, she lost her dreams, her reputation, and her heart. However, she never gives up the hope of finding her friend, so when she learns of Ben's whereabouts, she leaves all that is familiar to convince him to return home.

But Eleanor isn't the only person searching for Ben. Hunters follow her trail. The thin veil of gossip and rumor may be their only chance of a future ... unless the Loch Ness Monster is real after all.

daniellegrandinetti.com/our-house

Harbored in Crow's Nest

Welcome to Crow's Nest,
where danger and romance meet at the water's edge.
daniellegrandinetti.com/harbored-in-crows-nest

Confessions to a Stranger

Harbored in Crow's Nest, #1
She's lost her future. He's sacrificed his.
Now they have a chance to reclaim it—together.

Refuge for the Archaeologist

Harbored in Crow's Nest, #2
Will uncovering the truth set them free
or destroy what they hold most dear?

Escape with the Prodigal

Harbored in Crow's Nest, #3
Only a Christmas miracle will save
an unwed mother and the lumberjack protecting her.

Relying on the Enemy

Harbored in Crow's Nest, #4
She's protecting her children.
He's redeeming his past.

Sheltered by the Doctor

Harbored in Crow's Nest, #5
A fake relationship might keep her safe,
but will it break their hearts?

Investigation of a Journalist

Harbored in Crow's Nest, #6
A second chance to set the record straight,
and rekindle a lost love.

ABOUT THE AUTHOR

Danielle Grandinetti is an award-winning author of 1930s historical romance, where mystery and suspense intertwine with hope. Her work has received recognition including a Distinguished Faith in Writing Award, two National Excellence in Storytelling Awards, and finalist honors in the FHLCW Reader's Choice, Selah, and Daphne du Maurier contests.

A second-generation Italian-American rooted in Midwest traditions, Danielle draws inspiration from tea, books, and the creative beauty of nature. Holding a master's in communication and culture, and driven by a lifelong love of stories, she crafts tales that celebrate resilience, diversity, and belonging. Danielle lives along Wisconsin's Lake Michigan shoreline with her husband and two sons. Find her online at daniellegrandinetti.com.